ENVY

Book Four in the Love is Cure, Vol. 1 - Vices & Virtues Series

Brookelyn Mosley

85 Media LLC

More By Brookelyn Mosley

Novellas/Series

No Fraternizing, Pt. 1
No Fraternizing, Pt 2
No Fraternizing, Pt. 3
First Came Love: The Love, Hate & Revenge Prequel
Love, Hate & Revenge, Pt. 1
Love, Hate & Revenge, Pt. 2
Love, Hate, & Revenge, Pt. 3
Girl Code
Mr. & Mrs. Jones
Forbidden: An Anthology
They Call Me Mello
A Love Deferred
Indecent Arrangement
Last Comes Love
Ebb & Flow
PRIDE
Meant To Be
LUST

Loveless
GREED
Rekindled
My First, My Last

Short Stories

Just Friends
Chateau Luxure
Lena's Ex-File
Dream Boss
Unsilent Knight
Twice In Love
Home For Christmas

MESSAGE FROM THE AUTHOR

Thank you for purchasing your copy of *ENVY* – the fourth book in the *Love is Cure, Vol. 1 – Vices & Virtues series*. This series comprises seven books in total.

This book, like the other books in this series, is a standalone. So if this is the first book you've stumbled on in this series and you want to start here, you can. But if you are reading the books in the order I am releasing them in, that's even better.

The stories released so far are *PRIDE*, *LUST*, and *GREED*.

If you want to read the stories in order, *LUST* is the story you'll want to start with before reading *ENVY*, since some characters who appear in this story also appear in *LUST*. But you can, of course, read the stories in reverse order (*ENVY* before *LUST*) as well.

Certain elements of this story deal with parental illness and verbal abuse, so if this is a sensitive subject matter for you, it is best that you browse my catalog for something else that will fit your reading experience. There is also sexual content in this book with a very light reference to bondage. And by light, I mean not even worth mentioning, but I'm still mentioning it here because it's mentioned in the story.

Thank you again for purchasing your copy of *ENVY*. Enjoy!

Love,
Brookelyn.

Acknowledgments

A loving thank you to my amazing husband who is without a doubt one of my biggest supporters. Your support is worth its weight in gold. A special thank you to my reading family and early supporters of my work. I'm sure you've noticed the growth, you've even commented on it. I thank you for sticking beside me and growing with me. You all have embraced my brand of writing and I'm beyond appreciative of it. Shout out to the readers who have reached out to me to share your thoughts regarding my books. I thank you for keeping me motivated and excited to create new projects for you. When I write, I keep you in mind. Thank you for your support. It's my soul food.

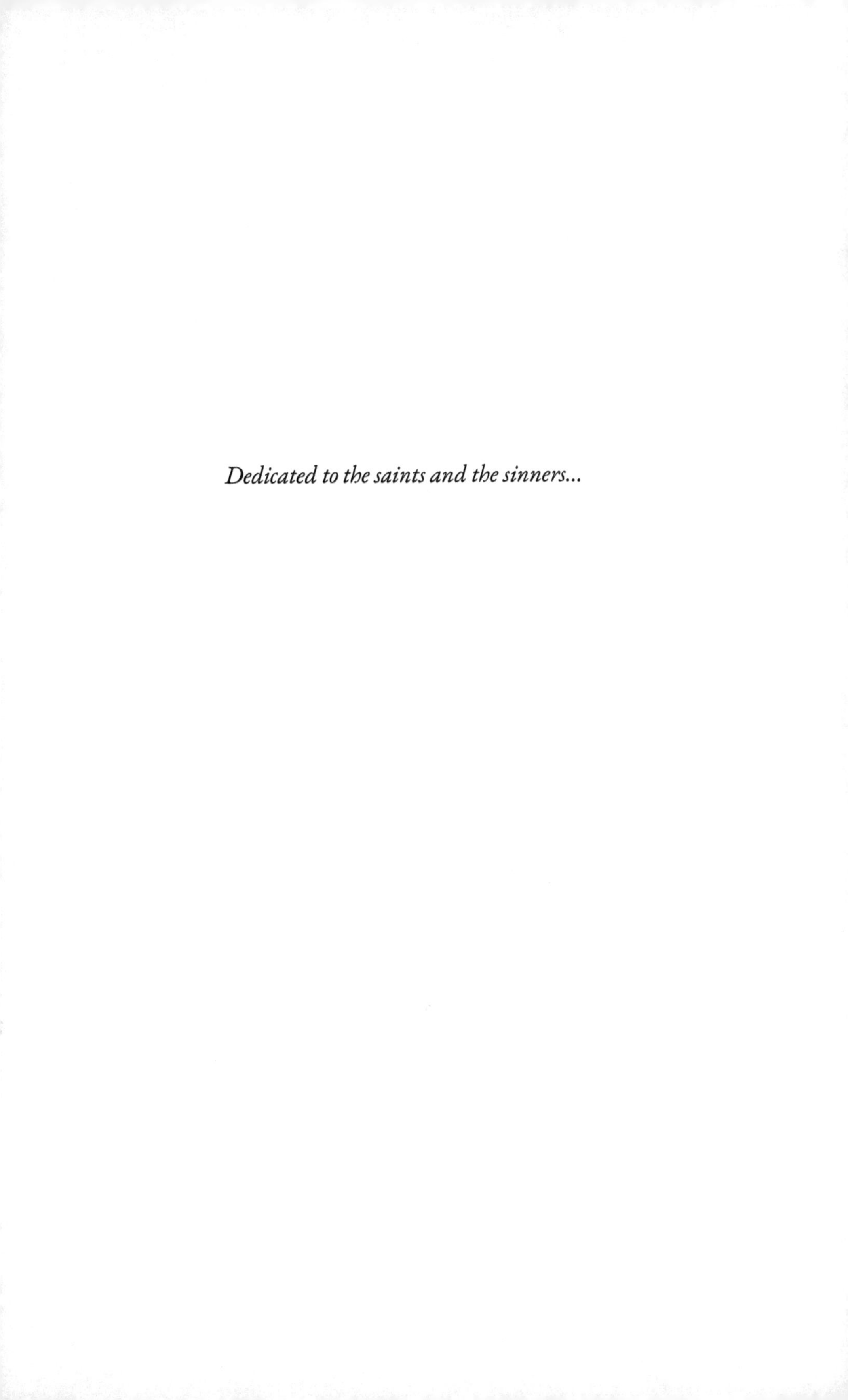

Dedicated to the saints and the sinners...

PROLOGUE

15-YEARS EARLIER...

MYKAL

I squeezed my eyes closed and belted out song lyrics about a home where love overflowed. My voice traveled around me, echoing off the restroom walls. I faced the mirror as I sang my solo. If I had the choice to do anything, singing in my performance arts high school bathroom wouldn't have been at the top of my list. I was practicing, moments away from performing "Home" from the musical, *The Wiz*, in front of my music teacher. She was organizing her version of the soulful musical. Ms. Wallace's *Wiz* had yet to debut, and half the school was already vying for any role they could get their hands on. I was going for the role of Dorothy. The lead. The damn star of the show. How ambitious, right? But my music teacher, Ms. Wallace, promised Dorothy's part was mine. Music was never really my thing. Movies were. My interest in cinema was the only reason I wanted enrollment at Bakeridge High. But news of this musical happening changed all that. Ms. Wallace told me to read for the role. That's all I had to do. She also promised I was born for this and had the pizzaz, the je ne sais quoi, as she said before punctuating her words with a chef's kiss.

I smiled to myself as I brought my voice up a vocal register in time to ease into the second verse in my a cappella.

I held a copy of the script in my grip as I continued singing to my reflection in the mirror. Having the script was unnecessary. I knew every moment in The Wiz by heart. Every line down to the unscripted sighs I could recreate even with the movie's volume on mute. My father had only watched the film a million times, easy. It was his favorite movie, the one film he indulged in for entertainment and comfort. A sight to see too, observing him watch the musical on VHS seated on his tattered armchair, an armchair reserved for viewing basketball games all season long. He'd smile from ear to ear as he mouthed all the song sequences from The Wiz. And if you saw my father, the big burly bear he was, you wouldn't even guess he'd be into such a thing.

I squared my shoulders and held my chin up high as I sang the lyrics louder.

The main reason I was even interested in the role was because of my father. Back then, we had nothing to talk about. He never seemed too thrilled when we dialogued and getting him to pay any attention to me was like waiting for paint to dry in a heatwave.

If it wasn't about a basketball or a hoop, he wasn't interested.

I bet he'd love me if I was a boy.

In fact, I know he'd love me if I were a boy.

I shake my head and refocus, inhaling a breath to exhale the last of the lyrics in the medley to completion. "Home" was my father's favorite song from the musical. Truth be told, according to my mother at least, Jedidiah Jones couldn't care less about the musical at all. Diana Ross caught his eye. He's had a lifelong crush on the former Supreme.

The bathroom's door swung opened, and I glanced to my right to glimpse my friend Nayla walking through.

"There you are," she said, gesturing with her hands in my direction. "I've been looking all over Bakeridge for you."

"Well, now you've found me," I told her while folding the stapled papers, that served as the script, lengthwise, then pushing the gathered papers into my back jean pocket. "Why were you looking for me, anyway?"

"To tell you what I just heard."

I shake my head and turn to face the mirror again, fingering the length of my bangs into place. "What did you hear, Ny?"

"That Cody Evans wants to ask you out."

I kiss my teeth. "I have better things to focus on than to be beside myself over Cody Evans. Didn't he just break up with Angel Suarez?"

"Old news." Nayla walked closer. She stopped a few inches next to me and leaned her backside against the lip of one sink. "And what were you doing in here, anyway? I could hear you hollering from outside."

I purse my lips, returning my attention to my reflection. "I was not hollering, and you know it. I was singing."

"That's different." She furrowed her naturally arched brows. "Why?"

I shrugged. "Just because."

"Just because?" She questioned. "Girl, your major is drama."

And I barely liked that.

Truth be told, I didn't like singing or acting, but my father did... so I figured, I could too.

"Singing can be drama."

"You hate singing, though," she insisted. "That's totally my lane."

"Well, I'm making it my lane for just a little, okay?"

She quirked a brow. "What aren't you saying?"

Nayla wasn't quite my friend back then. Our mothers became situational acquaintances and so were Nayla and I. Nayla was the child of a single mother who worked two jobs and when Nayla and I were in grade school, her mother would drop her off at the bus stop then race off to work leaving Nayla in the care of my mother who would wait with me and Nayla until the school bus arrived. My mother, unlike Nayla's mom, was a homemaker, unfortunately, and didn't have a job to run off to. Annoying to me, but great for Nayla and her mother, because being the sweetheart my mother was, she'd volunteer our house to our situational acquaintances, so Nayla could have a home away from home. Nayla would often spend the night at my house because her mother got off work late into the morning hours. So, my mother would walk Nayla and me to the bus stop for school and pick us up at that same stop when school let out. After months and then years of this, Nayla and I had no choice but to find something in common and to become friends.

"Just because, huh?" Nayla challenged. She leaned forward and reached behind me, pulling the folded script out of my pocket quicker than I could stop her.

"Hey!" I shouted.

That didn't keep her from unfolding the script and skimming through the black words.

"Wait, what is this?"

"Nothing," I lied, reaching for the script only for her to yank the pages back and closer in her view.

She batted her long lashes a few times before shooting a surprised glare my way. "Is this for The Wiz?!"

I swallowed hard.

"Oh my God, this is! This is Dorothy's lines..." Her slender jaw dropped. "I didn't even know Ms. Wallace was casting for this yet!"

"She isn't." I snatched the script from her hand before she tightened her grip around the gathered papers. "The role is mine."

"What role is yours?"

"Dorothy's."

"Yeah, right! Says who?"

"Ms. Wallace?"

Nayla folded her arms tight. "Impossible."

"She told me I'm perfect for the role and that the part is mine." I walked closer to the mirror and flipped the strands of my pressed hair over my shoulders. "All I have to do is read for it today."

"She's holding auditions?!" Nayla's voice echoed around us. "Where the hell was this even posted?"

"She isn't holding auditions, Nayla. She's simply making an exception for me. I already told you." I smiled with pride. "She said I'm perfect for the role and for the third time, it's mine."

Nayla twisted her lips to one side. "Why are you just telling me about this? And how did you memorize an entire script enough to read for the role?"

"She already knows I can act, so she only wants for me to sing "Home." I'm meeting with her today in the auditorium at 3pm. I stopped by her classroom earlier to confirm." I turned to the mirror again and continued feathering my bangs with my fingertips. "The role is literally mine. That's

the reason I didn't bother mentioning it. There will be other roles you can try for though, so don't trip."

I turned to face Nayla and caught when she lessened the tension in her jaw and the squint in her eyes. That should have been the telltale sign of how much of a friend she wasn't. Who wouldn't be happy for their friend? She knew the significance of that film to my father... I mean, to me.

I was naïve back then. Completely not prepared for what would happen next.

She exchanged the glare of contempt quickly for something else. Something I couldn't quite identify at 15-years-old.

"You should do a quick French braid to pull your hair out of your face," she suggested.

I furrowed my brows. "Why?"

"Well, Diana Ross's hair in The Wiz was short, and yours is long. I'm sure Ms. Wallace will have you wear a wig for the show, but you want her to visualize you in the role."

"She already said the role is mine—"

"I know," Nayla interjected. "But what's the harm in fitting the image just a little more? It's like Mrs. Reiner said in drama, to be cast, you must emulate. Look as close to the role as possible so the casting director can see you in it."

I stared at her for a moment, processing her words. This school musical was nowhere near that serious for me to use Mrs. Reiner's useful advice.

"Anyway..." Nayla shrugged a shoulder. " It's only a suggestion. You can do whatever you want."

I turned to face the mirror, seesawing my head from left to right, observing and analyzing my hair and face. In that instance, I started second guessing myself.

After some thought, I figured there was no harm in pulling my hair out of my face like Nayla suggested. The role was mine. There was no big deal in being extra prepared to audition for it.

"Fine." I raked my fingers through my bangs, pushing the strands toward the crown of my head to ready my hair for plaiting. "Can you help me?"

"I have to go lock my locker," she answered in haste. "I left it unlocked *after I overheard Cody's friends talking in the hall. Then I went looking for you and forgot all about closing my combination lock."*

I sighed and refocused on the mirror. "It's fine. I'll just do a quick braid. How long could it take, anyway?"

"Not long at all." Nayla said as she turned on her heels. "I'll catch you later."

She was out the door before I even thought to utter a farewell.

As I worked on my hair, I hummed "Home," working quick so I wasn't late getting to the auditorium.

I hummed the entire time, in fact. Hummed until I plaited down to the ends of my hair, stepped out of the bathroom door, and made my way down the school's hall en route to the auditorium.

One glance at the gold-plated wristwatch I wore offered false confidence. The time was 2:43 pm, which meant I had more than enough time to practice a little more in the auditorium before Ms. Wallace's arrival.

Bakeridge High School was the biggest in the city. Indoor elevators and escalators connected the building and led to a stadium sized auditorium, our shining star of our school. The creme de la creme honed their skills between the walls of that eight-story building before acting in motion picture films or accepting Grammy's on stage... or both. That was one reason I wanted to study at Bakeridge High School. My father was a cinephile. Loved all things filmography. And honestly? I wanted to be a part of anything that would get his approval.

I was on the second verse of my "Home" hum when I heard the piano accompaniment to the very song I hummed. The instrumental played on a piano, and floated down the hall, bouncing off the ceilings, and invading my listening space. My wrist was up in front of my eyes before I could think of lifting it. I glanced at the time to see it was only 2:45 pm.

"What?" I whispered to myself as I moved toward the music. The more distance I closed, the more prominent in sound the melody became. That melody was coming from Ms. Wallace's classroom.

I was within inches from the classroom's door when I narrowed my eyes and peered through the door's window. My brows relaxed and my jaw slowly hinged opened at the sight of Nayla standing on the mini-platform stage in Ms. Wallace's classroom. Ms. Wallace parked herself on her piano bench in front of her black baby grand, her red manicured nails dancing along the black and white keys as Nayla eased into the second verse of "Home."

All the air I had in me expelled through my slacked jaw as I witnessed my friend belt the lyrics to "Home" with such passion and elegance. She emphasized each song lyric with the extension of her arms, every wrinkle in her brows, and both dimples in her cheeks.

My heart raced as my eyes darted away from Nayla's very dramatic performance, landing on Ms. Wallace, who couldn't take her eyes off my friend. I recognized the adoring smile that pulled at the corners of Ms. Wallace's lips, the admiration in her gaze as she watched in awe as my friend Nayla betrayed me right before my eyes.

"Sneaky bitch," I whispered to myself.

Nayla went from being my friend that day to becoming Dorothy a week later after landing the leading role in the musical. More like stealing the role from right under me. I sang "Home" right after her that day, at 3pm as scheduled, but seeing her perform the song before me threw me off and messed with my head. I fumbled over the lyrics and was careless with my pitch. I sang off key and with trembling vocals as I tried my hardest not to cry angry tears while I auditioned.

Nayla became the shining star pupil at Bakeridge after her Wiz performance and I couldn't escape the echoes of her praise, not even at home. My father raved about Nayla's performance long after the show ended. He actually still raves about it to this day.

Some would say what Nayla did to me was a tiny insignificant thing, but her actions pushed me to form an unhealthy relationship with feeling sorrow at the good fortunes of others. And because I believed I had reason to feel that way, it became an emotion I nursed and nurtured foolishly for years. Went from a habit to a trait whiles becoming my motivation and my defeat. That, however, was until I met someone who changed me in more ways than they'll ever know...

ONE
PRESENT DAY

MYKAL

"Ugh, I can't *stand* her," I mumble to myself. I stare down at my phone, eyes fixed on a photo of Pryce Williams - the man who I thought would be mine - and the woman he chose over me.

The picture annoying me is of him and his wife, Leelah, photoed at an event. They dressed cute in their color coordinated all-black outfits, her a bodycon black mini-dress and him a black button up with slacks and shiny black loafers.

Photos of them have been circulating around a lot lately since they married secretly on some exotic island last month. I roll my eyes at the thought and click out of my safari app to venture somewhere else on my phone.

My text app.

I scroll down once and stop on the name Lucas, a guy I met at a Chinatown restaurant close to a month ago. A Wall Street type, he talked fast and climaxed even faster. Not a minute man. *The* minute man. He wasn't one of my best but I needed a confidence boost after seeing what I just saw on my phone's screen.

Me: Hey you, what's up?

Lucas: Who's this?

I twist my lips to one side.

Me: Mykal

No response.

Me: We met at Mr. Won Ton in July.

Still no response.

I roll my eyes and walk up in line.

Me: And hooked up two nights later in the back of your Bentley.

Lucas: Mykal, hey! Yeah, you were great.

I bet.

Lucas: How have you been?

Lucas: I hope well

Lucas: I miss you

Lucas: Got any plans tonight?

My phone chimes in my hand with each message he sends within the minute.

Lucas promised he would buy me the new Yves Saint Laurent pumps as I rode him in the back seat of his car. I should've known better than to fall for that bullshit. He didn't even have the decency to save my phone number to know when I reached out to him again.

I'm bothered.

I shouldn't be bothered.

So much for that confidence boost.

I click out of the text window and inhale the air sharply through my nose.

The scent of ground coffee beans engulfs me when I do. I stand in line at Groundhouse, waiting to place my order for a large hot cup of caffeine close to the middle of August. I usually bought coffee an hour before I stepped into work. During my broke days, I always dreamed of sipping coffee at the window of a luxurious coffeehouse, resembling a doll in the window while I watch the bold and the beautiful specimens of New York City go about their fabulous days like I would do after sipping on my espresso. I imagined I too would have somewhere important to go. A casting call, on the set of my newest movie, or a table read in a studio office somewhere.

I scoff at myself as I walk up in line, getting closer to the register.

I'm kind of happy I didn't get what I wanted. I'm sure my father would have been proud had I become a starlet but the movie industry wasn't for me, I learned.

So, no, the life of glitz and glamor didn't really find me. Instead of table reads, I pitched ideas at the start of every day at the magazine I worked. My cousin, Amir Jones, started For The Culture with a business friend and I begged him to green-light me interning there. I've had to beg to have many things in my life, so it was familiar territory for me. Anyway, beg I did and an offer I finally got and now with our current editor pregnant and choosing the family life over her career, I now anticipated stepping comfortably into her former role at the magazine.

The line inches up a little more, and I follow in tow as the last person in line, at least for now. Entrepreneurs and their laptops pack Groundhouse. They always flock to this place by the pound. The boutique coffeehouse is one of the cutest 24-hour coffeehouses in New York City. Two heiresses who wanted a place they could escape to, to get caffeinated after clubbing every night, owned Groundhouse. Plus, they needed at least one place to put their money to watch that money grow, and Groundhouse became that place.

"Two shots of espresso," the barista shouts up ahead. "Extra hot."

For some people, life is just that easy, and I will know what that feels like, even if it's just a slight glimpse. Because with that editor position open, I can secure that spot and elevate my lifestyle. Once I step into my role as editor, I can get closer to the people I adore and rub shoulders with the rich and famous a little more. As a former intern and current staff writer, there's very little respect in my title. I'm seen as disposable and replaceable. So being around the people I want to be around requires some leverage.

Writing is a career I happened upon while trying to find my way around the existence God gave me. Sometimes I feel like I'm in the wrong life.

My cousin Amir, now he's living the life that's supposed to be mine, through and through, at least *now* he is. As an internationally known R&B singer, his life was once upon a time somewhat appealing. But now, as a blockbuster golden boy in Hollywood, I would do anything to trade with him.

"Caramel Macchiato with two caramel chews?" the barista shouts next from her station.

I glance ahead to see how many more patrons are in front of me. Only three, finally. I've been in line for close to ten minutes and like every day, I'm getting annoyed being the last person to be served.

I wouldn't need to deal with this as editor. I'll send one of the interns down here to fetch my coffee tomorrow morning. Thankfully, I never had to do it for any of the higher-ups at For The Culture when I interned two years ago. Perks of my big cousin, I'm sure.

Since I still have some time before I can place my order, I return on my phone with a goal to check out For The Culture's website.

Daily, it's like a rush to see if I've made the homepage. Getting a feature on the glossy mag's front cover is damn near impossible, although I achieved it last autumn, to my surprise. For me and all the other staff writers, getting on the magazine's homepage is a more achievable goal.

For The Culture is a monthly lifestyle magazine that covers culture, entertainment, fashion, and beauty. My area of focus has always been entertainment. Attending red carpet events, interviewing celebrities, writing about the latest movie and song releases, while injecting just a small dose of gossip is where my byline appears. The most popular section in the magazine isn't entertainment at all, to my horror. It's the culture section and mostly lifestyle topics. And for the past few months, a writer, Dee Ellis, has been showing her ass by showing me up on the online site's carousel.

I roll my eyes when I see her byline, yet again on the homepage. Never even met her. That's because she doesn't show up at the office. No one has met her as I discovered through my internal investigation. She's this incognito do-gooder who prefers to remain faceless as not to steal attention from the stories she covers.

"Large black coffee with two sugars," the barista shouts this time.

Technically, Dee didn't even write her published pieces. I mean, she *writes them*, of course, but there isn't any creativity to them. She speaks to random black women around the city, allows them to tell their stories which are usually of triumph or survival, and all Dee does is curate them. The articles are only 1000 words, and the photos of these Plain Jane women look like a grade schooler shot them with a cracked screen flip phone. But yet, her articles get the front page.

I take a deep breath and try not to scream.

Dee can literally sneeze on an article and the thing will go viral. I can slave over an interview, transcribe it word for word, perfectly, which takes me hours by the way, and all I get is a text ad-size appearance below the carousel. Not even a photo to accompany my shit.

But that was okay.

In an hour, all that would change.

The editor position belonged to me. I know as much since the last editor hinted at it before her departure from the magazine. And I would not get the job because my cousin co-owns For The Culture, although that helps a lot. I'd be getting it because I worked for it and earned that position.

So, Dee could have the front carousel. I'm moving on to bigger and better things.

"I might not allow your articles to be on the carousel when I'm editor-in-chief, anyway." I whisper to myself, a sly smile accompanying my words.

I'm next in line, and smile at the barista. She knows what I'll order because I've been ordering the same thing for the last three years. All I plan to do is greet her.

The moment I lift my foot to step forward, the scent of something more heavenly than coffee invades my space.

It's cologne, a scent I've never smelled before and that smells expensive. The expensive you can't just swing by the store to "pick up." Appointments only, and they serve you champagne and chocolate truffles on arrival because they want you so comfortable, you'll want to stay longer and spend more. Because not only the cologne is expensive, in fact, the cologne is the cheapest thing in the store. But none of that will matter if you're too financially insecure to step a foot through the door even though the salespeople are beautiful with their welcoming smiles and—

"Excuse me," the deep voice starts, putting a stop to my retail fantasy. "I apologize for doing this but..." He shifts his eyes off me and onto the cashier. "Can I get two large black coffees? I can add the milk and sweetener myself. I'm running late."

I glance at him, then to the cashier, then back at him again.

He is *gorgeous*. Absolutely a work of fine art. Collector's piece. All the facial makings of a black male soap opera icon to rival Shemar Moore and Kristoff St. John in their youths. Dark black curly hair faded on the sides; deep brown eyes so dark they appear black. Skin the shade of milk and coffee I like my cup of caffeine to resemble when I'm preparing it. He's several inches taller and towers over all 5'3 of me. He is a walking and talking fine ass mannequin too. He wore a simple dress shirt and slacks, with his sleeves rolled up, of course, because how else would an Adonis dress?

His only flaw?

His ass *skipped* the line.

"*'Excuse me'* nothing," I bark.

He turns to me, and we lock eyes.

"I'm sure everyone who stood in front of me was running late before they ordered." I lower my shades down the bridge of my nose and look him up then down. "What makes you the damn exception?"

For a moment, he says nothing. Crushed ice and coffee are blending. Fresh ground coffee beans are brewing as silence settles between us.

"Two large black coffees," the cashier says, breaking my focus.

When I point my eyes in her direction, she's holding out two paper cups with lids on them in each hand, waiting for this guy to take them.

My jaw drops at the sight of her disloyalty.

She's not even taking note of my shock. How can she? Her focus is entirely on him, and she practically has hearts in her eyes.

"Eboni!" I stage whisper. It's like I said, I come here all the time and she's usually the one who takes my order.

"Thank you so much," the gentleman says to her. He accepts the cups from her hands and places them down on the counter below him.

"I'll pay for her order too," he adds, using his thumb to gesture at me over his shoulder. "How much is everything?"

"You will not pay for my order, thank you," I grit out. *The audacity of him to be this fine and rude.* "You can't buy *me*. Like you can't buy the class you clearly lack."

He glances at me over his shoulder before turning to face me again. The gentleman dips his hand into his slacks' back pocket, retrieves his slim leather wallet, slides out a gold Amex card, and hands the stainless-steel credit card to the cashier while still maintaining eye contact with me.

And then he does the one thing that forces me to take an extra breath to remain upright on my feet. He smiles, and the brother has a smile like Rome Flynn. Dare I say even better than Rome Flynn's?

"I meant no disrespect," he says, studying my expression. "I'm running late to an important meeting. I only needed two plain coffees." His eyes abandon mine and are now coasting. Moving over my breasts, hips, and thighs in the most respectful but lustful way, and it is heating me up instead of pissing me off.

The fuck?!

"I'd be more than happy to buy you whatever you want."

And he's speaking my love language?

I'd orgasm if I wasn't in a room full of people, I'm sure.

I shut my eyes tight to refocus. He's disrupting my frame of thought.

I can't even find the words to respond.

I can't even think straight!

His face, his smile, what he's just said - honestly, his entire being is throwing me off in a way I'm not used to.

His card is back in hand, and he slides it into his wallet, dropping the wallet back in his pocket while turning to pick up the cups of coffee. He says to me, "I really have to go. I apologize."

And with that, he's off. Swaggering toward the area of Ground-house that has the various options of milk and sweeteners to choose from.

Even his walk is attractive.

Okay, who the hell is this guy? And what the hell did he just do to me?

I peel my eyes off him and focus on Eboni.

"Hey, Mykal." She smiles, pecking at the keys with her fingertips on the touchscreen that operates the cash register. "A medium cocoa and espresso with a dollop of chocolate whipped cream on top, right?"

"Well, yes, *that's* right, but *you're* wrong." I place a hand on my hip. "How could you let that man skip me like that?!"

"Girl, did you see him?!"

Yes, I did. He was...

"Gorgeous," she adds. "He was *ab-so-lute-ly* gorgeous. Now *that* right there? Is a man."

"Eboni, please." I run my fingers through my short tresses. "There wasn't a thing special about him."

Big lies.

"Ha! Yeah right. That man was unreal, and you know it," she insists.

And I can't argue with that.

"You should have let him buy your coffee," she continued. "He clearly has it. The credit card he gave me is not like the plastic ones you hand over. It's metal and heavy and..."

I tune her out as she moves about, making my order. Since I'm the last person in line, she ventures from the register to handle it herself like she usually does.

As I wait, I play back what just happened, trying to figure out why I'm intrigued instead of pissed off at that very fine gentleman who seems to have materialized out of nowhere.

Damn. I can't wait to see him again.

Two

"Corey," I say the moment I see him sitting at the edge of his seat on a long white couch. He's writing on a large legal notepad he balances on a wooden coffee table inches below him. Corey glances up and does a double take when he recognizes me. "Dez!"

In my hand are two paper cups of coffee. Before he can stand to greet me, I extend one hand in his direction. "I remember you saying you were just stepping off your jet and heading straight here when we last spoke, and I figured you might not have had time to pick up a cup of coffee. Black with a splash of milk and two sugars, right?"

"Man," he replies, accepting the cup from me, "people would never guess who you are or where you come from based on the things you do for others."

"Oh, stop it."

"I'm serious. I wish my interns had even a pinch of your generosity. This was thoughtful." He takes a sip. "I needed this for real."

"No doubt and no problem." I sip mine and revel for only a

moment over how soothing it is as the liquid caffeine blankets my insides and offers that warm hug feeling I know and love. "I'm familiar with what jet lag and an early morning start can feel like."

"Well, thank you, this is beyond appreciated." Corey extends a hand and I follow the length of his arm, which gestures out into the office. "Welcome to For The Culture."

The space is large, with long tables and sleek chairs on either side. Opened laptops sit atop those tables with writers in front of them, either tapping at the keys or conversing with each other through the gaps between the lines of computers. Overhead, pendant lights hang from the white cement barreled ceilings. The conference room with walls made of glass is straight ahead and a few feet to the left and spaced apart are two offices, one big, the other considerably smaller.

"The larger one is yours," Corey says, standing from his seat on the couch.

"I really appreciate the offer," I tell him. "I've watched the growth of this magazine skyrocket since you launched it five years ago and I'm proud of what it's become."

"Thank you, brother." He smiles with pride. "I'm happy with what it's matured into, too. And I'm confident with your ideas, it'll move in the direction I've always envisioned since Woodson prep."

Corey and I attended the same private high school and became fast friends during our sophomore years. He was a fan of my father's, which was par for the course in my youth, and I loved hearing Corey's innovative ideas since he had so many at such a young age. Besides the magazine, Corey has investments in a women's basketball team, rental basketball courts, a chain of seafood restaurants, and is currently working on a plan to build an elementary school. And all at 33-years-old. He is the ancestors' dream in wakeful form, and I consider myself blessed to witness it all.

"How's your dad doing?" Corey asks.

"He's great," I answer quick so Corey won't find the truth in my eyes. "Writing, as always."

"Even when retired," Corey adds, smiling widely. "I've read a few of his entries on his blog. It's so impressive that he's gotten with the times.

A lot of writers in his tenure wouldn't even consider touching a blog, much less have their byline appear atop a blog post."

I inhale a deep breath. "That is true. I gather he just knows it's a way to keep the cogs moving, you know? Just to continue to hone his skills with words."

"I'm here for it all." Corey claps once. "Every entry is a treat."

I nod, swallowing hard while avoiding eye contact.

"Anyway, let me show you around."

Corey leads the way, the leather bottoms of our shoes tapping against the dark cement floors.

"How many writers work here?"

"About twenty," Corey answers. "Five of which are interns. We'd love to expand and add on new writers in Q1 of the new year but we may need to upgrade the space first."

I glance around myself, eyes falling on melanin skin tones of various shades creating at their desks. This is exactly what my father envisioned when he was once just a writer like them. He worked at the Holidae Press, one of the largest newspapers in the country, in the same league as the New York Times. He covered stories relative to black culture and found much success covering a news story that practically got swept under the rug by major media outlets. It was a raw piece about a black girl kidnapped by a family friend and held for ransom. She was missing for days. Her parents and friends were looking for her, after the authorities abandoned their search. Her family hoped and prayed her picture would make the news so that finding her would be easier but it never happened until my father got wind of it and published a piece in his column. A day later, the story got traction, everyone curious as to where this little girl was. Interest grew. Her picture made major news. Neighbors near an abandoned property recognized the assailant's face from his mug shot and gave a tip to the cops who tracked the assailant and the little girl down. The whole thing made national news and was the flint stone that lit up my father's career. After that, the most respected journalists referred to him as a living legend.

"By 'we', you mean Amir?"

Corey nods as we continue down an aisle in the office. "Despite how busy he is - new baby at home, working on a new album, and plans to star in a new film - he's always checking in on his investment."

"Stand up guy."

"Extremely," Corey adds. "When he agreed to go half on this mag, I thought he was doing it just to have an avenue to promote himself and his projects, but he hasn't had a single thing featured. Hasn't requested he be on a cover or have one journalist here interview him. He operates as a silent partner, but he's very hands on, requesting nothing in return. He is as stand up if not even more stand up than most people believe."

I nod, impressed; although I knew all of this already. Amir and I have been close friends for years. "Sounds like the Amir I know."

"Well, you know what they say – 'birds of a feather flock together.'" He chuckles. "Facts, since you also have experience with working silently even when you are doing so much good."

"Can't imagine doing it any other way."

We stop in front of one of the two offices I spotted when I first walked in.

I point. "Your office?"

"I don't have an office here. I always work from the couch where you found me because I like to stay out of the hairs of the people who make this magazine possible."

I glance at the office again, then back at him. "So, this is—"

"Your office."

I turn to the office encased between glass walls. The door is glass as well and from where I stand, outside of it, I can view the entire office, including the incredible view of Midtown New York City.

"This is amazing."

An Apple computer sits on top of a glass office desk, a prominent leather chair behind it. Someone positioned two leather armchairs on the opposite side of the desk. Already I've decided how I will have it decorated but will request the help of my interior decorator to ensure my vision for the space comes to life on short notice.

"I'm glad you like it." Corey says with his signature wide smile. He pats my back and adds, "Now let's go introduce you to the staff."

THREE

The elevator pings and the doors peel apart on the 17th floor. Instantly, a wave of fingertips colliding with computer keys reaches my ears. I step off and keep straight, heading for my desk.

As always, natural light pours in through the warehouse-sized windows. The backs of heads and tips of shoulders are visible at practically every computer.

For The Culture started in 2015, created by my cousin Amir Jones and his close acquaintance and rich friend Corey Barnes. They wanted a magazine that covered black entertainment and lifestyle topics viewed through our lens and told with our voice. African Americans control less than five percent of broadcasted and printed media but African Americans are most likely to trust the media more than their racial counterparts. And for that reason, For The Culture's purpose is to protect the black image, nurture, cultivate, and promote it by our rules and in the brightest of lights. A literal ancestors' dream.

If you can't tell already, I *love* it here.

"Hey girl, hey," Asha greets when I'm feet away from my desk.

"Hey, hey, hey," I reply, removing the gold chain strap of my purse off my shoulder to place the quilted accessory on my table.

My desk has always faced the editor's office. Those glass walls and door with the windows that act like a picture frame for the view, taunted me every day. I've wanted the editor's position since I started here three years ago as an intern and today as a staff writer, all my hard work would pay off.

"Tell me about last night," Asha insists.

I crack a smile. "I literally just walked in."

Asha Davis is the coworker-friend everyone wanted. Funny, reliable, and always down for drinks after we clocked out. Happily married with three kids, she loved inquiring about my adventures and single girl escapades. One of which being my visits to this exclusive property out in Long Island - Chateau Luxure.

"I know you went to CL last night."

I smirk while sliding into my seat. "And how do *you* know that?"

"It was singles night and you never miss singles night."

"Hmph." I lift my laptop's lid. I am less than an hour away from having a desktop computer. I hated my laptop and always wanted to sit at a proper desk, in a real chair, and type on a real computer.

"So spill it," Asha insists.

I twist in my seat to face her. Not swivel because this stationary desk chair never swiveled, unlike the editor's chair.

"His name was Byron," I start whispering, to her delight. "He was a jerk like most of them, but hung and wild. Used his hands to bound my wrists so he could eat me out to his content long after he made me come."

Her jaw dropped.

"He secured the crimson room," I continued, balancing my elbow on the table to lean my cheek into my hand. "He was an ass man, couldn't keep his hands off mine. Instructed me to get on all fours all so he could run his hands up and down my ass, wiggle my cheeks back and forth, and slide his finger down my crack extra slow. Thank God I waxed."

Asha snorted a laugh. "And the sex?"

"*Meh.*" I fan my hand in the air once. "It's always *meh*. Any man who can afford to enter CL is pretentious, paid, and they rarely prioritize satisfying the women they're with. They're the ones often getting satisfied because members of the opposite sex want to break their back, sprain their jaws, then jump through hoops to please them all so they can get chosen. You already know. I rode him most of the time." I shrug. "Used him as a sex toy and got off twice."

Asha nodded. "Makes sense."

"Now I know for a *fact* that if Pryce and I went all the way the night we ran into each other, that would have been the first time someone blew my mind to epic proportions at CL. That man vibrates big dick energy and seems like he's all about people pleasing in the bedroom."

"Hmph," Asha huffs.

"You know he was almost mine, right?"

She sighs, annoyed. "*I know* Mykal. You've only told me one hundred times. This being the one hundredth and one..."

"I was this close." I pinch my fingers partially closed, then roll my eyes. "I saw a photo of him and his wife this morning and they're decent together, but I know I would have been better on his arm. She's practically a troll."

"A troll?" Asha hollers a laugh. "His wife is gorgeous and a really sweet person. I saw this interview with her on BET the other night. She's extremely genuine. Like an authentic human being. She's refreshing."

"Please." I suck my back teeth. "Take away the gray eyes, big hair, and curves, and you've got a regular ass woman who tries way too hard."

Asha pinches the bridge of her nose. "Can we talk about something else? *Anything* else? I hate having this conversation with you. Which has been occurring too much as of late."

"I'm just saying." I focus elsewhere.

"Let's talk about this promotion and what you plan to do with that office."

A smile pulls at my lips.

"I already know you're going to hook it up like you've hooked up your apartment downtown." Asha's brown eyes lighten up, the apples of her cheeks rise as her lips reveal a sparkling smile. My work friend, as I like to call her, is beautiful with dark black hair she never wears down and a body she refuses to show off. She handled the accounting at the magazine and although we work in different departments, we clicked upon first meeting years ago in the break room on my first day. She's older by three years and doesn't judge me for my youthful choices. One of the sweetest people at For The Culture who I actually enjoy hanging around outside of work, too. Her family always comes first though, and she will cut an outing short quicker than Usain Bolt reaching a finish line if she's needed at home. She has the life I admire, but that I know can't be my reality. Not with my big plans.

"Oh, you already know I'm going to beautify that space." I turned to face my computer. "I ordered a palm tree plant to place in the corner, right beside the window. So much light pours in through that window. I'm pretty sure it'll grow a few feet by Christmas. Then I'll get a few more plants so it resembles an oasis."

She inhales a deep breath and closes her eyes briefly. "I can't wait to see it and to have a new place to escape to."

I giggle, tapping into my email. The second I access the mail system, I spot the correspondence from Corey Barnes requesting my presence in the conference room.

"When is the meeting, anyway?"

"Right now." I push my seat back to stand. "Just received the email."

Asha squeals with excitement.

I giggle. "I know!" I point my attention at my desk. "Farewell, desk and laptop. Wish I could say it's been real, but I'm too happy to leave your raggedy ass."

Asha's amusement echoes around us when she stands to her feet too. "I'll walk with you. I have to send out a few emails from my desk."

"Cool."

"Will you act surprised?"

"Oh, of course." I peer her way. "I've been practicing my stunned face all morning."

I drop my jaw and press my hand to my cheek. "See, there's that one. And this is the other one." I cover my mouth with my hand and gasp loudly.

Asha chuckles. "You are too much."

I snicker as we near her desk. "I'll read the room and will decide which surprised reaction is appropriate for the moment."

"Stop by and see me after. I wanna hear all about it and then check out your new office. Lunch is on me to celebrate after."

"Done and done," I promise. "See you then."

I continue down the walkway alone, closing the space between myself and the glass conference room door that's only a few feet away. The closer I get, the more in view Corey becomes as he sits on one side of the conference room table. I immediately notice the body sitting beside him.

I approach the door and pull it open, and my eyes widen with familiarity and shock.

"You!" I utter, pausing in step, absolutely stunned.

FOUR

I settle in my seat at the sight of her. Down at the coffee shop, she caught my eye. Petite but statuesque with a face that resembled a brown porcelain doll. She intrigued me before we exchanged a single word, so to see her standing only feet away from me again caused my heart to beat a little harder and a smile to pull at my lips.

I watched as Corey's eyes bounced between her and I. They finally landed on me again as he pointed a finger at her.

He asked, "You two have met?"

"Briefly," I answer, eyes still locked with hers.

Her mouth puckers at the sides and if steam could whistle from her ears like a kettle, it would.

"Down at the coffee shop." I break eye contact with her to focus on Corey. "I was rude *and late*," I add, glancing at her, then refocusing on him. "I needed to grab coffee for you and myself and I skipped the line."

Corey snorts a laugh before covering his lips with his hand, then holding up that same hand in apology to her for laughing.

"Well, let me do the honors of formerly introducing you two." Corey gestured her way. "Mykal, this is Desmond Ellis III, Desmond, this is Mykal Jones."

"A pleasure," I say, bowing my head.

She says nothing. Only remains at the door, this time with folded arms. If her eyes could shoot daggers, they would've done so and right through my eyes in that moment.

"Mykal," Corey says to her, "will you come in and join us?"

"Of course," she answers. Mykal inhales a breath next and takes steps toward a seat, two chairs down from mine on the opposite end of the table. And when she sits down, she points her beautiful browns back on me.

As far as I knew, the meeting would only be us three. Corey gave me the heads up days before scheduling our sit down.

"Thank you both for joining me today," Corey says while folding his hands on the conference table. "You two have been very instrumental in For The Culture's success this past year, so I couldn't imagine having this meeting with anyone else."

Her brows furrow when she shifts her eyes off Corey to me before refocusing on Corey.

"This has been an exceptionally fiscal quarter," Corey continues, "And I know neither one of you as writers care for the logistics of it all, but I want you two to know that your words have translated into higher revenue by subscribers to our print editions and increased page views on our webpages. Excellent work."

I found it impossible to pull my attention away from Mykal. Even with my father's voice echoing from the corners of my mind.

Stay focused, son. Everything in order and time. Women are to be enjoyed, not to distract you.

But this one who sat before me might have to be the exception.

Her skin is flawless. Cocoa brown hue without a single blemish. She wore a pair of high-waisted black jeans, and a silk black v-neck tank tucked in the waist. A long bright yellow blazer covers it all, but she would need a cloak to hide that ass. She is thick *everywhere* it counts. Mykal has some spice to her too, something I noticed from the coffee shop. A chic haircut that reminds me of Halle Berry's mushroom pixie from the movie *Strictly Business* completes her look. The woman is stunning.

"I'm sorry, what?!" she asks Corey, her eyes widening. "I couldn't have heard you correctly."

I direct my attention his way, grateful for the opportunity to tune back in.

Focus.

"I said Desmond has been writing under the pen name Dee Ellis," Corey repeats. "And since his articles have appeared on our magazine's website, readership has increased significantly. Tripled even."

"*You're* Dee Ellis?" Mykal looks my way. "*The* Dee Ellis." She jerks her head back. "Dee Ellis is a *man*?!"

That makes me chuckle. It's funny because that's exactly what I've wanted to conceal. I've intentionally worked toward making a name for myself, wanting readers to be attracted to my content through my words and not my name. I am my father's junior, and his reputation proceeded him and sometimes me. So a pen name only seemed right.

Returning to the present, I felt a searing gaze on me before I spied Mykal's way again to find her eyes piercing mine. She is an intense presence that most people would likely find intimidating. *I* am a fan.

"Mykal, as an intern, you went above and beyond to best your peers," Corey says, smiling widely. "I'll be honest with you. When your cousin recommended you for the intern position three years ago, I wanted to say no because I thought *you* thought you would skate by here on just your relationship with the co-owner of this magazine. But you worked harder than the other interns when you interned. So hard, you turned your credit-based internship into one that was paid, an exception FTC made only for you. And you earned every penny back then."

She smiles with pride while perking up in her seat. Her neck is long and model-esque. She has great posture. Like a woman who took etiquette classes religiously as a little girl.

Focus, Dez.

"As a staff writer, Mykal," Corey adds, "you've doubled your efforts and for that, you've earned your seat in this meeting today."

"Thank you," she replies softly.

"I called this meeting because I wanted you two to meet formerly," he continues. "You two will work closely together in your new positions."

I got a position I'd like to work with her in.

Focus!

I pinch the bridge of my nose, hoping to release those thoughts.

When I lift my gaze again, I see that Mykal's eyes are lit up. She is attentive and deeply engaged in what Corey is saying. Dare I say excited? My eyes wander down to the curves in her breasts. The peaks tease me from the view in her v-neck.

Shit.

I shut my eyes for only a second.

I'm in trouble with this one.

"I'll start with you, again, Mykal." Corey opens a folder sitting on the desk beside his legal notepad. "It is unheard of for a staff writer to move up as quickly as you. But exceptional work deserves exceptional rewards."

She bites her lip while smiling.

"Therefore, the team and I have agreed to promote you to assistant editor."

She shoots up from her seat with her hands clasped to her chest. "Oh my God, thank—" She pauses. Her head tilts to her right, and she blinks twice. "Wait." Mykal giggles nervously. "I don't think I heard you correctly for the second time today. *What* did you say?"

"I said we have agreed to promote you to assistant editor," Corey repeats. "Congratulations!"

"*Assistant* editor," she repeats, doing her best to hold her smile. But as hard as she tries, it cannot reach her eyes.

"Yes, congrats!" Corey says once more. He turns to me briefly and gestures toward her. "She's so excited, she's stunned."

But I know that's not the case. It's something else. Personally, moving from staff writer to assistant editor in two years without working in other lower level positions in between is rare and damn near unheard of, but I've read her articles and can see there's a reason she's experiencing such a level up in her tenure at the magazine.

"I just thought... but everyone's been telling me that *I*..." She pauses again and shakes her head. "If I'm an assistant editor, who's the editor-in-chief?"

I clear my throat and slowly raise a hand, waving when we lock eyes again. "*That* would be me."

FIVE

That thing I said at the coffeehouse about how I can't wait to see him again? I take that back. All of it. I most definitely could have waited. In fact, if I *never* saw him again and, in the capacity, I now must see him, it would've been too soon.

My thighs swallow the impact of every step I take as I stomp my way back to my desk. This is *not* how I envisioned the day. I planned to return to my old desk glowing. Smiling ear to ear so hard my cheeks ache. But the ache would have been okay. It would have been temporary and soothed by the view from my new office.

I exhale all the air in me when I finally reach my desk and drop myself down on my chair.

It's hard to choose which emotion to grant access to in the moment. I want to trash my desk. Just swipe my hand across the surface and knock everything to the ground, but I also want to cry, like *really* cry until my eyes burn and are red rimmed.

"Son of a *bitch*," I hiss while slamming my fist atop my desk.

"Hey there editor-in-chief," Asha sings, pulling my attention away from my fury for only a second. "You didn't stop by my desk as promised."

I glance her way and the smile she wears slowly melts off her lips. "Oh no. What the hell happened?"

"New guy happened," I sneer. "New guy *happened* all over my hopes and dreams."

"Oh, shit! You know I saw him shortly before you got in, right? He's certified eye candy."

"Yeah, well." I throw my pen across my desk. "His ass is giving me a toothache. That asshole stole my job! *He's* the new editor-in-chief."

She gasps. "Say what?! So, you didn't get promoted?"

"I did," I whine while folding my arms and briefly pouting my bottom lip. "I just didn't get promoted to editor. I got *assistant* editor."

Asha clutches her chest and stifles an elated scream. "Mykal, oh my God! That's still awesome!"

"No, it isn't." I shake my head. "*No*, it is not! I wanted editor. I've been aiming for *editor*."

"Girl, do you know how uncommon it is to go from staff writer to editor in under five years? I didn't want to say anything but, you seemed so sure—"

"It's happened before," I argue. "Maybe not at For The Culture, but it's happened... before... somewhere... on this planet for sure. It's happened."

She sighs and smiles slyly. "You're acting like a spoiled brat, you know that, right? You might as well throw yourself on this floor and flail your arms and legs like an ungrateful child in the cereal aisle."

"I would." I pout for only a moment longer before lifting my eyes to her from my seat. "But I'm wearing Chanel and don't want to wrinkle my blazer."

"Oh my God, Mykal." Asha howls a laugh. "You got assistant editor. This is good news."

"But it isn't *great* news, and my father—" I stop myself and pinch the bridge of my nose. "Assistant editor is second best. Assistant editor wasn't what I was aiming for at all."

"Shoot for the moon and even if you miss, at least you'd be amongst the stars," she quoted. "Ever heard of that?"

"Please don't start," I snap back. "I don't need one of your internet quotes right now."

"Okay, so how about this?" She beams. "You are going to be working under one of the *finest* men in this office."

"Ha!" I release a short laugh. "He is *not* that fine."

Lies.

Big lies.

"Right." Asha grins. "He's fucking gorgeous. Don't even try to act otherwise. That's one of the first things I noticed when he walked in. One of the first things *every* woman here noticed. We've all been talking about him and his fine ass in the break room."

I huff. "Asha, married much?"

She cackles then slaps her hand over her mouth to mute her loud reaction.

Nearly two seconds later, my desk phone rings.

I peek down at the caller ID window, grit my teeth, then snatch the phone off it's dock to answer. "Yes?"

"Can I meet with you in my office in five?" Desmond asks on the other end of my line.

"Do I have a choice?"

He chuckles and my God, even that's sexy. "Bring a pen and pad with you."

Before I could say anything else, he ends the call.

I slam the phone down on the dock and drop my head back.

Screaming is what I want to do.

"What's up?" Asha asks.

"I have to go meet with your office crush," I reply, pushing my chair back from my desk to stand up. "*Can I meet with you in five?*" I try to mock in his deep voice. "*Ugh*, I hate him already."

"Mykal, play nice," Asha reminds in a serious tone. "You may not have gotten the position you wanted, but you got promoted. Gratitude is your genuine thank you to God."

"Oh?" I arch my brows and lean in. "And where do I place my complaint? Because this is *not* what I prayed for."

"Mykal," Asha warns. "You better not play with the most high."

I roll my eyes. "I have to go. I'll catch you later."

The walk to Desmond's office is long, even though his office is only a few steps away. On my stroll over, at least three colleagues congratulate me on my promotion. I'm sure they'd trade places with me in a heartbeat, but to me, assistant editor is a B position. Assistant editor isn't what I've envisioned, not what I was aiming for.

I'm feet away from Desmond's office, what would have been my office, when the view of the city comes into focus. My heart nearly sinks down to my toes. It's the most beautiful sight. A sight I've wanted for my own since I started interning at For The Culture. I push open the glass office door and almost shatter the glass as the door slams against the steel bar that holds up the glass walls behind it.

"That was fast," he says from behind the desk; correction, *my* desk.

He sits beautifully behind it though. With his squared shoulders and dark, diamond-like eyes. He is eye candy all right, a delight to feast my eyes on. Not a single flaw detected. And now with this office, he might as well call Vogue and inform them their next cover story is available to be photographed - him.

"Where's your notepad and pen?" he queries next.

I ignore him, walking further into the office, the glass door closing behind me. My eyes are everywhere after I've ripped them off him. I glance at the corner where I planned to sit my palm plant. The shipment with the greenery arrives in a couple of days, so I can't cancel the order, nor do I plan to. I'll have to figure out how to keep the plant alive in my office.

This office, though, is a sight to behold. Three hundred square feet of decadent space. Present is a wooden desk where an Apple iMac lives. Pendant lights hang above the desk, giving added space to an already large room. But it's the view of Manhattan for me. One that looks over the globe green heads of trees. I can see the taillights of yellow taxis and luxury black vehicles as they beep their way down the city's black asphalt. Farther in the distance is a view of skyscrapers and the beautiful Freedom Tower. At night, the glow-in-the-dark landscape is even more gorgeous.

Yeah, I'm going to cry.

"Mykal."

I turn to glare at him.

He smiles that warm, genuine smile.

I've analyzed his smile enough times to know it's genuine and from the heart. It reaches his eyes and makes them slant a little and does things to me that a simple smile shouldn't do.

"Care to take a seat?" He gestures with his hand to one of the leather armchairs positioned across from his desk.

He's comfortable here. I don't like that.

"Like you *took* my job?"

His brows wrinkle.

"I planned for this to be *my* office," I blurt. "This *is my* office."

His eyebrows arch this time. "Oh?"

"*Uh-huh.*" I nod. "But just like my place in line at Groundhouse, you have skipped me in line with this too."

Desmond leans back in his seat and pays me even more attention.

"I have been working toward editor for months. I've never seen you walk these halls, sit in a writer's seat, burn the midnight oil penning an article, only stopping when the cleaning company arrives. Hell, I've never even seen you until today. I would've remembered if I had."

He nods slowly.

"I *slaved* in my intern position and I have been breaking my back as a staff writer. Doing my job and everyone else's and here you come on day one, after walking through these doors once and you become the head honcho? How?"

He parts his lips to answer and I stop him.

"I know *how*. I *know* who you are."

"Okay, and who am I?"

"Your father is Desmond Ellis II. Famed journalist for the Holidae Press. I see he started his own blog to keep up with the changing times."

I can't believe my journalistic eye missed the obvious. Dee Ellis, *Desmond Ellis*. I didn't put two and two together until I learned Desmond wrote under a pen name.

Desmond's father is a living legend, a culture king who has created a brand of sophisticated journalism covering black culture. Everything from black fine art, current events, and politics, Mr. Ellis's byline has graced. No one has seen him in years, but he keeps his byline fresh in recent news articles, and his culture blog that several publications have mentioned and quoted since he started it only a year ago.

"You could have gotten a job anywhere, but you come here to step on the toes of us little people who have to earn our keep—"

"Need I remind you," Desmond cuts in calmly, "of who your cousin is and his role in getting you an internship here at this magazine?"

I kiss my teeth.

"Not to mention how unheard of it is for a staff writer of two years to move so swiftly up the ranks to become assistant editor in such a short time."

I approach his desk, lie my hands flat against the surface, and lean in. "I *am* the exception, *Desmond*," I snarl. "The last thing on my mind is who did what or what they didn't do before me. They're not me, and I pity them because of it."

His eyes drop from mine and land between the hills of my cleavage. I can feel his attention there, visually caressing the peaks while moseying even lower into the shadows. My nipples harden. I stand up tall immediately.

"I called you in here to discuss our first assignment," he explains, paying me every second of his attention. "I'd like us to hit the ground running in our new positions."

I blink repeatedly in response.

I wouldn't have thought about doing that. Honestly, I didn't have any story ideas if Corey put me in that editor chair. I just wanted editor and reasoned I had time to figure all that other stuff out when I take my seat behind the desk. Desmond's responsible and clearly has a plan for the magazine. It's commendable. I wouldn't tell him that, though.

"Don't get too comfortable," I instruct instead. "Don't bother changing this office. Don't even buy shit for your desk because I'm coming for this office and your position starting right now."

He smirks.

"Everyone knows assistant editor is *second* best. It's *second* in line, *second* in command, and I don't accept *seconds* in any form. I busted my *ass* from day one, writing articles under my God given name, not some *pseudonym* like *you*."

He chuckles.

"So hell yeah, I deserve editor. And I'll get it. So stay ready."

I thought for sure I'd shatter his cool veneer with that and he'd do me the favor of caving. I believed my aggressiveness would cause him to tighten his jaw, square his eyes, something, anything. Instead, his eyes are coasting again, south of my neck. Rolling over the curves of my breasts, wrapping around the width of my hips, before he lifts those eyes to greet mine again.

Silence falls between us for only a moment.

Desmond licks his lips, then folds the bottom one into his mouth, only to drag his white teeth over the fullest part.

"Okay, if that's what you want," he whispers. "Game on, Mykal."

My jaw drops and I blink a few times, stunned.

"Because I can see why you want this office so badly." He swivels in his chair to turn away from me so he can face the view out of his window. "This view is stunning. And you want to know the best part about it? It's all mine." He moans and I grow weak in the knees, needing to grab the neck of the armchair below me to stay on my feet.

Without turning to meet my eyes again, he tells me, "You can go, you are dismissed. We're obviously done here."

I want to snap. Charge at him and strangle him with his own silk necktie, but I'm too afraid of the jail time or worse, losing the position they have promoted me to. I also can't get wanting him out of my system despite being furious with him. So, I turn on my heels and storm out, slamming his door closed behind me as I leave.

Six

My car's wheels roll over the stone paved driveway. I lean my foot on the brakes to bring the vehicle to a stop. Manhattan and the promotion I've received at For The Culture is a memory now, especially since I've arrived here. I'm twenty-nine miles away from the office and in Old Westbury, Long Island, parked in front of the home I grew up in. The copper statue and fountain that once was a decorative statement piece my father purchased for my mother, sits at the center of the driveway, now a rusted green after patination occurred years ago. It sticks out like a sore thumb on the property. We have not turned the fountain on in years, decades, but its presence matters and is a reminder of a woman who was such a powerful force in our lives.

I shut off the car and inhale a deep breath. I glance at the colonial property, my eyes moving to one of the windows on the top floor. That's the master bedroom where my father spends most of his time. The light is on, so I know he's awake.

I'm out of the car and walking up the stone paved walkway. This property is my father's pride and joy and for a substantial reason. My mother came from money, never really having to work a day of her life, although she chose to. My father was the complete opposite. Raised in a two bedroom apartment in East Brooklyn, having to share his bedroom with three older brothers. He had to share everything. The only things that belonged to only him were his dreams. This home was his everything, his dream in waking life. His blood, sweat, and tears have gone into making every square footage of the property a home. Writing at his computer, penning first drafts that would blossom into some of the best pieces of his career with just a pen and spiraled notebook. Investigating reporting, interviewing the people many were too afraid to speak with. Asking the tough questions no one would dare ask. He was a journalist in its truest form with every fiber in his being. One who cared only for the facts and left his opinion out of the mix. Respected by many and imitated by most. A genuine writer. A man who parlayed all of that into something lucrative. He is the American dream and I couldn't be any prouder to be his namesake.

I have the key to the property and let myself in. It's dimly lit inside but not dark, so I can still see my way around. Honestly, I could close my eyes and still know where to go and what to avoid to get there. A Basquiat painting artfully greets me at the door like always. Abstract line art guide my eyes to the double banister stairs. In the air there is a faint married scent of cedar wood and gold amber. My father had this property built from the ground up when I was three. Two stories, five bedrooms with amenities like an in ground pool outback and a huge study with tall bookshelves that might as well kiss the ceiling. Obviously, I don't remember a time when I didn't live here, but I have the photos of when I was an infant, swaddled in blankets and cradled in my mother's arms in a studio apartment in Brooklyn.

I stop by the library, a vast study my father has penned most of his articles in. The room is also dimly lit, the curtains barely ever drawn back. The desk in the room is bare, with only a photo album on top of it.

"Mr. Ellis?" I hear behind me.

My lips curl into a smile before I can turn to the voice.

Mali stands there in her navy blue scrubs, matching blue Crocs on her feet, smiling back at me. "I didn't even hear you come in."

"I was quiet," I tell her, while sliding the album off the desk and making my way toward her. "How are you?"

"Great," she answers. "My daughter will be in town next week from Georgia, so I'm just planning for her arrival. I've already arranged for my stand-in. She'll be here to train with me starting tomorrow."

"Great," I tell her. "How was he today?"

"Good," she replies, her voice elevating an octave.

I know that isn't the whole truth. I know she says *good* not to worry me. As much as I didn't want to face the absolute truth, my father hasn't been good in some time.

"Great," I say, playing along. "Is he awake?"

"Very much so," she answers, gesturing toward the staircase. "He's just had a late lunch and is now catching up on the news."

"Then I'm right on time." I nod my exit, clutching the album in my hand as I make my way up the stairs.

The news anchor's voice grows louder the closer I get to my father's bedroom door. The hallway leading to the master bedroom is dark because it has no windows. The only light available is the sunlight shining through his window which lights my way to him.

The door is open, so I walk in. I find my father sitting upright in bed, his back flush against the black leather headboard.

"There is a lottery underway for housing in Greene Gardens," the anchor reports. "Representatives for the building project confirm that beginning in December, they will start accepting applications from black business owners who have an interest in opening shops in the new community scheduled to begin building in 2021. The Greene Gardens project is the brainchild of multi-billionaire Bryant Greene who has heavily invested in..."

"Hey Senior."

The moment my father hears my voice, he peels his eyes away from the mounted flatscreen. His brows knit at the sight of me, his eyes telling me the same thing they told me the day before, and the day before that, really for the past year whenever I visited. It's painful to deal with and honestly, some days I stay away so as not to feel like this. It's selfish and I know it's selfish, but it's my truth.

I swallow the knot in my throat and do my very best to maintain the smile on my lips.

"Your nurse, Mali, told me you did good today," I continue, approaching his computer desk chair and pulling it closer to his bedside. "That's great."

The second I take my seat, he sighs roughly. "And who are you?"

"A gentleman and a scholar," I reply, like always, without hesitation.

It's one of his favorite quotes from one of his most beloved books.

"Hmph," he huffs, a smile appearing slowly through the course salt and pepper hairs of his wiry beard. "The Catcher in the Rye is one of my favorite books. I used to read it when I was a child every night."

"I know." I balance the leather photo album in my hand and open the album's cover with the other. "You used to read it to me when I was five."

I open the album to four photos, all of which are of my father and mother. Each photo is a capture of them on their wedding day in the 80s. They're both wearing all white, in a church, beneath an arch covered in red roses.

My father's eyes light up and he smiles widely.

"My Phyllis," he starts, before laughing. "I bet that woman of mine is downstairs right now, just standing at the threshold gazing at that copper fountain outside."

"You know it," I lie, while turning to the next page. I don't have the heart to tell him otherwise, and that isn't the focus now. "Do you remember this?"

He stares at the new selection of photos, this one of himself holding me. I'm only hours old and wrapped in a hospital blanket. His gaze is entirely on me in the photo, smiling with all his teeth. The other three pictures are of me and my mother, me still an infant. One of those photos is of me swaddled in a blue blanket cradled in my mother's arms as she sits with me in that studio apartment in Brooklyn.

My father first started showing signs of Alzheimer's disease during my final year in college. He was working on a news story out of town and couldn't remember what hotel he was staying in. When his memory lapsed into more severe things, like forgetting his name and the year of his birth, he transferred everything into my name, including this estate. Family and friends had advised me to put him in a nursing facility, but I would never. Could never. This man was fifty percent responsible for the man I've become. The other credit goes to my mother. May she rest. She passed when I was seven, but I wouldn't tell my father that this evening. The way he smiles when he speaks of her warms me too deeply to freeze that over with truth.

Instead of putting him in a home as suggested, I hired a nurse to provide 24-hour care. Insurance wouldn't cover it, so I'm paying out of pocket, partially with funds from my trust fund I was granted full control over at 21-years-old. My father set the trust up for me when I was only one week old and when my mother passed, he added the funds, granted to him as the beneficiary of her life insurance policy, to a bank account he set up in my name. He never touched it, only added to it with his own hard earned money. So, I will continue to use his hard earned money, my mother's insurance policy money, and whatever difference I'll need to add to pay for his care for however long I need to.

To jog his memory whenever I visited, I always started our visits by showing him photos from the album. For a time, only showing him the page of his and my mother's wedding was enough. As of late, after my father's Alzheimer's transitioned from mild to moderate, I've had to show more pictures.

His eyes bounce from the photo to me to the photo again. I say nothing. Like always, I just sit there, ready to turn to the next page until he recognizes me. His son, the one who has every intention of continuing his legacy. That is the only reason I would start a blog and ghost-write posts under his name to keep his byline alive. The sole reason I accepted the editor-in-chief position at For The Culture so that I could gain as much experience heading a publication so I can start the next black-owned newspaper, something my father has wanted to do since he earned his degree in mass communication at Langston University. I wait for him to recognize me on his own, to show him as many photos as possible for him to put the pieces together, because I've learned to convince him of who I am, has never worked.

He examines the album photos again, stares for another second longer before locking eyes with me again.

"Son," he greets, extending his arms. And I go to him, laying the photo album at the foot of his bed.

"Hey dad." I wrap my arms around his shoulders, bringing him close to my heart.

SEVEN

Hours after my promotion, I couldn't wait to get out of work. The moment the clock struck 4 pm, I gathered my stuff and hightailed out of there to hail a cab to Tribeca.

"Hey Mo," I greet the moment I walk through the loft building's turnstile doors.

The security guard on duty glances up from what he's reading. "What's up Mykal!" He holds up what he's reading, and it's this month's For The Culture. Pryce Williams is the cover story again for the third time. I didn't conduct his interview for this one, but he looks the fuck good on it, like he always does.

"This is a good issue," Mo tells me. "Y'all have been putting y'all foot in these stories, man, I swear."

"I appreciate you, Mo." I point at the elevator. "Is my cousin in?"

"Sure is." He chucks his chin in that direction before looking at me again. "You can head up."

And I do. The smile I had to plaster on my lips for Mo, slowly releases as my mouth twitches into a sneer.

I am beyond pissed. I can feel the pressure in my jawline as I clench it tightly. I've wanted to scream since my meeting with Desmond and Corey where I received a promotion to assistant editor.

Assistant editor, tuh!

My disappointment is so immense I'd have to buy it its own seat on an airplane.

The elevator arrives on the floor I need, and I stomp off. Usually, my cousin's security takes shifts outside the door if they aren't inside, but knowing him, he wants to be alone with his little family and has sent them on their way for the remainder of the day.

I'm in front of the metal sliding door when I bang on it with my fist. Three seconds later, I hear the click of a lock and the steel loft door slides open next.

He's wearing a big, beautiful smile when he greets me with a, "Hey cuzzo."

"What the fuck, Amir?" I shout.

His smile falls off his lips immediately, and his eyes squint. He shakes his head and wags a finger for emphasis. "Nah, see, because there ain't no way I just opened my door to this. Let me try this again."

With that, he slides the metal door closed, right in my face.

I jump back and gasp.

"No you didn't!"

"Yes, *I* did," he taunts on the other side.

I approach again and start banging on the surface once more.

Amir slides the door open again, wearing the same Academy-award winning smile like moments ago. He repeats, "Hey Cuzzo!"

I suck my back teeth and push past him to enter his loft.

It's enormous, his loft. High ceilings and stone columns to hold those ceilings up. Gorgeous black art paintings adorn the walls and glass stairs guide the eyes up to the bedrooms. My eyes move into the living room, instead, to find his wife, Melodee, seated on the couch with my baby cousin wrapped in a blue swaddle blanket.

"Melodee!" I run to her. "The only cousin I love and who I know loves me back."

"Oh wow," I hear Amir whisper behind me. "It's like that?"

Melodee laughs as I wrap one arm around her and she does the same around me. I lean forward to place a gentle kiss on my baby cousin's forehead next, who is resting in her arms.

He is the sweetest little thing. We've all settled into calling him AJ Junior, although I think the name is a mouthful. He has the same light brown eyes and bow like lips as my cousin, Amir. His nose is all Melodee though.

"What's got you so turned up?" Melodee asks, brows furrowed with curiosity.

I sigh and fall back against the couch pillows. "This new guy at work stole my office and my job."

The wrinkles in her brows deepen.

"I got promoted today."

Melodee's eyes light up.

"But they, and by *they* this includes your husband, promoted me to a position I wasn't aiming for. I deserve more than assistant editor for all I've done at FTC."

Amir kisses his teeth as he swaggers past Melodee and me to head into the kitchen. "Ungrateful."

"Unappreciated," I snipe back. "I've busted my ass at the magazine."

"Which was why the team and I agreed on assistant editor," Amir explains to my back. "There was no way you were going to go from staff writer of two years to editor, Mykal. That kind of jump in position would've screamed nepotism and I don't get down like that."

I roll my eyes. "You *own* the magazine."

"Co-own " he corrects.

"And it would've been clear that I earned my seat as editor."

"Hmm, no." He stresses. "Desmond is more qualified. He's been writing for several years. At 33, he's accomplished a lot in the writing world."

"Under a pen name," I assert.

"Writing nonetheless," he emphasizes. "He knows journalism through and through. His father—"

"Aha!" I yell, turning in my seat to point at him. "I've been waiting for you to bring up that point. Will Desmond be editor under his pen name?"

Amir folds his arms. "Of course not."

"And I bet that was another reason you made him editor-in-chief. Because of his *father* and the fact Desmond is his *father's* namesake. When people read his byline on the monthly *letter from the editor*, it will remind them of his father and on that alone, the magazine will sell issues."

"At the end of the day." Amir plants his palms flat on the black granite counter in his kitchen. "Desmond is more qualified."

"More qualified, my black ass," I mumble.

"And yes, having his name appear as editor in the magazine will attract the right attention to For The Culture, which should matter the very most, right?"

"*Ugh*!"

"*Ugh*, back at you, too." Amir turns to his SubZero refrigerator, pulling out sandwich ingredients. "And yes, his recognizable name was *one* reason he got editor..."

"*The* reason, you mean," I interject.

"But," he adds, "to keep it real with you, Mykal, even if Desmond didn't get promoted to editor, it still wouldn't have been you."

I ball my lips and twist in my seat, turning my back to him again. Next, I fold my arms and pout out my bottom lip. I feel defeated and literally seconds away from punching the air.

"Now I know you've been working hard, cuz," he continues. "Desmond may have accomplished a lot by 33, but at 29, my cousin has earned her keep and is doing the damn thing too." By the sound of his words I can tell he's smiling without me looking at him. "That's the only reason I mentioned your name for the assistant editor position in a room you were not in. You are family and I love you, but business is business kid. I ain't gon' hook you up like that. There are people at the magazine who would question that decision. For The Culture is still a baby. We're just getting started. Stick around, and editor could be your next move."

"I hate it here," I whine, dropping my head back in defeat.

"You'll be aight," he replies. "Want a sandwich? I'm making a couple for Mel and me."

"Can't eat right now."

"Suit yourself, big baby."

As he returns to stating his case while preparing lunch for him and Melodee, Melodee scoots closer to me on the couch.

"So," she whispers, shouldering me. "Do you find him cute?"

I glare at her from the side of my eyes, really wanting to be pissed at her too, only for being married to Amir, but I can't. Melodee is one of those people who you just can't be mad with. Her big beautiful brown eyes always appear sincere and she has a smile that could melt the coldest attitude, especially mine.

"No," I whisper back. "He's not cute to me... he's hideous."

She purses her lips and I snort a laugh.

"You know I know that's a lie, right?" She asks.

"It's a big lie," I admit, dropping my head into my hands. "He's gorgeous. He's the fine that ain't even fair."

Her smile grows wider.

I press my fingertips to each of my eyelids. "He has the jaw structure and height of a model, voice of an actor, physique of a God... and that's with his clothes *on*." I lick my lips. "Someone said he's unreal and honestly, that's the best way I'd describe him too."

The apples of her cheeks glow from smiling so hard. She peeks down at AJ Junior to fix the swaddle blanket that is partially covering his face. "Do you think that's part of your frustration and another reason you're bothered by him, along with the obvious of him getting the position you wanted?"

I sit with the thought for a moment, wanting to lie some more but can't. "Absolutely. I can already see how working under him will be a challenge."

"Hmph." She shrugs a shoulder, swiping her hand against her face to clear it of one of her clumped coily curls. "What are you going to do? Assistant editor is an excellent position too."

"It's second best and I don't *do* second best," I explain as calmly as I can. "And since I can't kill him with my bare hands since that's frowned down upon, I guess I'm at a loss at what to do."

Melodee giggles and that makes me laugh too.

"I don't really know what I'm going to do." I twist my lips to one side of my mouth. "But what *I know* is that I'm going to get the editor position from him if I have to die trying."

Amir joins us shortly after placing a plate down on the coffee table in front of Melodee. "She's over here talking shit about me, huh, Mel?"

"Ain't nobody even thinking about you," I say, while holding back a smile.

"*Mm-hmm,*" Amir answers while leaning forward to place a kiss against AJ Junior's forehead then pecking Melodee once on her lips. That ends up not being enough, because he pecks her again before taking her chin between his pointer finger and thumb, then parting her lips with his to take their kiss deeper.

"Wow, right in front of company?" I wrinkle my nose before grabbing my bag. "It never fails with you two, even during *my* crisis."

They laugh on each other's lips before throwing a look my way.

Amir and Melodee's relationship has always been goals from the moment it started. The only reason I even cared about their relationship is because I adore Melodee just as much as I do Amir... I'll never tell him that, though. They are the most affectionate and sweetest couple. Some said marriage ruined things, but with them, things just seemed to keep getting better. Their relationship is the relationship I want to have with a special someone of my own, but I know it could never happen. No time soon, at least. Not with my goals.

"I'm out," I announce, standing to my feet. "Amir, thanks for nothing."

"Oh, word?"

"Love you though." I turn to the door to leave. "Love you too, Melodee. I'll call you later this weekend. Amir, I'm never talking to you ever again."

"Aight." He bites into his sandwich and with a full mouth, mumbles, "So, next week, right?"

"Shut up!"

"Love you back, Mykal," Melodee says through her laugh right before I step out. "And be kind to Desmond!"

"Okay, I won't," I promise as I slide the door closed behind me.

EIGHT

I arrive at my new office at For The Culture and I'm in here for all of five minutes when my desk phone rings. The desk is metal, the chair a mesh and leather cheap combo, and my view a direct look into someone else's office in the neighboring building across from ours.

I shut my eyes to keep from screaming. I did my best to see the bright side of the situation. Tried my hardest to find the blessing in all this so I could show gratitude for how far I've come in such a short time at FTC, but I just keep coming up short on that.

I peep down at the call window to see the familiar extension that should've been mine.

I click speaker and through my teeth ask, "Yes?"

"Good morning, Mykal," Desmond's honeyed bass booms through my phone's intercom speakers. "Can we meet in my office in five?"

"No," I answer, pausing for reaction.

"Great," he says instead. "I'll see you in five."

"I said—" The click on the line indicating he'd hung up left my words hanging in limbo.

I grunt. "This is bullshit."

I return to analyzing my new space. The office sucks; no way around denying that. There's no brighter side to see. Literally. The office gets no sunlight. That plant I ordered won't survive its first week here.

I scan the office once more, noticing that my desk can barely fit in the space. The office chair appears used as if they plucked the piece of furniture from one of the writer's desks. The only thing appealing about the space are the glass walls.

I check my watch and decide I will be three minutes late for no other reason than to get under Desmond's skin.

It's been three days since my promotion, and I'm still not over being snubbed. I got what Amir was getting at. And even though I didn't want to admit it, he was right. Promoting me to the editor position would have raised red flags for a lot of the other writers. Competition at For The Culture is real between us writers. We all want front page or at the very least a spot on the carousel on our magazine's homepage online. But only a selected few made it on that platform. And fine, it may have been a tad easier for me considering my cousin co-owned the magazine. I wanted editor though. Since I started interning at FTC, I wanted editor. The only thing I wanted more than editor was to write and star in my own musical off-Broadway. But since that will never happen, the editor position is a goal I know I can achieve.

I take another skim around the office, knowing I shouldn't because it'll piss me off some more.

"This is the ghetto," I mumble, pushing my seat back to stand up and exit my office.

The walk to Desmond's office is heavy footed. I'm practically dragging my feet to his front door.

The For The Culture HQ is quiet. It's always quiet at this hour. It's 6:30 in the morning. Most of the writers have been in since six. We start early because we are constantly catching up on overnight topics. Doing our best to stay on top of breaking news, evolving trends, and growing discussions about topics that matter to our readers. Not one day is the same in journalism and that drew me to this career. The unpredictability was my motivation behind me studying journalism and mass communication in city college. My father, however, thought studying journalism was a foolish career choice.

"Who writes for a living and actually earns a living doing it?" He'd ask in his usual condescending tone during dinner. The man owned a library of books that overflowed from the shelves, and he didn't miss a day of reading the morning paper. But my father would fix his lips to ask me such a question when most of his entertainment came from reading.

I inhale a sharp breath and exhale the air just as hard. I'll have to breathe the same air as him, my father, soon for dinner. I always ate at my parents' home at least once a month to appease to my mother's request for me to visit. If I had the choice, though, I wouldn't step foot in that house as often as I did. Especially after not getting editor. I'm sure that would be the discussion at dinner.

I'm steps in front of Desmond's office door when I see he did exactly what I told him not to do - get comfortable.

He's decked the office out in greenery. A plant sits on his desk. Another in the corner where most of the sunlight shines through. A smaller potted plant drinks the sun on a bookshelf that wasn't present three days ago, and a tall plant to the right of his office's entrance is waiting to greet me at the door.

If I wasn't pissed before, I am now.

I push through the door. He glances up from his computer screen to glimpse my way. The second I'm in sight, his eyes darken with something I haven't figured out yet while a smile tugs at the corners of his lips.

I'm going to need him not to smile at me. His smile makes it hard to hate him when he smiles at me like this.

The man's got style from the way he's set up this office in such a short time to his style of dress. He's clothed in a white linen button-down shirt he's tucked into perfectly pressed black dress pants. I only know this because, upon entering, he rolled his chair back to stand from his seat. And when he does, I realize his entire outfit is accentuated by these dope ass suspenders that only he can pull off. Of course, he rolled his sleeves up to show off the vein-lined muscles in his forearms. I hate myself for noticing.

"Mykal," he greets, gesturing to the leather armchair opposite his desk. "Please have a seat."

They can afford to give him a leather armchair for his guests, but I get stuck with the raggedy office chair that's a hybrid cross between cheap and tacky?!

I don't argue today because I'm so full of a feeling I haven't felt since my freshman year in high school when my friend stole the starring role in our school musical, from right under me. This feeling, like the one in high school, burns me inside and makes my heartbeat triple time. It's a feeling that has traces of betrayal, even though I know Desmond owes me nothing. The feeling is at war with something else, something I've never had to process before and it's throwing me off.

"I called you in here today because like I said last Friday, I want to hit the ground running in our new roles." He takes his seat behind his desk so easily and casually you'd assume he's been in this office since For The Culture printed its first magazine issue.

"I've been reading the articles you've had published since the start of your internship," he continues. "You're an exceptional writer."

My eyes soften at his compliment.

"You don't just write what you're told to write in interviews. You have a way of setting the scene, tapping into the five senses, giving the reader the feeling of being right in the room with the subject you're interviewing." He smiles while nodding. "You have a knack for story-telling and it shows. You'll be perfect to lead this next project."

I say nothing on purpose. I'm trying to control my breathing. It's one thing to hate someone, but it's another to maintain that hate while they are pouring into me so easily. I want to stay mad at him, but my resolve is thinning.

"You're not using your storytelling ability at its highest capacity though and I know how you can and beneficially for us both." He leans back in his seat and my eyes fall to the outline of his pecs against his linen shirt. The sight of just that sends a zing between my legs that I have to shift in my seat to calm.

"For the project, I want for you and the writers to create articles that all tie into the theme of unsung black entertainers. The actors, musicians, and vocalists overlooked by the broader entertainment-appreciating public, but who helped pave the way for the celebrated superstars of today. The Jefferey Daniels's, the George Cables, the Nina Mae McKinneys."

My breath hitches at the last-mentioned name. Along with being a bookworm, my father is a cinephile and loves watching old films. Nina Mae was one actress I remember falling in love with when I watched her in one of those films. It surprised me to learn from my father she was the first African American ever to secure a contract with a major studio.

I like Desmond's idea, I like it a lot. I wouldn't show it though.

"It'll take a lot of research and sourcing to pull this all together and I know it's a venture out of what you usually write for the magazine, but I have a hunch you and the team can execute this flawlessly."

He's assertive and forward thinking. It's only day three, and he's bursting through the gates, swinging. I'm impressed and annoyed and I guess I can't keep it under wraps, nor do I want to.

Desmond stops speaking and just stares at me from his seat. After a few seconds of silence, he asks, "Am I in this meeting alone?"

I clench my jaw and release the tension slowly. "I'm clearly here."

"Are you?" he challenges, leaning forward in his seat and closer in my direction. "I've presented to you a fully fleshed out idea and the only feedback I'm getting are crickets."

"You called the meeting," I retort while crossing my legs.

Desmond's eyes drop to them. My thigh, to be specific. My lemon-yellow pencil skirt rides up my leg and gather at my hip in my leg's crossed position. His eyes roll up from my calves and they are smoldering. I blink twice when I notice and try to swallow back my arousal when I recognize the look. To my surprise, I'm breathing heavier now and that zing from earlier has returned, causing me to involuntarily pull in my walls.

"Mykal, do we have a problem?"

"A *big* one," I shoot back.

He licks his lips slowly, and I make the glass wall my interest, sucking in a breath through my lips, wishing his tongue could lick me anywhere instead.

Get it together.

"So, the tension I'm sensing between you and me isn't all in my head?"

"No, it's not all in your head." I smile. "I hate you. *Very* much."

"Wow." He barks a laughs. "That's harsh."

"Most truths are and I have my reasons. For one, I thought I told you not to get comfortable here." I point around his office. "You've added things."

"It's my office."

"Subjective."

"Not really?" He points at the nameplate on his desk. "Not according to this name plate. It's labeled "editor" below my full name because *I'm* the editor. Which makes me your boss and whether or not you like it, or hate me as you've revealed, you are my subordinate and I expect you to act as such, respectfully."

I ball my lips together.

"Now you don't have to like the fact I'm the editor, but I need for you to respect it. We have a magazine to run here and it's imperative we run FTC right."

I inhale sharply.

"Now, give me some feedback," he orders. "Please."

I square my eyes at him, equally turned on and pissed at how direct he is and how much of a turn on it is to me. I squeeze my thighs together in my crossed legs position to calm the pounding happening between them.

"It's a great idea," I grind out. "The readers will love it."

Desmond stares for a second longer and I am damn near melting under his gaze and praying he doesn't notice.

"We should have dinner," he suggests. "To break the ice. We met under less than ideal circumstances, and first impressions materialized out of our controls. I'd like to fix that."

I consider it for a few breaths. How we met wasn't in the most ideal circumstance, I'll admit. But now I have something else distracting me.

I'm attracted to him when I should just hate him. He has something I want and I can't have anything distract me from getting it.

Dinner might kick-start something I wouldn't be able to control. We are in a work environment, so I have no choice but to behave. Alone,

I might not be so responsible. I want editor and can't have anything jeopardize getting it. Especially not something as simple as my attraction to a man I must make my enemy.

"You've already ruined my plans of becoming editor," I tell him. "I won't allow you to ruin food for me too."

He scoffs a laugh.

"Your unsung idea is great," I repeat. "I look forward to working on it." I stand from my seat, smoothing my skirt down, his eyes catching everything. "If that's all, I'm going to return to my small ass office to lick my wounds and regroup. It's taking a lot to sit on the other side of a desk I promised myself would be mine. Plus I have to go figure out how to keep a plant I ordered, and that arrives today, alive in an office that offers practically no sunlight and might as well be a windowless closet."

He leans back in his seat again, resting his right leg by the ankle on his left knee. Both of his elbows rest on each armrest as he brings his hands together and steeple his fingers over his lips. I'm waiting for him to dismiss me. I'm direct and I'm pissed but I'm not rude, so I don't want to walk out without being dismissed.

His eyes lock with mine when he says, "You know the writers here better than I do right now. Send me at least seven who you think can bring out the best in my idea and we'll take everything from there." He gestures to the door before focusing on his computer screen. "You're free to go."

I turn on my heels fast to leave.

"Thank you for meeting with me, Mykal," he says to my back and I pause in my steps. "Like I said, you're an excellent writer, and I'm sure you'll be a stellar assistant editor. I'm looking forward to working on this with you."

I glance at him over my shoulder, and he peeks up from his computer screen to meet my eyes and to offer a genuine smile.

I blink away and focus forward to pull open the door. Out of his office and walking to mine, I'm completely flabbergasted by how kind Desmond is to me, despite how unkind I've been to him from the start.

He's unreal, for real.

NINE

I pull over to the curb of my parents' home. It's 8pm exactly and I'm late. I'd be on time in any other household, but to my father, arriving at the time agreed upon, is arriving late.

I inhale the air in my car and release it like a lion's breath. I then lean forward to slam my forehead against the horn on my steering wheel. To say I've been dreading this dinner tonight with my parents would be an understatement. When it was clear I wouldn't get editor, I'd been dreading it. Dreading it because I've talked endlessly about getting the position. I still don't understand why I didn't get it when everyone around the office promised I was a shoo-in for it.

I roll my forehead against the steering wheel to look toward the house. It's a two story property in south Brooklyn. Your usual asphalt shingle roof and rusted metal fence framing the outside of the house with the lights on.

Even though I haven't told my father I didn't get editor, I'm sure my mother has, which is why I told her instead of him. I just couldn't bring myself to admit to him I got second best. So knowing she would deliver the news the moment she heard it, I played telephone with her.

I look to the passenger seat in my rental to grab my purse. Owning a car in New York is difficult. Aside from parking, insurance is a pain and so is having the money to buy it. I loved being able to rent a Mercedes on a Monday and a Ferrari on a Friday. It allowed me to dip my toe in the feeling of being rich and famous, since the actuality of that happening is close to none.

I inhale another deep encouraging breath, then grab a hold of the car's door handle to open the door and step out. The air is warm and slightly muggy, characteristic of summer in New York. Bright green leaves create a frame over my parents' home from the giant tree that has been there all my life. I take my sweet time climbing the weathered porch stairs. And when I arrive on the straw welcome mat in front of the house door, I press the doorbell, hoping my mother is the one who answers because I just can't deal with my father first on arrival.

"Mykie," she greets when she opens the door. "Come here."

Her arms are outstretched and I walk between them, closing my eyes the second her arms encase me.

My mother, Talia Jones, is what most would call the mom of all moms. It's like she read the handbook on how to be a mom several times and from cover to cover. She bakes cookies, she told me bedtime stories every night when I was younger, prepared and still prepares a warm meal every night, and she tucked me into bed at the end of every day until I told her to stop when I was a freshman in high school. She has always been around, always there for every milestone in my life. She is amazing... and everything I didn't want to be.

As picture perfect of a mother she is, she's also the picture perfect wife and that picture is only as perfect as the frame will allow. My mother is the quintessential wife who respects her husband and believes his word is final, even when he's wrong. This meant she barely stuck up for me whenever my father threw his insult parades in my honor. I can never remember a time when she stood in my corner and spoke out against any criticism my father dealt me. She was a great mom but also the submissive, dutiful wife and it seems I can't get one without the other.

I gag at the thought of following in her footsteps, but I love her so much for her big heart.

It conflicts me.

She runs her hand down my face and pulls me close to give me a kiss on both cheeks, one at a time.

"You look beautiful, Mykie," she gleams.

And so does she. At her 60 years of age, my mother doesn't appear older than 40. Her smile is radiant, her face plump, youthful and free of lines, and her spirit is as lively and calming as it was when I was a child. She is perfect, albeit for her lack of a voice. How she ended up with my father and still maintains her vows to him for over 30 years baffles me.

"You look beautiful too, ma," I return, inhaling the smell of food from the threshold. "Chicken piccata?"

She nods. "You're favorite. To celebrate."

I force a smile. "Ma, you didn't have to do that."

"I know I didn't *have to*. I wanted to." She takes me by the hand and ushers me inside. I wish we can just stand and talk outside for the rest of the time, but I know that isn't possible. She points at my pumps. "You know the drill. Shoes off, regardless of how cute they are."

I kick off my designer heels and sit them at the side of the door. The floor creaks when I walk on it en route to the living room. My parents never fixed the floors, they never repaired most things around the house. Just like the floors, every door in the house squeaked no matter how much WD40 they sprayed on the rusted hinges. My mother loves design and decor. She's who I get it from and why I've designed my apartment to rival clipped pages from home décor magazines. But as much as she loves to spruce things up, she doesn't, because my father finds anything that isn't a bill or basketball related, not worth spending money on.

The closer I get to the living room, the louder the game gets on TV. I spot my father seated on his tattered leather recliner watching a basket-ball game. It's the Bronx Ballers against the Golden State Warriors. Pryce Williams is on the court.

My father is a basketball fanatic, has been since before I was born. He's a new fan of Pryce, though, ever since Pryce started playing with the Ballers. There is no doubt Pryce and I would've thrilled my father had Pryce and I became a thing.

"Hey daddy," I greet at the entrance of the living room. "I see the Ballers are in the lead."

His eyes remain on the screen when he says, "And *I see* you're late."

I inhale confidence and exhale annoyance. "I was actually out in my car gathering my things."

And my sanity.

"You mean the rental car?" He asks, finally peeling his eyes off the TV screen. "That is not *your* car Mykal, so you shouldn't call something borrowed yours."

"You're right." I tighten my lips. "And I apologize for being late daddy."

"Hmph," he huffs.

Jedidiah Jones. Growing up under his roof was like living on a military base. Up at a certain hour always before the sun, addressing him in the proper way or suffer the consequence of belittlement. Failing is a crime and so is achieving anything that is second best. You're either number one or nothing at all.

He looks me up and down, taking in my silk deep v-neck top tucked into my lemon-yellow pencil skirt I wear beneath a contoured black blazer with the sleeves pushed up. I could've gone home to change after work, but I guess this is the only power I know I have over him. Being a woman and loving it.

I was supposed to be a boy...

Well, that's what my father told me on the days when I did something he hated, and he admonished me for it. An experienced doula known as the human sonogram in the labor and delivery community promised my parents they would have a son based on the way my mother carried me. My father was totally against sonogram machines in the late 80s and 90s because of alleged radiation risk claims, so he forbade the use of them during my mother's pregnancy with me. And like the dutiful wife she's always been, she never protested, only agreed to his quack wishes. So they trusted the doula who told them my alleged sex. And common sense wasn't so common because they believed her, convinced she had to know what she was talking about having supported hundreds of pregnancies before my mother was even pregnant with me. So, daddy picked the name, deciding to name his son after his favorite basketball player, of course. They foolishly decked the nursery out in blue. My parents naively purchased baby boy clothes, so much clothing some of the chest's drawers couldn't close properly, according to aunts and uncles who confirmed.

And then on November 26, 1990, I arrived, healthy with a head full of hair... and a vagina.

Me having a vagina devastated my father. He wouldn't talk for a month according to family.

Instead of being named Michael Jordan Jones, I became Mykal Jordin Jones, and the rest is history, or shall I say herstory?

My father has hated me for who I am since the day I was born. I don't know him to be anything other than this. Occasionally, an opportunity pops up for me to see a different side of him and out of curiosity of experiencing what love feels like from him, I go for it. But every time I put my hopes and my efforts into achieving that one thing I know would make him proud, it always backfires and never goes as expected. When I was younger, it was the role as Dorothy in my high school musical. A fail. Present day, the editor's position at FTC. Also a fail.

"Table is set," my mother's sweet voice cuts the tension between my father and I.

He grunts before using his rough hands to lift himself off the couch. My father has slimmed down since his heart attack three years prior. It was a scary feeling, believing that would be it for him. That he would leave this earth and our relationship be no better than it's always been. And you would think a life-threatening event like that would bring us closer. But it just made him colder, more sharp tongued, and even more anti-Mykal than ever.

We walk into the dining room and my face lights up. My mother has made all of my favorites down to the key lime pie.

"Wow, ma!" I squeal. "You didn't have to do all this."

"You really didn't, Talia," my father adds as he takes his seat at the head of the table. "These are the fixings for a celebration. Are we celebrating something?"

"Of course we are." She's beaming. "Our daughter has just received an amazing promotion. That is cause for celebration for sure."

I blush, if I can blush.

"Hmph," he huffs, sliding his chair closer to the table. "Not a promotion to editor like she's been talking our ears off about for the past few months."

"Intern to staff writer then to assistant editor in three years is unheard of, daddy," I correct as respectfully as I can, considering what I really want to tell him which is to fuck off. "It's the first time the magazine has done this."

"Please. The magazine is still an infant compared to the other active, grandfathered publications," he states, reaching for the piccata. "So them doing this for the first time isn't something to write home about, and you know it."

I shut my eyes briefly to keep from rolling them.

"I'm still trying to wrap my mind around why your cousin would even risk his illustrious, and might I add a solid reputation by allowing you to get this promotion when everyone knows you're indecisive and flaky," he adds. My father utters that so casually, it is as if he's commenting on the weather and not being unsupportive and rude. "Amir is always giving you charity, putting his neck out on the line for you, and for what? You claim you want to model, he puts you in his music video and you decide you don't want to do *that* anymore."

"Uh, yeah. After I attended an industry party and was almost roofied," I shoot back.

"You've always dressed provocatively, like you're dressed now. What were you expecting?"

"Wow."

"You say you want to write," he continues, "and Amir allows you to intern at your grown age at the magazine. This is after you took a three year break from schooling following your high school graduation to model, which you eventually quit, right? Only to stay in community college for five years, struggling to get your journalism degree of all things, which I still think was a waste. And even with that, I just know you'll decide soon that *this,* journalism, isn't for you either. I'm just waiting for the phone call because you never can be consistent with anything. I just hope you don't turn around and embarrass Amir one of these days. He's worked so hard to get to where he is. I would hate to see you ruin everything. Like always."

I catch sight of my mom, who's seated across from me. She shakes her head, then leans forward to place a warm hand on the back of mine. "I'm proud of you, Mykie. Your dad might not see how huge this is," she acknowledges, shooting daggers with her eyes his way when his focus is his food, "but I see how incredible all this is. I've seen how hard you've worked for this position. You've earned it."

"You're always coddling her, Talia," he chastises between bites. "That's probably why she lacks drive."

"I have plenty of *drive*, daddy," I grind out.

"Hmph."

"The only reason I'm not editor is because Amir and his partner see what value having the son of a superstar journalist would have on For The Culture. But the job *was* mine, through and through."

"*Was*, not *is*," he claps back before taking a sip of his water. I must cross my ankles beneath the table to anchor myself to my seat, so I don't lean to my right to slap the glass out of his hand.

Typical dinner at the Joneses. And this was a light night.

I pinch the bridge of my nose to gain some kind of composure.

The daddy-daughter relationships I would hear about never existed in this household. I can't remember a time my father has hugged me or showed any sign of affection. Tough as nails and there financially was all I got, nothing more.

We eat in silence for the next few minutes.

Maybe I'm a masochist because I still seek my father's validation. Even as I sit here hurt and bruised by his insults, I still have hope I can change things between us for the better.

I swallow my food and what little confidence I have left and announce, "I'm working on a piece for the magazine covering unsung entertainers. Nina Mae McKinney may be one subject."

My father's head lifts from his plate and interest brightens his eyes. "Is that right?"

Like I said, my father's a cinephile. A huge fan of musicals and old black and white films. Nina Mae McKinney appeared in *Hallelujah*, one of his favorite drama musicals he owned on VHS, so I knew that would bait his attention.

"Now *that's* fascinating." He lays his fork against the edge of his plate and threads his fingers together. "When do you work on that?"

"Soon," I answer. "I just had a meeting about it earlier today."

"Very nice." He nods with approval and for a split second, I feel... good.

"Whose idea was it to work on this?" he asks. "Yours?"

Well, that didn't last long.

"It was Desmond's," I mumble. "The new editor."

"Figured as much," my father blurts as he lifts his fork again to stab at his food. He takes another bite of his chicken piccata and adds, "You'll have to introduce me to him. I'm a fan of his father's writing. I know the junior must be an amazing writer too."

"He told me my writing is exceptional," I blurt, sounding as desperate as I felt.

"He more than likely was just being polite, Mykal."

I want to slam my fist on the table. Cry, scream, something to get this tension out of my heart and off my chest, but I just smile... more like grin and bear. I blink back my tears, and force myself to enjoy my favorite meal or what *was* my favorite meal until tonight.

At that moment, I'm quite decided.

Desmond's got to go.

TEN

The sun is bright and there isn't a cloud in sight as I dine outdoors. I'm at Blyss, a lounge and restaurant with a rooftop and outdoor street view seating, popular amongst the 9-5 crowd and celebrities who want to be unseen. Street view dining is a new offering at the restaurant and I'm all for it. Beneath a giant green umbrella and seated on a wood and wicker chair, I slice into my char-broiled sirloin, forking a piece of the well done meat into my mouth.

I'm not alone.

Across from me is R&B royalty and what many media mavens are calling Hollywood's new golden boy. But you couldn't tell by how easy-going he is.

"How's the steak?" Amir asks.

He's a great guy and a genuine friend. I met him at an event years ago when his star just begun to shine. I'd gained entry to a red carpet party for no other reason besides being my father's son and having his well-known name. No idea what I wanted to do with life. I was just floating from club to club in the New York party scene. Amir and I met through a mutual friend and I asked him if I could interview him and he agreed, granting me an unplanned and unstructured Q&A recorded on my cellphone. I had no magazine to shop the piece to. I was simply free-lancing, to my father's annoyance. My father couldn't stand freelance writers, convinced they were taking trained journalists out the job because of their cheaper rates and flexible schedules, but I always believed there was room for both.

The impromptu interview Amir granted me was the start of my journalism career. A now debunked magazine I shopped the interview to published the piece under my pen name Dee Ellis and I've made sure that all articles after received the same treatment. I struggled and still do to make a name for myself and I wanted to do it on my own and not as Desmond Ellis III.

"The steak is great." I take another bite. "You should've ordered it."

"My wife is doing this no meat for a month shit." He chuckles. "She wants to lose some of the baby weight and eat healthier, so to support I'm doing it with her."

I smile. "That's real dope. I like that."

"Thanks." He spools his linguini in marinara sauce around his fork and shovels the food into his mouth.

Amir is a stand-up guy. A family man these days, he doesn't make it out as much. He travels back and forth between California and New York and in both places, he's barely seen out and about without his little family. It's nice and admirable.

"You know what I like?" he asks, reaching for his napkin to clean his mouth. "This unsung entertainers idea."

I nod with pride. "Thanks, I appreciate that."

"You're always paying homage in innovative ways. I'm hoping you can maintain your column as editor too. On the low of course. You can continue to publish your column under your pen name, but I truly think it should stay. It's what For The Culture is all about."

"Oh for sure," I agree. "I would love to continue. I actually have a few new subjects lined up."

When I approached Amir to tell the stories of black women through photography and dialogue, he agreed to give me a platform at For The Culture. The magazine was fairly new, and I wanted to work my way up the humble way, give me something to build my platform off of. Photographing random black women on the streets of New York City and having them tell their stories of wins, losses, heartbreak, and triumph has given me so much purpose in and out of For The Culture. My mother would've been proud for sure, and that gives me peace.

"I hope Mykal isn't making things difficult for you, though," Amir comments.

My dick twitches at the mention of her name.

"My cousin can be a lot," he continues, "but she's a hard worker and delivers on all her assignments."

"Oh no, she's been no trouble." I move my eyes down to my plate. "Mykal's all right. She's been…"

I pause in speech when I lift my gaze in time to catch Amir's *yeah right* stare.

"Okay, yes, she's been a handful," I admit. "She's been more than a handful, actually."

Amir laughs, and I do, too.

"See," he starts, "if you would have said otherwise I would think something was wrong with her."

A flash goes off to my right, Amir's left. We glance that way to see three photogs in the distance, producing flashes from their cameras aimed at Amir. One of his security guards head off in that direction, covering the distance with large steps.

Amir points his fork in that path. "Sorry about that. Hopefully you don't mind being photographed."

"I expected it," I assure in response. "You're always so cool about it though."

He shrugs. "It doesn't bother me too much when it's just me but when I'm with my wife and my son, it's a problem, at least these days."

I glance that way again to see Amir's security guard flashing a flashlight in the path of the photogs' cameras, a tactic to cause a glare in their lenses and blur every photo they take. Two other guards remain within feet of Amir and me.

"Speaking of which, how is fatherhood?" I take another bite of my steak, adding the veggies to my fork this time.

"Bliss." He taps on the Blyss logo napkin beside my plate. I chuckle.

"Nah, but seriously," he adds, "fatherhood is a blessing I thank God for every day. It's wonderful when you're ready for it all even when you're really *not* ready for it all."

"I can imagine," I beam. "My father would tell me always how being a father was his favorite job."

"I feel him on that. My father and my relationship isn't as great as yours is with your father, but I appreciate my pops for the lessons. It's because of him, I knew exactly the kind of father I wanted to be to my son – a better one."

"That's real." I sip my drink. "Is your father brothers with Mykal's father?"

"Yup, but my father and uncle don't get along," Amir reveals. "They barely speak, if at all. They're different."

"Is that so?"

"Yeah, my dad's the artist type, flaky, inconsistent in relationships. He's flaky with everything, really. Whereas my uncle, Mykal's father, is super militant and disciplined even though he's fought in no man's army a day in his life."

"Interesting."

"That's part of the reason Mykal is as *difficult* as she is, for lack of a better word."

I lean in, intrigued by the prospect of learning more about a woman I haven't stopped daydreaming about since the day we met.

"She'll never admit it, but I know she works as hard as she does to make him proud." He shakes his head. "He doesn't take it easy with his only daughter and it shows. I know they swear pressure makes diamonds, but I suspect too much pressure pulverizes the stone before it can become anything beautiful to anyone."

"Hmph," I say low.

"But standing up for herself with him is something she has to take on for herself whenever she's ready, of course."

There's something about Mykal I like a lot. And I know what it is, but then I don't. She's beautiful, but I've been with tons of beautiful women. There's this vulnerability about her that I find impossible to pinpoint by name but that I clearly see she tries to hide and attempts to mask by being difficult, as her cousin Amir puts it. I almost feel compelled to protect it although I'm positive she'd never allow me close enough to do it. She wears a hard exterior but there's this softness in her eyes that tells me there's more to her story and the intrigue of it all, the fact she's not so easy to read gives me a rise at just the mention of her name.

And it shouldn't, not in our new positions. I've gotten into way too many affairs with women I shouldn't have even looked twice at. My father's secretary, one of his maids, an English major I tutored in college, and the list goes on with the violations. It's like I'm committed to shitting where I eat. The one thing that's been a disappointment to my father and the only blemish on my character he has repeatedly warned me about.

"Were any of them worth the risk? Because life happens after you know what, Desmond. Only risk it if she has potential, like we have discussed."

But I always knew they didn't. So, I made a promise to him years ago to do better and I've done well, but with Mykal and I preparing to work so closely as colleagues, I really couldn't tell if my word would remain bond.

"Is she seeing anyone?"

Amir's attention remains down on his plate as he spools another mountain of linguini around his fork's silver prongs. "Is who seeing anyone?"

"Mykal."

He stops spooling and his eyes slowly rise out of his plate to lock with mine.

I clear my throat. "Asking for work," I claim. "I'm going to be working her." I shut my eyes tightly, then open them again. "I mean working *with* her during late hours to bring this project to fruition in time to meet the approaching deadline and I don't want to keep her away from anyone if she is seeing someone."

"Oh." Amir shrugs again and resumes spooling. "Mykal doesn't share too much about her personal life with me, so I really don't know. Shorty got her secrets like no other."

"*Hmm.*" I nod. "Well, she's beautiful, so I wouldn't imagine her being without someone to tell her that often."

I regret the words the moment the final one leaves my mouth.

Amir stares at me for what feels like forever before he lays his fork against the rim of his plate, leans back in his seat, and places his elbows on each of the armrests on his chair. "Dez, are you feeling my cousin?"

I sputter a laugh, and he smirks.

"Because if you *are*, you know you can just *tell me* that, right?"

I lick my lips and look away, knowing that if I answer that, I'll admit something not only to him but to myself that I really am not ready to admit yet.

"Mykal's stunning," I acknowledge before refocusing on him. "That goes without stating. But I was just asking because of the long hours I plan to invest in this unsung project. That's all."

That's a lie. That isn't all. That is far from all.

Mykal has been living in my head rent free. She's been there for so long she's making a home there and I am more than willing to make her stay comfortable, too. Her petite but still statuesque figure is appetizing to the eyes, and I just knew she wouldn't disappoint if we took things there. I'm sure we'll set off alarms with the fire we have the potential to create.

"Aight." Amir leans forward to resume eating. "Be careful with her either way. She is not like other women and not to tell my family business, but she got baggage, a whole bell cart full of them. You're my friend so of course I gotta warn you if you're planning to step to her."

"Not to worry because I *plan* to keep things strictly professional between Mykal and I," I assured, but more to myself than to Amir.

ELEVEN

Heavy bass paired with light percussions pulse from the small speaker system in my living room as I stand in front of my full-length mirror. I press the dress I plan to wear against my frame and tilt my head from left to right examining. I know the dress will lay good on me. I spend an hour and a half, five days out of the week at the gym to ensure this. What I'm doing is trying to decide on the pink hue of the dress and if it's the color I want to go with for the night.

To say I am stressed is for lack of a more exact term. I'm beyond that and to make matters worse, I'm severely backed up. It's been an entire month since someone has bent me over something and penetrated me to the point of exhaustion and I need a release of any kind.

I peek over at the pink strappy heels with the rose that adorns the top of the shoe. The mirror is my focus when I bounce my head from left to right to analyze the dress against my frame once more.

"Hmm." I twist my lips to one side. "Too matchy, matchy."

I turn on my white pedicured toes and return to my walk-in to sift through my rack of clothing. I slide the black velvet-wrapped hangers against the smooth sliver rod, searching.

My apartment is my pride and joy, my haven. Out of all the things in my life, this place that I've turned into my very own palace is the most ideal charging station. It's tucked away in downtown Manhattan. An under 15-minute taxi ride away from For The Culture's office. My apartment's rent is astronomically high, but you can't honestly put a price on sophistication and style.

My walk-in is actually a second bedroom I've converted into a closet. I had a decision to make when I first signed the lease - turn the room into an office or an open space to store my clothes. Since I loved fashion just a little more than work, the choice was simple.

I pass the white love seat and white leather studded coffee table on my way to the opposite standing silver rack. I sort through the plastic garment bags, hunting for the white mini-dress I know will get me the attention I'm preying over. My eyes land on the all white off-the-shoulder masterpiece that will hopefully decorate the carpet at the residence I plan to spend most of my night tonight.

After rolling up the plastic and removing the garment bag, I walk the dress to the large white picture framed mirror in my walk-in this time and press the garment to my form and smile.

"Yes." I hold the dress out in front of me to admire. "It's you and me tonight, Snow White."

I quickly test the holdings on the back of the garment. It's a zip up paired with a hook and eye fastening.

"Any man with a pulse should know how to undo you, no problem."

Where am I going?

I'm headed to an exclusive spot for the night to an event that's held on the first Thursday of every month. Not anyone can get in and those who can are top tiered, always.

With my dress selected and the shoes to complement it, waiting for my feet to occupy them, I examine my hair. I'm due for a hair appointment, but I don't have enough time to book one tonight. I'll make this work.

I comb my fingers through my pressed strands, smoothing the hairs back. I decide I'll add a little gel to keep them in place.

A little foundation, a dust of coral blush, three dabs of concealer, several heavy upward swipes of mascara, and a lacquer of gloss later, and I'm done and out the door and headed to my destination.

When I originally heard of this place, it was by accident. I'd overheard a journalist at a red-carpet event discussing how her colleague was planning to pen an exposé. The existence of the place that was the subject of the exposé was mentioned by several outsiders. However, no one really knew where to find it.

That's because Chateau Luxure is off the grid. No traffic signals or streetlights to guide your way. Street signs don't exist for at least ten miles and you need gps coordinates to get to the castle's front door. That's only if you know the password.

An hour later, my rental car's wheels roll over fallen leaves and clipped branches. I press gently on the brakes to bring the car to a stop adjacent to the intercom.

"Password," the voice demands from the small black box mended to the tall wrought-iron gates.

"Red and gold," I offer.

The gates fold outward, creaking an old iron sound, revealing more about the age of the castle than anyone ever could.

Speaking of the castle, it comes into view the closer I drive to the winding driveway.

After learning of the plans to print the exposé, I went searching for the place on my own. It took a few wrong turns to find the right one and to find my way into the office of MiMi, Chateau Luxure's owner. Pleased and grateful for snitching, MiMi gave me a lifetime membership to Chateau Luxure events, which I've used extensively since receiving. I don't attend every first Thursday night, but I attend enough.

I park alongside a domino row of vehicles and step out. All the cars are upscale, not a single one economy. Not even my rental, which is a white Corvette tonight, you know, to match my dress.

I ran into Pryce Williams here last year. Thought it would have been my lucky night and it could've had he not cockblocked himself.

"Welcome to Chateau Luxure," the gentleman greets, as I climb the last step to arrive at the castle's doors. He's outfitted in a tailor-made suit that molds to every groove and defined line in his muscles. In his hand he holds a gold serving tray that's balancing stemless glasses of champagne with floating topless strawberries.

"Thank you." I lift a glass off the tray, holding it in his view for him to see. "I'll take this one."

I step in.

Music plays from a distance behind heavy gold-plated doors. Rouge red carpet leads the way to the grand ballroom which I follow like a yellow brick road. When I arrive at the doors to the ballroom, two gentlemen, both dressed in a similar all black suit as the Adonis who served me champagne upon my arrival, grip the Art Deco-styled handles of their respective doors and pull, allowing my view to fall on more beauty that awaits inside the ballroom.

As always, the bar is the room's centerpiece even though it's posted up in the corner. The counters expand from one end of the room to the other, with top shelf liquor lining rows and rows of shelves. A giant chandelier hangs at the center of the room and tall circular tables without chairs orbit a dance floor no one ever uses.

The place is at capacity. Wall-to-wall attendees. This area of the castle tonight and every other first Thursday of the month is brimming with people.

Their voices scatter like cicadas posing as background noise to the music that plays at a volume loud enough to enjoy but not to intrude on conversation.

I'm searching, mentally reviewing tonight's inventory. I have been attending singles Thursday for well over a few months and I'm still baffled by how many fresh faces I see whenever I attend. Though my experience with another single isn't always a moment to remember, it's an experience if hardly ever I regret, if ever.

I raise the rim of my glass to my lips and sip, eyes still scanning the room for a suitor.

Singles Thursday is all about the thrill of a hookup. No strings attached. Hell, you don't even have to give your real name if you don't care to. As long as you practice safe sex with a person, you know, is upstanding enough to make it through the front door, there is no harm and no foul. Just a good time. Dope clean fun with someone you didn't have to speak to the next morning.

I needed all that tonight.

My heels click against the floor beneath me as I make my way around the room. I've caught the eye of a few, but they don't give me the zing between my legs I'm desperate for to inspire me to spread my thighs for them.

The last time I felt that was the night I ran into Pryce Williams. I couldn't believe my eyes when I spotted him entering the room. Nearly broke a heel trying to get to him before another woman could recognize him. Thought I'd hit the jackpot when he agreed to follow me up to the room I had booked for the night.

I swallow the last of my champagne and gulp the drink, clenching my teeth as I reminisce.

I was a hair close, more like a literal inch, away from having Pryce in the palm of my hand when he reneged and said he had to leave. I wanted to be pissed because I knew he was leaving because of guilt. When I interviewed him last summer, he excused himself to take a call, a call I could tell was with a woman based on the bashfulness in his smile as he spoke on his phone. After that night at Chateau Luxure, I knew for sure that he would be back, or at the very least come to his senses regarding me soon enough.

Never happened.

Five months after we ran into each other at Chateau Luxure, gossip mongers reported he proposed to his high school sweetheart. That zing has been missing ever since.

With an empty glass and a search to continue, I turn to the bar and make my way there to order a stiffer drink.

I sway my hips to the music and walk to the beat intentionally, hoping it'll be the bait for the right catch. There are a lot of skills I don't have that a pick-me is certainly better at. I don't cook, I hire outside help to clean, and I'm probably not the ideal woman to invite home to mom. But I know if nothing else, my sex appeal and what I offer behind closed doors is enough to hook a man and have him crawling back for more. Fuck all that other shit.

I arrived at the bar with my focus on the top shelf. I needed something strong to awaken the social butterfly in me.

"Gin and tonic for the lady," the deep voice instructed beside me.

I peer up to see his eyes fixed on me.

"We meet again," I say when I recognize his deep brown eyes and prominent neck. His name is Byron, and I held that neck in the grip of my hands while I rode him to a screaming orgasm the month before. I did a good bulk of the work for my release, but that wasn't new. Most men over sold their capabilities in bed and had a hard time keeping up, so it was to be expected.

"We got so caught up the last time with me pleasing you that you didn't get a chance to return the favor and taste me too," Byron reminds.

I look away to keep from rolling my eyes.

Because we didn't get so caught up on nothing. I just didn't bother to make returning the *favor* a priority.

So typical though. Consistently putting themselves first.

That's the reason I make it a priority to get off first. I used to concern myself most with being a giver until I realized I was giving more than I received. The men who frequent Chateau Luxure were more selfish than anything else, although I'm sure Pryce would have been the exception.

"I have a room, the crimson," Byron informs. "I just need to pick up the key from the front."

The most basic room of them all, again.

"Why not the gold?" I ask, accepting my drink from the bartender. "We did it in the crimson the last time. Didn't you tell me you're a doctor?"

"A plastic surgeon, yes," he answers.

"Well, I'm sure you can do better than the crimson room." I sip my drink. "Since you haven't picked up your key yet, you still have time to upgrade."

Everyone knew the gold room was the standard. Top tier with the finest gold upholstered walls, Italian marble floors, and silk bedding. The view is magical. I only knew this from word-of-mouth, though. I've yet to see for myself, unfortunately.

He says, "But who really cares about the room when we're just in there for a limited time?"

Translation: I can't afford it.

"Can't see the room if your eyes are closed most of the time, anyway, right?" Byron adds.

I force a smile. "Right."

"Perhaps tonight you can prove why the gold room should be our meeting spot the next time we're here together."

Prove? Please.

This time I do roll my eyes, but away from him to hide my annoyance. I should pass on him, but the prospects tonight are minimal. I've been here for all of ten minutes and I've yet to see better. Might as well go with what I already know.

"So I'll be back with the key," he says, moving in closer to my ear. "I can't wait to get between your lips. Both of them."

I move my eyes to one corner, glancing at him from the side of my eyes. I'm so unenthused. "*Mm-Hmm.*"

I have no intention of giving this man anything close to head. It would take a lot of man to bring me to my knees and he isn't even half of one.

The moment he leaves my side to retrieve the key, I place my drink on the counter and open my clutch to pull out my phone. I'm skimming through emails to occupy the wait time when I feel a warm body behind me less than two minutes later.

"That was fast." I finish my drink, then twist in my seat. "You left for the key only seconds ago—"

I nearly swallow my tongue when I gasp.

"This world is too small," Desmond says before sipping his champagne.

I blink, hoping to clear my vision because there is no way he is here in front of me.

"Impossible," I whisper.

TWELVE

"Tell me something, Desmond, is there *anywhere* in New York you aren't?"

I chuckle at her response.

"I have literally crossed a bridge and drove to a place with no street signs, and yet, somehow, here you are, in a place where I am and where *you* shouldn't be?"

She's stunning tonight. She's stunning every other day I've seen her, but tonight she's emanating all the things I'm tuned into. The hills of her shoulder blades glisten under the gleam of the mini light fixtures that surround the hulking chandelier in the room. Mykal dressed herself in white and the contrast of the color against her skin is making my mouth water. She glows and I'm attracted to her light.

"You seem upset," I tease, sipping my drink soon after.

"*How*," she stresses through her teeth, "are you *here* right now?"

"This is my second time attending," I answer, placing my drink down at the bar. "The first time was almost two years ago. I haven't felt a need to return until recently."

Since I've been working with you, actually.

"It's something to do for the night," I state instead. "But I'm preaching to the choir. I'm sure you already know what I mean."

"I don't *know* what you mean." She jumps up from her seat. "*I* am not the choir. I'm only here for the drinks."

"Pretty expensive drink."

"I like the atmosphere."

"Is that what we're calling it these days?"

"*Ugh*!" She drops her head into her hands and grunts.

"Mykal, there's nothing to be ashamed of." I gesture around myself. "We're all grown here. We all know what Chateau Luxure is all about."

"*We* work together. *You're* my boss. I'm *not* ashamed. *I'm mortified.* Do me the favor of not confusing the two."

I laugh this time.

"And it isn't funny." She moves in closer. "And can we just pretend you didn't see me here? Please?"

If only the situation were that simple.

The irony too. The only reason I dipped into the deepest part of my closet to pull out the bespoke ash gray suit to enter this place was to find a distraction that would get my mind off Mykal. And here she is.

Fate?

"I don't even know why I'm asking. Listen here, you will *not* tell anyone you saw me here. Got it?" Her tone is firm but her eyes are pleading for something she need not plead for.

There's that vulnerability again that I spoke of. The one she can hide from others but not from me, and that I feel an odd pull to protect.

I step closer and into her space. "If I tell people I saw you here, I'll have to admit to being here too, wouldn't I? Besides, it's like I said, there's absolutely nothing to be ashamed of, anyway."

"Oh please! You know damn well it's *different* if you reveal you were here versus if I did."

"I fully support a woman's freedom to express her sexuality in whatever way she sees fit." I shrug a shoulder. "Most men are sleeping with women and they expect that woman to be sexual for his pleasure, so I don't see why a woman can't embrace her sensuality and seek fulfillment of her own wants and pleasures, too. Seems unfair to expect otherwise."

She stares at me with squinted eyes, analyzing me for a second more.

"So no, I don't see how it's different or how we're different when we're in the same place for the same thing."

Mykal pushes the tip of her tongue against the inside of her cheek. "You're saying all the right things but I still don't like you, Desmond."

I smile and she looks away.

"And why do you dislike me so much, Mykal?"

She snaps her head back in my direction. "As if it isn't obvious."

"It's not."

"You stole *my* job!"

"You mean I accepted a promotion I *earned*?" I push my hands into my suit's pant pockets and wait for an answer.

"Earned?" she mocks. "You got editor-in-chief because of your father."

"Did I?"

"Yes, " she answers through her teeth.

"How? I'm listening."

She turns to face me. "If you were not who you are and your father was some regular journalist writing for whatever no name publication, the position would be mine."

"You seem sure," I challenge.

"One hundred percent sure." She steps closer. "You've been writing under a pen name."

"A decision I made to make a name for myself and not as my father's junior."

"Your columns are basic."

I bark a laugh. "My columns are phenomenal and you know it."

She clenches her teeth and her protruding jawline is proof of this.

"That's probably why my promotion pisses you off so much, huh?" I smirk. "Here I am, penning phenomenally evergreen content in less words and under a pseudonym, but you... you're drumming up word salads under your precious byline about mundane things like what so-and-so wore to lunch, and you're writing them under your name no less, and you're not given half the accolades as me. Shit, I get it. That would upset me too."

She balls her lips.

I unbutton my suit jacket and slide my arms out one at a time. "Unfortunately for you, your problem with me sounds like a *you* problem with yourself and for that reason, it's best I stay out of it."

Her eyes follow my movements as I remove my jacket, her view landing on the hills of my biceps before coasting down my forearms. She exhales through her mouth, chest rising and falling as her eyes move past my fingertips and stops at the bulge in my pants.

I tilt my head when I recognize something I can't believe I've missed before.

"I hate you," she sneers.

The wonderful thing about a form-fitting dress on a woman is that you see everything. Every curve of her hip, the muscles in her abs, and, in Mykal's case, the pebbling of her nipples.

I observe her arousal for a minute longer, treating myself to the view.

I gesture at myself. "*You* hate *me?*"

"Yes."

"Are you sure?"

"*Very* much so."

"Interesting," I whisper, then point at her chest. "Because your girls are telling me otherwise."

She gasps while stepping back.

"I got the key," I hear over her shoulder.

She quickly twists her head in the voice's direction.

His suit reeks of off-the-rack and is in need of a tailor. I can see why she'll go for his deep voice and pronounced jawline, but I know she can do better.

Me, better.

His eyes bounce between her and I. She runs her palm down the back of her neck in response.

"Ready?" he asks her before refocusing on me.

I sneak a peek at the key chain attached to the key ring he's holding. It's red, indicating the type of room he's booked.

I'm amused.

"The crimson room?" I finish my drink. "Cute."

"I'll be up in fifteen minutes, Byron," she says to him, her eyes on me before she turns to face him. "Meet you there."

He hesitates for a moment, eyes bouncing again between Mykal and I.

"I just need to wrap up this business conversation—"

"Oh, it's a wrap," I confirm, challenging her. "We're done. You can go enjoy your night in the crimson room. I hear the view of the forest is worth every bit of the room's cheap rate."

"Shut up," she hisses.

I laugh.

If this guy is anything more than what I sized up, it isn't even a question where she'll spend her night and with whom. What I see before me is proof she has no intention of spending another minute of her time with this guy.

"And we are *far* from done," she points out to me before turning to address the gentleman. "Fifteen minutes."

"My man," I call to him. "I don't think she'll be joining you tonight."

I walk away before he can even respond, and head toward the balcony of the grand ballroom, knowing I wouldn't be alone for long.

"And where are you going?" she barks from behind me.

I lay my suit jacket behind the crook of my elbow and remove the cuff links on my sleeves, dropping them into my pocket. I roll up my first sleeve and step out onto the balcony, working on the other sleeve. I'm hoping she doesn't follow me out here like I'm predicting, but I'm also hoping she does. Because if she *does*, I'm not sure how much self-control I can practice when we're alone and without an audience. But I'm also curious to see what happens when it's finally just us two with no one to interrupt.

Thirteen

"Desmond!" I call to his back. He doesn't stop, just continues to take steps out onto the balcony.

I turn to glance over my shoulder to see if Byron is within sight. He's gone, likely up to the room.

At the thought of the room, I cringe at Desmond's reaction when he learned of the type of room I'm staying in tonight. I don't even know why I care about his opinion. I shouldn't care what he thinks.

I hate him...

... right?

"Desmond," I repeat the second both my heels with me in them are out on the balcony. Ahead of me and past the balcony is darkness which spills into a view of the East River and New York City. Manhattan glitters on the other side of the water. The lights from the buildings make my borough from miles away appear so inviting.

I peep the suit jacket he wore, draped over the cement slab of the balcony and turn my head to my right to see no one there but a cement wall. As I twist my head to my left, he takes me off guard, wrapping a hand around my bicep and pulling me to the closest wall in that direction. Desmond closes the space between us once he has me where he wants me.

My knees buckle, but he catches me before I can collide with the cement behind me.

"*Yes*, Mykal?" he asks within inches of my lips.

I pull my arm free and he lets it go, pressing his hands to the wall behind me one at a time. He's positioned me in a way where I stand out of view of the partygoers inside and where there's no space for me to escape. I can still hear the music, and shards of light from the lighting fixtures in the ballroom illuminate the outer areas of the balcony, but not where I stand.

I swallow hard at his presence. This is the closest we've ever been. I imagined what it would be like to be in his space like this but even my wildest imagination wasn't vivid enough to capture this feeling. He's arresting but not overbearing. Domineering but fluid. I'm comfortable here in his space and I can't understand why.

I can't control my breathing either. My chest rises and falls against his as I struggle to maintain eye contact with him. Desmond towers over me, but he isn't intense. I'm not afraid, but I don't take for granted the energy he exudes.

I part my lips to say something, but the words get stuck in my throat when he gently takes me by the jaw and tilts my head backwards so that our eyes meet.

"I will destroy you in ways you'll enjoy fantasizing about, days after we're done here." He states each word slowly and with weighted breath. "You have my word."

My walls pull in.

"Just say the word." he instructs.

I dart my eyes across his face, stunned by what he's just said and that he's not only touching me, but in this way. It's far from professional. It's intimidatingly intimate. His warm grip seers the skin along my jawline and I welcome it. My exhales are audible, my mind cluttered by my thoughts in this moment. It's a wonder how I'm even able to remain upright on my feet with the amount of oxygen I'm finding difficult to inhale.

"Just tell me..." He tilts his head to one side, moving in even closer. "... what you want from me."

"Your job," I whisper.

He chuckles softly. The scent of mint mixed with scotch on his breath sends my temperature up two notches.

"Right now," he starts, "in this instance, what you *want* is my *job*?"

Of course not. I want what I came to Chateau Luxure for, why I even stalked him out onto this balcony.

I know better, understand if I know what is good for me, I will excuse myself and meet Byron up in one of the cheapest rooms in this castle and fuck him like he's Desmond because it's the wise thing to do. But I am here, outside alone with Desmond, a man I claimed to hate, and yet his hand is on my jaw and it is the sweetest feeling.

Speaking of which, he releases his grip on my face and runs his hand down my neck. "Well, Mykal, I hate to tell you no but you cannot have my job while I still have it. You knew that already."

I tilt my head further back as a reaction to his touch.

"So what *else* do you want?"

The scatter of voices drops even lower, which means fewer people are in the ballroom and more people are making their ways to their rooms.

He moves his lips closer to me, leans in, and whispers in the maze of my ear, "If you don't start talking I will have to send you upstairs."

"Send me?" I finally question.

"You heard exactly what I said." He pulls back so I can see his smirk. "Because if you wanted to be up there with him, you wouldn't have walked out here searching for me."

I take another breath.

"You should go, actually," he suggests next.

I level my head so I can see his eyes.

"You should definitely go," he continues, "because I don't have the good sense to walk away from this."

I lick my lips slow, but still say nothing in response.

His hand glides down my neck and lingers at my collarbone. "You can tell me to stop if you want me to stop. You know that, right?"

I know I can, and would have told him to stop a long time ago, but the urge to walk away hasn't occurred to me either. Instead, I'm curious how far we're going to take this and what it will be like if we do.

"Do you want me to stop?"

He uses his fingertip to glide down the side of my right breast. The act sends a chill racing down my spine, causing me to involuntarily shiver.

I could end this right now. Back away or instruct him to give me five feet, but I don't. Instead, I push myself off the wall gently and more into his space. He doesn't hesitate to lay his hands on each of my breasts, cupping the globe of them in his palm. One hand rubs the right one while the other releases the left to continue its journey south. With me close, Desmond leans in and brushes his lips against mine.

It isn't a kiss, it's a caress with lips. Open mouths with tongues that want to engage. It's a restraint that speaks volumes on both our parts.

I feel the warmth of his fingers above my pubic bone, behind my white dress. I tilt my hips and lean forward on the arches of my satin heels with the goal of moving closer to that heat. I want him to continue. So far, I like what he's doing to me, and he has done little.

"Mykal," he whispers.

"Keep going," I tell him.

His eyes lock on mine as he lowers his fingers even more and ever so lightly cups his hand against me. His hand molds to the shape of my pussy and just the idea of having a part of him there makes me close my eyes.

In one breath, he hikes the hem of my dress effortlessly and slides four fingers down and into my panties.

"Can I touch you here?" Desmond asks against my lips.

I press my hands to the wall behind me and nod slowly.

His touch sends electric charges through my body. Desmond leaves fiery trails down the valley between my lower lips. And when the pads of his middle and ring fingers contact my swollen clit, I release my exhale and take another sharp breath in when I inhale.

He's creating slow circles over the pearl of my clit now, applying pressure where it matters most and it is making my pulse race. I spread my thighs wider, giving him more access, eager to see what he does with it.

His expression is even and observing the whole time. He's watching me as if I'm a moment he can't miss. Recording my every reaction to memory. I try to hold back my moan, but that goes to hell when he replaces his two fingers against my clit with his thumb to dip those same two fingers inside of me.

My body deceives me, my moan escaping my lips, head falling back, and eyelids fluttering closed.

I can't believe this is happening and I hate myself a little for allowing it to take so long to happen.

The muscles inside me clench to the width of his digits.

Desmond moves in closer, pressing his body to mine and his lips to my neck.

"I need to be in here tonight," he says against me, curving his fingers and angling them upward.

And then he groans, and I lose it. Completely.

The bass in his voice travels down my chest and lands in the spot inside me that causes me to moan in response.

His finger thrusts paired with the pressure and dozens of circles he's drawn against my clit with his thumb, topped by his groan, triggers a release that knocks me off my feet.

He catches me, of course, and leans me back against the wall as his fingers never lose the rhythm they've created.

I clutch my hands to the sides of his shoulders to hold on, leaning my head forward to bite his shoulder to keep from screaming my orgasm. I come so hard in his hand I feel like I can rocket off the balcony ledge.

Once I come down from whatever high he's taken me on, I open my eyes to his. I'm panting, trying my hardest to gain some composure when he lifts the same two fingers he originally caressed my clit with, the same two fingers he then dipped inside me. He raises those fingers to his lips and licks them clean with his tongue in my direct view.

My eyes widen, and I'm breathing hard again.

"That guy from earlier, his name is Byron, correct?"

I'm mulling over what to respond with in this moment. Because what just happened, what we just did, has to be bad... right?

"Go to his room and thank him on my behalf for keeping you

company until I arrived," Desmond instructs, breaking the silence. His voice is deeper than usual and I like it. I like it a lot. He lifts my chin so that my mouth is in line with his. "Then meet me in the gold room," he concludes on my lips, punctuating his words with a kiss.

Desmond walks off and my eyes follow his exit. I press my hands to the cement wall behind me to keep myself on my feet. He leaves before I can say anything in retort and really, what is there more to say? I either do as he orders, or I don't.

But I will, and I hope like hell I don't regret it.

FOURTEEN

"Where were you last night?" Faith's voice booms from my telephone's speaker. "I called your phone, but you didn't answer."

I pad my apartment, barefoot, shirtless, with only a pair of black sweatpants slung low at my hips. The wood floors creak under the weight of my walk to my kitchen cabinet.

"I had a business meeting," I answer.

"At midnight?"

I chuckle to myself lowly when I realize how absurd that sounds.

It's Friday, around 5 am. The sky is dark outside since dawn has yet to break. I'm on the phone with Faith, who I sometimes referred to as Faye, a model "friend" I met at an industry party years ago.

Honestly, she is more than a friend, but I always found it appropriate to refer to her as my friend so not to confuse what we really are - fuck buddies.

"I haven't seen you in weeks," she continues. Her voice elevates an octave, a tone short of whining.

My relationship with Faith has always been everything but a relationship. She calls when she's free and I do the same and if our schedules line up, we meet up for drinks or to catch a movie with the unspoken understanding that we'll retire to my apartment, a walking distance from Central Park. She always follows me home under the false pretense of a nightcap, which always ends with us sleeping in the same bed. Even if we never do actually only sleep in my bed. We're the epitome of friends with benefits. We both live our lives, but when we are together, we're together, just not as of late.

I pull open my kitchen cabinet and grab a can of tuna off the shelf. Noticing only one remains after removing the other, I make a mental note to pick more up from the market or to have the cans delivered.

I turn toward the living room, and make my way there en route to my window. My attention falls on the arm of my couch where my necktie lays. I wore it only hours ago.

That necktie was just a necktie until last night. On sight, I clench my teeth at the memory it elicits.

I could barely keep my eyes open, completely distracted by the gradual tightening of her pussy walls around my dick. Mykal squeezed me with her thighs, and the sound her wetness made as I slid in and out between her legs wasn't helping my efforts to focus at all. I watched her like TV, watching as Mykal folded her lower lip into a bite between her top and bottom teeth. She held onto me inside and out, her nails digging into the flesh of my backside as she guided me deeper into her while grinding her pelvis against me. Tired of her trying to lead, I stopped mid-stroke and grabbed my tie off the floor to secure her hands to the bedpost behind her head. I've been wanting to bind her since she stepped into the room, but waited patiently for a good enough time to do it, unsure if it would freak her out. She shocked the hell out of me when she didn't protest. I think I even saw a smirk when I tied the last knot around her wrists. And when I plunged back inside of her, she didn't run or cave into the pressure. Instead, she arched her back and angled her hips, spread her thighs even wider, rolled her head back against the pillow and took her pummeling like the good girl I knew she could be—

"Desmond!" Faith shouts into my ear.

I pause in step and lift my hand to pinch the bridge of my nose, grounding me back in the now.

If my father were cognizant, I just know he'd give me one of his lectures. About how disappointed he is in my lack of foresight and for making a career costing decision without weighing the consequences. What I wouldn't do to hear one of his lectures right now, though. To not only realign me with my focus, but just for old times' sake.

Mykal should've been untouchable, completely off limits to me, and she had been... for a month. All I know, she was the reason I'd visited Chateau Luxure last night to begin with. I planned to escape thoughts of her. What good that did me because the one thing I'd been avoiding between us ended up happening, anyway. And I tried to talk myself out of it. I even rehearsed the speech I would give her when she arrived in the room. I intended to apologize for what happened between us on the balcony while promising to keep things professional between us starting in that moment. But then she walked in and undressed without instruction. The last of my doubt to hookup fell to the floor along with the bra she unhooked. At that very moment, the moonlight outside the gold room's window shone a light through the billowing curtains and reflected off her left nipple. I pounced after seeing that.

Hours later, I run my hand down the side of my lips and outline my beard while shaking my head at myself.

"Dez, are you still there?"

"I'm here."

"Maybe now you are, but you can't tell me you were here on this line with me the whole time. You said nothing to what I just asked you."

"Sorry, Faye, my fault." I peek at my wall of sneakers in search of a distraction. I'd become an avid sneaker collector at 16. Invested so much on what my father called "fancy rubber with laces." He eventually forced me to invest in Nike stock at 18. I've never touched it. My stock has been growing and so has my sneaker collection. I am officially up to my 35th pair.

I walk to it when I notice I need to center my Jordan Retros on their platform. Not unusual since I often took my kicks off the shelf. And never to wear, always to admire.

She grunts. "I said, what are you doing next weekend? I would love to catch a live show or *something* with you."

I know that's code for I'd like to spend the night at your place. It's like I said, we both knew the drill whenever we hung out.

Faith was never direct and maybe that's why she's remained just a friend and nothing more. I like a woman who goes for hers. A woman bold enough to put herself out there fearlessly and with a brave heart. She'll only take the risk if she knows it's safe to do so. I don't like that. Faith was the type to wait for things to happen and life isn't that neat. She's beautiful though, and I enjoy our time together, but I know it can never be more than that between us.

I leave my wall of sneakers and move toward the window. This window leads to my fire escape. I lift the metal latch, raise the hatch, and slide the steel gate to my left.

"It's been too long," Faith insists. I lick my lips at what she implies.

I won't deny her even though the last thing on my mind is being with her next weekend.

I want to be balls deep in Mykal Jones again, despite knowing how horrible an idea that is. What I wouldn't give to watch her hide her lips in her mouth to conceal her moan as not to show me she's in bliss with me inside her. But that's only second to feeling as her walls clench to the column of my dick again as she tries her hardest but fails horribly at controlling her body that's completely submissive under my command.

A gust of crisp air pushes below the window when I lift it opened. Mornings from this side of Manhattan are always magical. My one-bedroom apartment faces the East and offers a stunning view of the park. So every morning I am treated to a view of the sunrise above the bushels of trees.

"I miss you too, Faith," I bass into the phone. "You'd save us a ton of time if you'd just say it too."

"Okay fine - I miss you Desmond," she softly obliges. "Terribly."

A familiar shadow slinks up the fire escape's stairs before its figure can become visible. The sunrises are always a beautiful view I'm lucky to catch, but it isn't the only reason I go through the trouble of opening my fire escape.

Her all black fur makes it almost impossible to see her in the morning's dark hour before the sunrise. Yellow-gold eyes glow beneath the sky that's breaking into dawn.

The cat peeks up at me as it takes its seat on the metal platform and waits.

"Good morning Sable," I whisper.

The usual tickle in my nose prompts me to step back an inch.

"What did you say?" Faith queries.

"Oh," I sniffle, more like stifle a sneeze. "Not you."

I place the can of tuna down, like always, and retreat into my apartment, closing the window behind me.

Faith kisses her teeth. "Feeding that stray again, huh?"

I chuckle.

"You know if you keep giving that damn cat food you'll never get rid of the thing, right?"

"It's cool."

"Aren't you allergic to them, anyway?"

I clear my throat. "I am."

"So why even bother?"

Sable has been appearing on my fire escape since I first moved in years ago. Faith's right, I'm allergic, which is why I never could touch Sable, much less pet her. Only discovered she was female after she birth a litter of kittens on this same fire escape three years prior. I've been setting out an open can of tuna every morning, ever since I found Sable sleeping on my fire escape my first night in this apartment five years ago.

"I like that I can always depend on the cat being there," I tell her. "Predictability in living things is cool sometimes."

"That's ironic because you're far from predictable," she mumbles. "Still haven't told me where you were last night when we meet up like every Thursday."

The mention of last night makes my dick jump.

"Where did you say you were?" She tests.

"I didn't say *where*," I answer. "I told you *what* I was doing - having a business meeting."

"Maintaining that, huh?"

I smirk and tell her, "Next Thursday. You and I can meet up at Gray-

Area for drinks, catch a play after then finish at my place with dinner. I'll cook."

"Desmond Ellis III if you think you can win me over by offering to prepare a meal for me... you're right."

I chuckle.

"I'll see you next Thursday."

Faith and I speak for another few minutes. Mostly she does the talking, though. That's because Mykal is still preoccupying my thoughts.

I'll have to see her later this morning, literally hours after what happened between her and I. And I'm praying we don't create an even bigger mess than we've created hooking up.

FIFTEEN

I bounce my eyes from left to right the second the elevator doors open to For The Culture HQ. My heart is beating at a rate that surprises me as I shoot straight to my new office, closing the door behind me once I'm inside.

When I had a desk outside of the editor's office, I always imagined what it would be like to see everything from my chair on the other side of that door. Since glass walls and a glass door made up the editor-in-chief's office construction, I thought it was like being all-seeing. Now in the assistant editor's office, also made of glass, I wish I could disappear.

My eyes still burn from only two hours of sleep, but there's another feeling overpowering that. It forces me to cross my legs beneath my desk so I can squeeze my thighs as tight as I can together. I drop my head into my hands and close my eyes, quickly opening them again when flashes of the night before return with little effort on my part.

I stood outside the gold room door for about two minutes before turning the knob to enter. The crimson room was a whole three floors down, but I'd only peeked in for a second to inform Byron I wouldn't be staying. He said something in retort, but I'd already shut the door to make my way upstairs. At the gold room's threshold, I turned the knob and stepped in, consciously inhaling an encouraging breath as my heels met white marble.

The first thing I noticed was the room was as amazing as rumored. Gold upholstered walls, a giant floor-to-ceiling window with heavy gold drapes framing them. The masterpiece was the gold framed canopy bed that took up most of the space. What bed size is larger than a king? Because I swear that was the size of that thing.

Desmond stood by the window, his hands in his pockets. I could barely make out his face and my thought at the time was that this was for the best. The less I could see him, the more gall I'd have to go through with this.

I knew I should've been anywhere but there. He's my boss, and I hated him. But here I was, in a room I'd always fantasized about being in with a man I couldn't stop fantasizing about being with since we met. My reasoning was, let me sleep with him, get it out of my system. Sex demystifies everything. Makes a reality out of the most hyped-up act ever. It'll be quick. The sex couldn't possibly last over fifteen minutes, anyway. This will be nothing but a blur in the morning.

With that in mind, I tossed my clutch on the floor and unhooked the hook-and-eye at the back of my white dress, then moved onto the zipper. It hissed down my spine, coming undone around my hips. Desmond walked closer, his gait poetic and smooth, much like the man himself. What he did to me downstairs, became a mental foreplay. I kept the scene between us on replay in my head since he exited the balcony. Suffice to say, I needed no additional warming up that night.

The air he brought with him on his way to me reached me first, and it carried a subtle scent of his cologne. I inhaled him, recalling the citrus woodsy notes in his cologne invading my senses as he rubbed me off to a muscle twitching orgasm several minutes earlier.

By the time Desmond stood inches in front of me, my bra was on the white marble floor and all I wore was my lace black thong.

He wasted no time picking up where we left off down on the ballroom's balcony, lifting me by the ass and carrying me to the bed.

We said nothing but showed a lot in our silence. I can speak for myself when I say I didn't want to ruin the moment with words.

He undressed over me. I leaned back on my elbows and watched from my incline as he removed every item of clothing without haste. When he got down to only his boxers, he pulled them down and his heavy dick buoyed from the waistband.

I inhaled a breath and rolled my eyes up to meet his. We both had that look of "we've come this far, might as well." So we did, in the most magnetic way.

From his first stroke into me, I knew fifteen minutes wouldn't be enough. And when he thrusted back and forth for the first time, the tip of his dick tapping a spot other men have taken forever and a day to find, but somehow he found within seconds, I realized that this was a mistake I would love making.

And I do love making it, every last minute of it. And damn, did it last.

He bounded my wrists to the bedpost, then moments later bounded them behind my back as he served me every inch of him at a different angle and with a rhythm that provided a pleasure I believed could last forever. The crash of my thighs against him was addictive, something I wanted more of after having the same thing only seconds earlier. His dick left me unapologetically greedy. My body did things with Desmond, it never did with anyone else. He differed from the rest too, more focused on my enjoyment. He allowed himself to come after he brought me to a screaming, convulsing, squirting orgasm that left the sheets damp and hanging off the bed with me on them, fighting to breathe in air that was of abundance all around—

"Hey, girl, hey!" Asha greets, pulling me out of my thoughts.

I sit up immediately, banging my knee below my new desk.

"Whoa." She stops in her stride. "You okay?!"

"I'm cool." I fix my posture. "I'm good. You startled me."

Her brows wrinkle. "Startled you?" She peeks behind her and points with her thumb. "You didn't see me coming? The entire room is glass."

I run my fingers through my crop cut.

"You should consider getting automatic curtains like Desmond did," she suggests, taking a seat across from me in the metal and mesh armchair. "I saw them setting it up in his office last night before I clocked out. I can barely see what's happening in his space. Don't even know if he's in there."

I take a breath through my mouth at the mention of his name and *last night*.

"So..." Asha wiggles her brows. "Yesterday was the first Thursday of the month. Got a story for me? *Hmmm?*"

A snapshot of Desmond's eyes rolling right before he shut them so he could focus on coming makes me salivate and my walls quake. I'm reminded of how even as he was getting his, he was angling his hips so that I could continue to come with him, stroking at a pace that was mindful and rehearsed.

I'm so lost in the moment I forget to swallow and instead of inhaling, I choke on what my mouth has produced while briefly reminiscing over last night.

Asha's brows shoot up and she almost shoots up out of her seat, too. I signal to her I'm fine with the lift of a hand.

"What is going on with you today?" She asks, concerned. "I walk in here. You're spaced out. You barely say a word but start choking right in front of me."

I press my fingers to my brow bone.

"Is this new office jitters? It's been a few weeks, you should be used to the space by now."

"He was there," I blurt, then close my eyes. "Desmond was at Chateau Luxure last night."

Her eyes widen and then she shakes her head, blinks, then refocuses on me. "I'm sorry, what?!"

"Girl!"

"No *fucking* way!" She shouts.

"*Shh*," I hiss, running my fingers through my hair once more.

My phone rings less than a second later. I peek down and almost lose my breath when I see Desmond's name appear in the call window.

Asha notices too and slaps her hand to her mouth.

I point at her. "Stop that. You said yourself this room is all glass and the last thing I need him seeing is your reaction right now."

"He has a whole curtain circling the perimeter in his office."

"I wouldn't put it past him. He still has eyes on us."

The phone continues to ring.

"Answer it, Mykal!"

I swallow hard and lift the phone off the dock.

"Good morning Mykal," he says before I can say anything and I damn near melt in my seat at the sound of his voice ear fucking me. It's clear within seconds I can't have him or his voice this close to my face this soon after what we did.

"Can I see you in my office in five?"

"Ye-yup-*mm-hmm*," I stutter, already regretting the unease in my response. "Sure."

"Thank you," he replies, then hangs up.

"I have to go," I tell Asha.

"What you *have* to do? Is let me know what time we are meeting up after work for drinks because I'm *buying*, and your ass is *telling me* every fucking detail."

"Asha." I stand from my seat. "I'm in the middle of a damn crisis and you want to talk about drinks and possibly the biggest mistake I've ever made in my life?!"

"*Um*," she contemplates exaggeratively, tilting her head a little for emphasis. "Absolutely!"

I grunt and head for the door.

"Okay, okay, okay." She stops me and places each hand on my shoulders. "It happened. Was it the wisest decision? It wasn't. But you two are adults, consenting adults who can have a working relationship even after *what* happened."

I nod, deep down, hoping she's right.

"Don't make it awkward," she advises, shaking her head. "Go in there and just let him lead the convo. Feel him out. Regardless of anything, work and what happened last night... *whatever* happened last night... did *something* happen last night? *What* exactly *happened* last night?"

"Asha!"

"Okay, sorry!" She shakes her head and refocuses. "Regardless of everything, you're here and have a job to do. You want editor, so prove that in your position as *assistant* editor. Don't let that man and what happened or *didn't* happen knock you off your block."

I nod again.

"The men can fuck their secretaries and coworkers and still are all business. They don't even use both sides of their brains at the same time the way we can. If they can fuck without feelings and be professional, you can too."

I exhale a sigh of relief. It isn't the best pep talk, but shit, I'll take it.

"Now go in there," she directs, stepping out of my way. "Then tell me *everything* tonight over drinks."

I shoot her a glare at the side of my eye and she laughs.

———

"You rang?" I ask at the threshold of Desmond's office door.

Just as Asha informed, a white light-block curtain drapes the perimeter inside Desmond's office. The curtain divides into two at the door and another two at the window with the view. For my arrival, he drew one side back to the nearest corner. I also notice he's added a few framed photos, some of which are with him and a couple of celebrities. I instantly recognize Wesley Sparks, a popular black playwright who writes, directs, and sings in his own musicals. Quiet as kept I admire him. When Hollywood refused to carve a space for him, he created his own lane almost a decade ago and has been thriving ever sense. It's respectable.

Desmond peeks up from his computer screen and I have to remind myself to breathe.

"Mykal, please come in and shut the door," he instructs, returning to typing on his computer's keyboard.

I do as told, then make my way to the armchair directly across from his desk.

Oddly enough, I'm not as bothered at the fact that Desmond has clearly made himself comfortable.

Along with a few personal items like a signed basketball, encased in a clear showcase that sits on one side of his enormous office desk, there are designer leather slippers parked beside the coat rack by his door.

"What do you have for me?" He quizzes.

I rip my eyes off the slippers and twist my head in his direction quick. "Huh?"

"Regarding plans for the piece we discussed a few weeks ago."

I wrinkle my brows. "What?"

"The unsung entertainers idea I ran by you." Desmond swivels his chair to face forward and he leans back, his chair leaning as well to accommodate his weight.

Is he serious right now?!

As if he didn't just blow my damn mind less than 24 hours earlier.

Or did I imagine the whole thing?

"Oh, yeah, uh." I recover though, quicker than I can figure out what's going on. Scratching my head, I tell him, "Franco Ramsey and Marie Martine are two of our, *um*, best entertainment writers at For The Culture. They both are familiar with your idea as well as penning evergreen content so they'll know what's needed to make your idea engaging for our reading market."

"Have you spoken to them about the project yet?"

"I can," I assure. "Today. I can set up a meeting with them to discuss expectations."

Desmond stares at me for a moment. The only thing that moves are his eyes as they scan me from the neck up.

"What?" I ask, running my hand down the back of my hair. "What is it?"

"Nothing." He clears his throat and sits up in his chair. "Please schedule a meeting with them and get back to me. If you need me to sit in as well, I can. Just let me know time and date. I need to assign writers as soon as possible since we're a little behind schedule." His eyes are back on his computer screen, his fingers sliding against his desk in search of his mouse. To think, two of those fingers were deep inside me hours ago.

I must have been staring at his hand for longer than I should have because when I finally look up at him, he's matching my gaze but with an arched brow.

"That'll be all," he dismisses without blinking an eye. "Thank you."

"That's... *all*?" I question.

"Yes." His attention is entirely on his screen again. "You're free to go.

There's a lot of ground we need to cover for this project so the sooner you can start, the better."

I observe him from my seat, confused. Wanting to fuss and throw a tantrum but I refuse to embarrass myself any further.

So, I exhale exaggeratively instead and press my hands into the arm of the chair to push myself up and onto my heels.

I steal another peek at Desmond, who directs his focus completely on his computer screen.

I feel stupid for wondering what's happening at this moment. What's going through his head. What was I expecting? Asha just said how men can *fuck without feelings*, differentiate work from all the other shit and here it is, playing out in front of me.

With this in mind, I straighten my posture and lift my chin, mentally checking myself. There is no way I am about to trip over some dick... regardless of how phenomenal it was because, my God, it was exceptional.

After paying one last glance at him typing on his computer, I pivot on the arches of my feet and head to the door.

There's a click and then a whir. I ignore it, knowing that it must be the curtains that he's drawing closed with a remote so the dense fabric can enclose around the office space the moment I exit. But when I reach the door and twist the knob to open it, I hear footsteps approach behind me, semi-muted by the newly carpeted floor.

I don't have time to turn around.

A gasp escapes my lips when I feel body heat against the back of my neck, along with the extension of an arm over my right shoulder. As quick as I opened the door, Desmond closes it with one hand and wraps his free arm around my waist. Before anyone else can see this play out, the curtains shroud us and conceal the interior of the office completely, including the door.

I close my eyes and settle my weight on his arm around me. My walls pull in when he moves in even closer, pressing his body to mine from behind. He's hard. It's the first thing I notice when he eliminates even more space between us and his stiffness pokes behind me.

"Fuck," he whispers to my back, leaning what feels to be his forehead against the back of my head.

All I see are curtain pleats inches in front of me when I open my eyes. He's taking deep breaths behind me, inhaling the scent of my hair and I want to say everything but nothing at the same time. I fear breaking the silence that has fallen between us. We take a few more breaths together. His arm tightens around my waist. My walls pull in even more and I flatten my hand against the curtained door in response.

"This is so bad." He grunts.

The longer I stand there, the higher my body temperature climbs.

Desmond slides his palm down the fabric and uses his fingers to create a split where the curtain naturally divides. His fingers pinch the lock above the knob and turns it to the left, locking the door.

He turns me next to face him and I hesitate with lifting my gaze, so he does it for me by angling my chin up so my head will tilt back.

His eyes reveal everything his words can't express. The same man I witnessed busy himself with his computer seconds ago did not stand in front of me. Replaced is the man I spent the night with. The familiarity in his aura tightens the skin around my nipples and makes them pebble.

"Fuck," he says again, but he doesn't whisper it this time. He shuts his eyes instead when he says it and holds them tightly closed for a moment longer. When he opens them, he opens them to mine and admits, "I didn't prepare for this plot twist in my plans."

A smirk tugs at the right corner of my lip, but doesn't materialize. That's because within milliseconds, Desmond cups his hand to the back of my head and uses the leverage to pull me to him so he can crash his mouth against mine.

And I give in, moaning when our lips make an impact. The softness of his lips and fearlessness to put them on me. And of all places in *here*, hours after the workday has started, causes me to lose my balance on my designer heels. Just like the night before at Chateau Luxure, he catches me by the curve of my ass, and with one arm lifts me to his waist. Desmond leans me back against the door and parts my lips with his, snaking his tongue into my mouth. With no desire to hold back, I hum a moan when our tongues touch and I wrap my legs around his waist to draw us closer.

It's insane that neither one of us is stopping this. Someone could knock on Desmond's office door at any moment. Anyone could interrupt us in this second and what would we say if one writer or worse Corey or my cousin, Amir, were to just show up and find Desmond and me with our clothes disheveled, lips red and plump from the kissing we're doing?

"Desmond." I force his name through my lips with desperation in my voice. He notices my pained tone, I'm sure, and pulls back in response, taking me by the legs and helping to lower me down to my feet. Desmond steps back an inch.

The man is so beautiful. His dark brown eyes are smoldering, heating me from the inside out. It's clear he knows this shouldn't happen again, especially not *here*.

His broad shoulders rise and fall in time with his breaths. I should continue to be the adult here and stop this. It's the responsible thing to do. It's irresponsible not to. But I don't know a damn thing about being responsible and I won't inconvenience myself by pretending to be now.

I close the little space he creates between us and take him by the tie he wears, pulling him the other half of the way.

Our noses are one breath away from touching at the tips when I catch his smirk. I balance myself on the arches of my feet, lean in, and say on his lips, "Fuck me."

He groans and I'm off my feet again and in his arms in seconds. He carries me to a vacant part of his desk. Desmond sits me on the surface and steps between my legs. I balance myself by placing my hands flat on his desk behind me.

Everything moves in swift motion. Like a well-choreographed dance between us. His hand sliding up my thighs, fingers hooking to the strings of my panties. As those panties came off, his slacks drop from his waist and circles his ankles.

A condom he retrieves from his wallet is in his hand and between the bite of his teeth as he rips the packaging opened.

The worry illustrated in his brows is no match to the lust darkening his eyes. Desmond glides me closer to him on the desk.

I'm so wet and him hard that when he slides me even closer, he tunnels right into me.

I gasp.

My walls adjust perfectly around him and quiver against his girth.

His head falls back as he sinks even deeper, his fingertips digging into the flesh of my thighs even more. Desmond's head remains slung back and his Adam's apple bobs when he swallows hard as he starts stroking. The friction overwhelms me. I'm still tender from our sex hours prior. The quivering of my walls intensifies and he must have noticed this because he levels his head and locks eyes with me.

I dart mine from his left to his right ones, rolling my hips intentionally. He removes a hand from my thigh and raises it to his lips. Drags the pad of his thumb down the tip of his tongue, then places his wet fingertip against my swollen clit.

I sigh when he circles the nub while maintaining his rhythm. It's my turn to drop my head back between my shoulders as the dual sensations he creates battle for dominance inside me. My jaw slacks when the warmth between my legs morphs into pulsing, then uncontrollable fluttering. A wave of pleasure crests and my heavy breaths become moans.

Desmond frees my other thigh and covers my mouth with his hand. My arms behind me are shaking, and I doubt I can continue to hold myself up.

He's grunting lowly each thrust into me and when his thumb circles my clit once more, I come undone completely. He snatches his hand off my mouth, wraps his arm behind me, and slams his mouth into mine.

We sound like animals as he pounds the last of his strokes in me and I roll my hips hungrily against him.

Coming.

Consuming every delicious glide he feeds me.

Goosebumps prickle my skin and my nails dig into the fabric of his dress shirt. I feel him harden and then the head of his hard-on mushroom inside me before he shudders once, then twice against me.

He gently pulls his hand from between my thighs and uses his palm to balance his weight on the desk. I take a couple more breaths against him before I unwrap my legs, then lower them from around his waist.

And when we make eyes again, we share the same expression of acknowledgment and shock at what we just did... again.

"Fuck," I say this time, tucking my lips into my mouth after.

Sixteen

I'm distracted.

I lightly tap my pen's projector against my desk as I do my best to stay present. This is exactly what I wanted to avoid, distraction. There is no room for it for what I have planned. Earlier, I drew my office's curtains completely to the origins of their individual rods, which led me to peeking through the glass wall at her...

Mykal.

She's in her office, several steps away at her desk, fingers moving about her keyboard like a seasoned typist. It's been almost two weeks since we christened the office I now sit in, watching her. Distracted.

I shut my eyes and force my head to twist away from her. She's said nothing since that day. As promised, Mykal arranged a sit down with the writers she suggested. Even cc'ed me in on the email with the date and time for the meeting. I never expected to be there, but she has been avoiding a conversation since that day in my office. I figured a dialogue would suffice, even if it were only work related. At said meeting, she kept it professional, although every time she looked my way or addressed me, her voice would drop an octave and so would her lids, giving her eyes a sultry appearance.

I lower the bridge of my nose into the pinch of my two fingers. I had one job to do - gain experience and relevant contacts in my position as editor at For The Culture so I can know what the hell I'm doing when I take on the ambitious goal of starting the next, and biggest, black-owned daily newspaper. My father's dream. What he worked his entire career for and probably would have brought to fruition had his health not betrayed him.

I scratch the back of my head while my eyes wander to the spot on my desk I sat Mykal only 10-days ago. It was apparent in her eyes while we were in the act that she was just as surprised and unsure about doing what we did in here. I heard it in her voice when we kissed at the door. Felt it in her hands as they shook from her nerves, getting the best of her.

I should've let her leave.

She was more than primed and ready to storm out and I just had to get out of my seat to stop her despite my mind telling me to sit the fuck down.

But if I did, I wouldn't have created an opportunity to have some of the best sex I've ever had... like, ever.

The office is quiet today, calm. Actually, the atmosphere is always calm around here, which is probably why Mykal and I could get away with what we did.

That day, when we finished, she hopped off the desk, fixing herself as she made her way to my office door.

"Mykal," I called to her before she could reach for the doorknob.

"Shh," she shushed, turning to face me soon after. "Let's just..." She ran her fingers through her short hair. "Just Shh."

Her hair was slightly out of place, skirt twisted a little to her left, lips a tad swollen from our kissing.

The moment I buckled my belt, I brought my hand to my mouth to run down my beard, a nervous habit. When I did this, I got a whiff of her scent on my fingers.

I grew hard again.

"Can I get you some water?" I asked, approaching. "Or anything else?"

"You've given me enough." She smirked. "I'm going to head back to my desk."

"We should talk," I insisted.

"Desmond." She sighed "I suspect we don't know how to talk, Desmond."

I didn't protest that. Didn't protest when she turned to exit my office. Or when she returned to her desk, and the day ended without us discussing what we let happen twice. Those were practically the last words we had that weren't about the piece I'd assigned to her, and I didn't like the silence between us.

My phone rings on my desk. It's my mobile and I sit up immediately when I notice the call is coming from inside of my father's property.

Glass crashing in the background is the first thing I hear when I press *answer*.

"Mali."

"Mr. Ellis," Mali says in a panicked tone. "Your father is having an episode."

I sigh in defeat, shutting my eyes briefly. This is not what I need right now.

"He's asking for your mother."

"Where the hell am I?" my father demands in the background of the call. "Why have you brought me here, you devil?!"

"Mr. Desmond, this is your home," she tries with him. "This is your room, I swear it. I am your nurse—"

"You're a fucking devil is what you are!" He shouts back. "Where is Phyllis? *Hmm*?" His voice gains more range. "Where is she? Tell me right now where my wife is!"

"Please don't tell him," I plead. I jump to my feet and round my desk in haste, heading to the coat rack at my door. "I'll be there in less than an hour."

"Please hurry."

I'm out of my office and taking giant steps toward Mykal's.

"I need a favor," I announce when I burst through her door.

She lifts her gaze from her laptop's screen, eyes scanning me the second I'm in her sights. "What's wrong?"

"I have a family emergency."

She wrinkles her brows.

"I'll probably be away from my desk for the rest of today. Can you supervise? Everything is off to print. I've edited all the online articles and scheduled them for posting tomorrow. I just need you to take any phone calls that may seem urgent. Paula, my assistant, can transfer all the unimportant ones to my voicemail. I'll call and brief her when I get in my car."

She rolls her eyes. "Will I get credit for sitting as acting editor for the day?"

"Please don't start," I say. "Not right now at least."

"It's the middle of the day, Desmond."

"Mykal, can you do this for me or not?"

She stares for a moment, then nods. "You owe me."

"Fine." I turn to leave.

"Let me hear you say it."

"Seriously?!" I huff. "For what purpose?"

"Clarity." She folds her hands on her desk. I peek down at her fingers interlocked and want to bind her wrists together and punish her for her insubordination, but mostly for my satisfaction.

Instead, I let it go... for now.

"I owe you."

———

"He's locked me out of his room," Mali informs as I enter the house. A cleaner from the maid service company that takes care of the property's cleaning daily is picking up shards of glass from the floor with a gloved hand and disposing of them in a bulging black trash bag.

I take a deep breath in and release it sharply, turning to the stairs to make my way up to the master bedroom.

In moments like this, all the doubts about keeping my father out of a nursing home come rushing in like a tsunami demolishing all the hope I have for his recovery.

Doctors have already confirmed that Alzheimer's isn't treatable or reversible and I've accepted that. It's these instances of relapse, when his dementia lightens and he remembers moments or important facts about his past while forgetting the present that takes a toll on my spirits.

I get by my father's room door and rap lightly on the wood surface.

"Senior?" I call lowly. "Can you open the door?"

"Who is it?"

I'm not clear on where in his recollection he is. With my father, the severity of his dementia seems to volley in extremes. So, I don't know in what time in the past he's currently in mentally. Clearly, he knows he's married, or was married, because he's under the guise of his wife, still living. But does he know me?

"It's me, dad," I try. "Open up."

There's silence for a second, but it feels more like minutes.

The door's lock finally clicks and the door flies open soon after.

"Desmond, where's your mother? What is this place? And who's this woman masquerading around here claiming to be my nurse?!"

His eyes are wild, his blue shirt wears the stain of his lunch around the collar. He's opened the door, and he's said my name, so I know he knows who I am, so there's no need to show him the photo album. I'm assured I made the right decision leaving the album in his study today.

Sunlight pours in from his bedroom's window, lighting the space behind him. He's pulled down the curtains in his fit of rage.

"Dad, can I come in?"

He doesn't move. "Not until you tell me where I am and where your mother is because I'm ready to get the hell out of here."

"This is your home, dad."

"Nonsense." He shakes his head. "Where's your mother?"

I shut my eyes tight and drop my head to run my hand across the back of my neck.

I'll admit, showing the photo album every time I visit never gets easy but this part, having to tell my father his wife is dead when he forgets takes a part of me each time. A part of myself I can't get back and that weakens me every time I tell him and witness his reaction.

"She's gone, dad," I remind him, moving closer to the door. "She died from a pulmonary embolism. Doctors said it was due to the several long flights she took around the world as a missionary. It happened when I was seven. Do you remember that?"

He stares in my direction, eyes moving erratically from left to right, visually recollecting.

"She died in Kenya, while there to help build a school with her spirit warriors, as she used to call them." I smile, but it never tugs hard enough to blossom into anything comforting to him or myself. "You cried when you told me. I'd never seen you cry until that day."

His wrinkled brows relax.

"It was days before Christmas. She planned to return on Christmas Eve. You told me the only peace you got from her passing was that she died while doing what she loved, helping people. You told me—"

"We should all be so blessed to spend our last days the same way, doing what we love," he finished.

I release a long exhale, both relieved that he's come to and that I don't have to continue down memory lane. I don't have to go into detail about her funeral and how it was beautiful despite the nightmare my father and my mother's relatives had to go through to get my mother's body back in the states to bury her. How for many nights my father would start his day with tears in his eyes that he had to force himself not to release because he was under the false assumption that men shouldn't do that. How he never grieved the way I now know is necessary when you lose a spouse, or anyone who meant anything to you. Instead, he poured himself into writing and working, leaving me in the care of nannies and babysitters so he could drown his loneliness in accolades and wallow in his new title of widower as he did the thing he loved and hoped to die doing it like his wife.

Tears cloud my father's brown eyes before he turns from me and takes steps away from the door. I follow him inside, visually digesting the mess he's created in his room. I lay a hand gently on his bicep to guide him to his bed. A pile of heavy drapes sit on the floor beneath the tall windows and the curtain rods hang off by the nails above the moldings. There are rips in the upholstery and food stains on the floors and walls.

It's like I said, in moments like this I wonder if my family members were right to doubt I could do this - keep my father out of an assisted living facility and in the home he's built and knows so he's comfortable.

"I need some water, son," he utters from his seat at the edge of his bed.

"Of course," I answer, turning to head out to get it.

"Did I ever remarry?" he asks to my back.

I turn to face him.

"She would've wanted that," he tells me, dropping his view to his ringless fingers. "She'd always say she'd want me to move on, be happy—"

"You were never really the listening type," I answer. "Not if you listening wasn't for an article, you had to write."

He chuckles to himself. His amusement is short lived though because his frown returns soon after.

"You married work," I remind. "And you did so without regret because you did it with a purpose."

He glances up.

"You covered a story that sets the tone for your career, and you rode that wave, which made you a living legend in journalism. Your reputation proceeds you to this day. So, you become happy. You satisfy her wish."

"Am I still doing that now? Writing and loving it? I must be." He stares at me, waiting for my answer, the desperation clear in his voice and his eyes. "Right?"

I stone in place, then swallow hard. The last time I was honest about this, my father fell into a mild depression. Telling him that his disease slowed him completely to the point he hadn't picked up a pen or a pad in years and that same disease had him bed-bound most days. It was the reason I started the blog under his name and ghostwrote articles as commentary on current events. Doing this helped in two ways - it offered false assurance to him he was still active in the writing world whenever I'd read what I claimed he wrote to him. Maintaining the blog also kept his name and brand fresh in everyone's mind.

"You are," I lie. "You're planning to start that daily paper you've been wanting to launch for forever."

His entire face brightens with a smile that slants his eyes. "How close am I to launch?"

I clench my teeth and take a deep breath. "Close."

That part is true - we are close, but I could jeopardize everything if I keep this thing up with Mykal, whatever this thing is. And my father wouldn't approve. He's always chastised me for sleeping with the wrong women in places I have higher influence over them which is just as wrong. But there is something about Mykal that transcends the physical. I'm pretty sure I know what that thing is. I'm just not all that sure... yet.

"Now that is great news." He nods to himself while turning in his seat to canvass the drape-less windows. "Phenomenal news."

"I'll be back with your water." I pivot on my feet and head toward the stairs. On my way to the kitchen, I decide that moving forward I will primarily focus on why I accepted the promotion at For The Culture - to make my father's dream come true. I refuse to get distracted by Mykal, but I doubt that's even possible.

Seventeen

“Now that everyone is present, let's get started!”

Melissa Borodin, the magazine's events manager, is at the front of the conference room, her arms clutching a thick black folder of papers over her chest.

I cross my legs in my seat and lean in her direction. In sight, at the far end of the table, is Desmond. He was one of the last people to walk into the meeting today. When he arrived, he made no eye contact with me. He's done little with me, including talk much. Come to think of it, we haven't exchanged more than a few words following the day he had to leave work early for what he claimed was a family emergency.

"As you all may know," Melissa starts, "we are coming up on our fifth year anniversary next weekend and this year the party will be bigger than ever."

Melissa is the magazine's events manager who has planned great soirées for the magazine since its inception five years ago. She started as a PR intern, then made her way up to coordinator, and now she is calling the shots as our sole events manager. And she is a damn good one at that. The magazine is small, so our PR team is even smaller. But what we lacked in quantity, we more than made up for in quality. Our events have received major press coverage every year and are one of the hottest tickets in town. I'm sure this year will be no different.

"Our guest list is growing by the day with a few confirmed attendees," Melissa announces. "I expect more confirmations before end of day."

"Who all gon' be there?" I ask which garners a few chuckles around the room. Even Desmond gives in to a little smirk.

"Well, we already know Corey and your cousin Amir will be there."

"Predictably," I mumble.

"But I've already received confirmation from Bryant Greene, Jolie Hart, and Pryce Williams, who is attending with his wife."

I straighten my back in my seat at the mention of Pryce's name. "Pryce confirmed?"

"Oh yes," Melissa replies, adding a nod. "He was one of the first to RSVP."

I try to calm my elation but I'm beyond happy after hearing this good news.

"Hmph," I add, "I'm surprised he had time to respond considering the basketball season is about to start and all."

Melissa shrugs and moves along with the details concerning the party.

The thought of being in the same room as Pryce again makes my heart patter with glee and lips twitch at the corners with a smile. I know it's foolish to have any expectations about him showing up, but I can't help looking forward to seeing him.

"We haven't established a dress code," Melissa informs. "Dana and I thought it would be a little offensive to instruct people on how they should dress for the event. But it is an anniversary event, so we're trusting that everyone gets the gist and dresses their best, including everyone here."

I'm mentally combing through my wardrobe, tallying up the outfits I'll pick through for the event. I know one thing, whatever I decide to wear, I must best Pryce's wife.

There was little published about Mrs. Leelah Waters-Williams.

Other than information about her being a psychotherapist and her owning a practice in the city, she maintained a clean digital footprint. I happened upon her social accounts, but she kept them private and only displayed random shit like moons and star clusters as her avatar.

I wonder if she's one of those fake *"I'm so woke"* types.

Melissa continues detailing information about the anniversary event when my eyes gloss over the other faces in the room and eventually collide with Desmond's. He holds his stare with me for all of three seconds when he casually checks out on me to refocus on Melissa.

He's been distant. We haven't known each other long enough for me to gauge when he's talkative and when he isn't, but I can tell when someone is keeping their distance. Not that I'm complaining. But I covered for him when he told me he needed to leave last Monday, and I hadn't so much as received a thank you for it. There wasn't anything to tend to during his absence at the magazine when he left early that day, but he could show some gratitude.

It didn't matter. The fact I am feeling some kind of way about him not talking to me much instead of celebrating over him speaking less to me is concerning, though.

The bright side is I'm hiding my conflicted feelings. I've done well with not making that moment at Chateau Luxure and the moment we shared in his office into anything other than what it was.

Sex.

It was just sex, and if he wasn't tripping over it, I sure as hell wouldn't either.

"Are there questions?" Melissa poses, her eyes scanning the room for a response.

"This is my first event with the magazine," Desmond starts. "So, I was wondering - can I bring a plus one?"

I whip my head in his direction before I can stop myself.

Who the hell would he bring?

I almost fix my lips to ask but bite my tongue to keep quiet.

Desmond, like I've explained, is a handsome man. I'm certain he has a Rolodex of women who are just pining away at home waiting, hopefully without bated breath, for him to call them. But hearing the possibility of someone taking up his time differs from *knowing* the possibility exists.

"Good question, Desmond," Melissa answers. "Yes, we encourage bringing plus ones, especially for the editor." She winks.

I clench my teeth hard.

"Perfect," he says. "I'll give you my plus one's name after the meeting."

To hell you will! You give her name now.

I train my eyes on his and break eye contact the second he pins his gaze to me.

He leans back in his chair and diverts his eyes off me and focuses on Melissa again.

I swing my jaw from left to right, annoyed by the prospect of him bringing a date.

Curiosity shrouds my thoughts as I wonder what his date will look like. Will she be taller? Smarter? Prettier than me?

I roll my eyes closed and force them off him when I lift my lids again.

Why am I even hung up over this right now?

Desmond and I should've never happened. Pryce and I should've. And with news of Pryce attending the party next weekend, that's who I should set my sights on. That's who should get my attention. And I focus on that, even if my focus reminds me his wife will be there too. But nothing is ever perfect in my world. There's always that one flaw, that one blemish on my plans. Why would my love life be any different?

So, I'll mentally prepare to see Pryce while hoping I'll have time to be alone with him, too.

Eighteen

"Well, this is very creepy of you," Mykal teases when she pulls open her apartment door and finds me standing on the other side. This is only after she made me wait all of five minutes outside after ringing her intercom from downstairs. Outside, when I announced myself, she delayed giving a response before she buzzed me in.

"Two questions," she starts, folding her arms. The breeze in the hallway billows the hem of her cherry blossom printed kimono.

"Shoot."

"How do you know where I live? And what *the hell* are you doing here?"

"Employee directory." I answer her former question, then lift the paper bag I'm holding in view. "And I bought you dinner."

Her brows furrow.

"Well, I bought *us* dinner."

"And, why?"

"We all have to eat, right? Hopefully, you haven't yet."

Her eyes shift from left to right, no doubt analyzing my response. I thought of this, ran through the scenario when I stood inside Sergio's, a popular Italian restaurant only three doors down from her apartment building. Restauranteurs touted the restaurant as one of the best Italian eateries in New York City. If my father taught me anything, it is that the way to a woman's heart is the same way to a man's. Food is a unifier, and I needed to smooth things out with Mykal. My plans depended on it.

"So." I scan from left to right. "Are we going to set up out here and eat or will you invite me inside?"

"That's mighty audacious of you to just pop up at my place and expect to be invited in, don't you think?"

I smile. "I knew if I called and asked if I could stop by, you'd tell me no before I could get my question out."

"When you know, you know."

It's amazing. Even dressed down with a face bare of makeup, and only a silk kimono clinging to her physique, Mykal is still stunning.

Stop.

I briefly shut my eyes tight, forcing myself to refocus.

"I'll only ask you once more," I tell her. "If you refuse, I'll completely understand. But I would really love to come in."

She remains at the doorway for almost a minute longer.

"I'm only asking to have dinner with you," I promise, studying her expression. "I swear."

She exhales loudly, then steps to the side so I can enter.

My nose is the first sense activated when I cross the threshold. Next, my eyes digest the layout of her abode. Her home smells of pachouli and lavender and is decorated like an interior designer's dreamland.

The place is small, tinier than mine in square footage despite there being two bedrooms and mine only a one-bedroom apartment. But her place is beautiful and has her style all over it.

White, black, and pink is everywhere. White on the couch and walls, black on the coffee table and side tables, and pink in the throw pillows with textures that range from silk to faux fur. Short-stemmed pink roses sit in small crystal vases on her coffee table and on a tiny table by her front door. She mounted painted portraits of fashion capitals around the world to her walls, including a landscape view of New

York City and a black and white cinematic capture of Paris's Eiffel Tower. Mykal has done well to make her home resemble a five-star hotel suite.

"Wow," I mouth as I make my way further into her apartment. "Who's your decorator?"

"West Elm and Home Goods," she answers. "Sometimes Target." Mykal maintains a distance as she folds her arms once more. "Not all of us hail from journalism royalty and can afford an interior decorator's invoice."

I chuckle while holding up the paper bag again. "Where did you say I could put this?"

"I *didn't* say." Mykal slightly tips her head to one side. "You can hold it for now. I haven't decided what to do with the man himself yet, much less the bag he holds."

"Okay..."

"Desmond, *what* are you doing here, honestly?"

"I want to fix things."

She arches a brow. "What broke?"

"Our professional relationship," I answer. "Things started off not how I would have liked between us. You hated me when we first met."

"Still do," she corrects.

I smile. "Allegedly."

She rolls her eyes.

"We've had sex twice and I don't even know your favorite color—"

"I take it sex is important to you?" she interjects. "It's something that's significant in your world?"

I chuckle lowly.

If only.

"You're probably the type who likes to wine and dine before you and a woman hookup. Meet her parents and buy them gifts during the holidays."

"I'm flattered. I wish I were that responsible."

"Oh?"

"I have a penchant for having sex with women I shouldn't even consider having sex with." I look away. "My maid when I was eighteen, a student I tutored while I was in college, my father's last secretary on her first day when I was 25. Oh, and now my assistant editor at my brand-new position where I'm her boss, no less."

Mykal raises both brows this time.

"So yeah, I don't choose women, wisely. No offense."

She purses her lips.

"Which is why I want to *fix* things." I walk a little closer to her. "I like you, Mykal, obviously. More important than that, I maintain that you're an incredible writer with a go-getter attitude I can use to create masterpieces that can benefit us both at the magazine. *This* meal..." I hold up the paper bag again for her to see. "... is a peace offering. My way of extending an olive branch and asking, with your cooperation, for us to start over."

She blinks a few times, then glances at the bag in my hand before moving her eyes on me again.

"Sex complicates things, especially when there isn't any discipline involved and where work needs to be done. I want to nurture a professional relationship that will benefit us both and not have a lack of self-control ruin it."

"The only *benefit* I see is with you in my position and me in yours."

I drop my head back and laugh.

"You *maintain* I'm an incredible writer? Well, I *maintain* you stole my job, Desmond."

"Christ, you're relentless."

"Extremely." She smirks. "And I'm just getting warmed up."

A smile settles on my lips.

"I hope you know I won't stop until I'm sitting in that office of yours with *my* name on the nameplate."

"Wow," I whisper.

"Until then, it will *always* be all guns a blazing when we're in the same room," she warns. "Understood?"

She does not know how sexy she is to me when she speaks like this. Mykal isn't one to be toyed with, and I like that. I like that she knows what she wants and isn't afraid to go after it... even if it's completely out of her range. It's a characteristic I see she wears beautifully, like a Chanel purse.

"I'll eat your food and will show appreciation for your little gesture."

She shrugs a shoulder. "Since the food is already here and all. But I don't accept it as a peace offering. This is still war, Desmond."

"Still war. Okay." A smile pulls at the side of my lips. "Just make sure you do your best, and please make me look good. If you can do those two things while hating me, I'll have no complaints. Deal?"

"I don't make deals with enemies." She places each hand on either sides of her waist. "I'll work with you because I have no choice but to and I'll do my best because I'm unaware of any other way to do things."

I lick my lips, enticed by her energy. It's in this moment I realize exactly what draws me to her - her potential. It's exactly the potential my father has always encouraged me to search for in the women I involve myself with. The potential that would keep giving. Right now, it is like a diamond in the rough and heavily misguided, but it's present in her and burns bright. A potential that is raw, useful, beneficial, and worth the risk. And Mykal's got it.

I take a breath to maintain an even expression when the realization occurs to me.

She wants so bad to convince me that she's this tough and bullish. It's defensive and hardheaded, and I want to strip her of this burden of maintaining it so she can let her guard down and be free. I can't help the feeling of wanting to penetrate this tough exterior with a purpose of meeting who lies inside.

"But," she states, holding up a finger. "Let's get one thing straight - the only reason I haven't kicked you out yet and why I'll eat with you is because this is from Sergio's and only a fool would turn down Sergio's... even if it's an enemy bringing the food over unannounced."

My laugh echoes around the room. She tightens her lips to keep from smiling but is failing horribly.

Mykal points toward her kitchen island. "Let's have this over there."

I nod to agree while extending a hand in front of us for her to lead the way. "Let's."

NINETEEN

I stand in front of my full-length mirror in my living room. It's the night of the For The Culture anniversary party, so I am all dolled up in my best. After much deliberation I've gone with the siren red long-sleeved dress that fits me snug from my breasts to my hips. The back is out with a scoop that dips to the middle of my back. The dress is a showstopper. Besides the color, the garment clings to my shape, accentuates my hour-glass figure, and elongates my petite legs. My goal is to do more than turn heads. I want to break necks tonight, a specific neck, to be honest.

Pryce Williams's.

I know he'll be there. I checked with the party coordinators regarding if anything had changed. Not only is he attending the event, he will do so with his wife, but I don't care too much about the latter. She isn't my focus. Pryce is. Plus, competition is nothing new. I've just learned to be more of a willing participant than a person who runs from it like a coward... at least now I am.

My smartphone chimes with a call. I peek at it on my bed to see my mother's name flash on the screen. The phone is in my grip a second later.

"Hey mom."

"Hey sweetie, quick question."

"What's up?" I wedge the phone between my head and shoulder to smooth out the slight wrinkles in my dress.

"Your father and I are heading out tonight, and I want to match purple and green. What do you think of those colors together?"

I smile. My mother isn't the dress up type or a fashionista, so she'll often consult with me in these areas, which is always flattering.

"Those colors are excellent... for Mardi gras."

She giggles and I do as well.

"What's green, and what's purple?"

"My dress is green and my shoes are purple."

"Which item of clothing do you want to wear most tonight?"

"Oh, the green dress. Absolutely."

"I recall you having a pair of camel brown suede boots. Riding boots, right?"

"I do, yes!"

"Pair the dress with that and you should look great."

"Aw, thank you, sweetie. My personal fashion consultant. How blessed am I?"

I blush. If I could blush.

"Where are you headed, anyway?" I ask.

"Out with your father to watch a show."

At the mention of my dad, I twist my lips to one side.

"He's right here, actually."

Oh God. I hope she doesn't ask if I'd like to speak with him.

"I'll put you on speaker so you can say, hey."

Even worse.

Before I can protest her suggestion, she does as promised and announces, "You're on speaker, sweetie."

I want to scream but I ball my lips and inhale a bulk of air through my nose and say, "Hey daddy, how's it going?"

"Mykal," he utters as dryly as he always does. You would think him saying my name was like passing a kidney stone to him.

There's an uncomfortable silence.

"So, I hear you and mom are heading out to a show?"

"We are," he starts. "Your old classmate Nayla sent us tickets to her performance. Remember her?"

I suck my back teeth before I can stop myself. How could I forget *Nayla*? It surprises me she isn't stewing in hell yet.

"She's making her debut in this musical off Broadway and she invited us," he continues. "Front row seats. Amazing or what?"

"Or what." I mumble.

"I just know she'll be spectacular," he gushes and I want to vomit. "She did such an exceptional job in your school's imitation of The Wiz. I haven't seen a better Dorothy since then, besides Diana, of course."

I don't know when it happened, but I'm clutching the fabric of the dress I'm wearing so roughly, the wrinkles I ironed out with my hand moments ago have returned.

The second I notice it, I release my grip and take a breath through my mouth.

I've followed Nayla's theater journey off and on throughout the years since our high school graduation. She'd continued her performance arts studies by attending The Juilliard School to study voice and drama. Nayla has done several musicals and plays as a swing actor and standby. It seems her patience and probably additional backstabbing and betrayals have led her to a permanent leading role. One she so graciously sent tickets to *my* parents to attend her performance.

I can't decide what is more offending, the fact she sent tickets to my parents and not me, or that she sent them tickets to watch her perform in a show she's probably in because she stole my moment of shine from me and has been capitalizing off it ever since.

That bitch.

We haven't spoken since high school. Since she stole the role of Dorothy from right under me. She is the reason I gave up drama all together. Honestly, I hated singing and acting, and only did the latter to impress my father. Funny enough, the only reason I ended up hating singing and acting was because of my father, too. After that incident with Nayla, I decided to bail on the whole performance idea. I remained at Bakeridge High but switched my major the next day to script writing.

That interest in writing evolved to journalism when I decided to go to college after taking three years off from schooling to model following my high school graduation. And here I am today. But the bug to perform creeps up in me every so often and I squash it before it can become a prevailing thought.

"I'm headed out myself to somewhere great," I blurt. My voice is wavering. It's impossible to mask the desperation. "For The Culture's anniversary party is tonight. We're celebrating five years."

Silence.

Too long of a silence if you ask me.

"Oh!" my mother forces out. "That's... *great*, sweetie."

"Please." My father sucks his teeth in the background. "Don't lie to the girl, Talia. There's nothing *great* about it. It's not like she owns the magazine or anything. She's not even the editor-in-chief."

I clench my teeth.

"Mykal, have an amazing time tonight, okay?" My mother says sweetly. "Enjoy yourself and take plenty of pictures. I'm sure you'll look beautiful as always."

I force a smile, hoping the expression will translate through my words. "Thanks mom, I will."

I end the call with them a few seconds later, then I throw my phone across the living room.

That scream I'd been holding in, I finally let it out. I let it out with so much energy, my vocal cords feel strained when I'm done. But I feel better. And I know what will make me feel even better. More like *who* – seeing Pryce.

———

The event planners have gone all out for the anniversary party. This is the first thing I notice upon my arrival.

I step out of my chauffeured black car for the night and my eyes light up at all the flashing lights. We've rented out a banquet hall and built a marquee that has "For The Culture Celebrates 5 Years!" spelled out in lit bold letters.

A red carpet leads to a backdrop that has the magazine's name and the sponsors for the event sprawled all over it. Photographers stand on the other side of the red velvet rope, snapping pictures of the people who walk the red carpet.

"Mykal!" Asha calls from the front door.

I smile with all my teeth and wave her way.

She points at the red carpet and strikes a pose. I wave her off, but she insists by gesturing for me to walk through it.

After the conversation I had with my parents an hour earlier, I need something to lift my spirits and boost my confidence, so I take the walk.

"Beautiful," one photographer shouts the moment I step on.

"Over here, please," another calls so that he can get a shot of me facing him.

The cameras go off like lightning, practically blinding me, but I'm okay with it. More than okay. My cheeks are aching from how hard I'm smiling. I'm hitting these poses like I'm PR trained. Less than a minute into it, I'm in love! My adrenaline is pumping, heart racing for all the right reasons. It's like a rush hearing photogs scream for my attention and fight to get the best photo... of me, and they don't even know who I am.

I wave bye to them when I reach the end of the carpet and make my way to the door where Asha is waiting for me. My vision is returning but I'm on so much of a high, the prolonged blur in my eyes caused by the camera flashes doesn't even bother me.

"Dope or what?" she asks, meeting my wide grin with one of her own.

"*That* shit..." I point behind me at the red carpet and photographers. "... is a drug."

She drops her head back to laugh, then takes my hand to pull me along. "Wait until you see what they did with inside."

My eyes grow wider with each step we take. Asha's enthusiasm is par for the course because the events team have outdone themselves yet again. I can describe the place in two words - a wonderland. Crystal chandeliers everywhere, pure white tables, no chairs of course, silk white drapes hang from the ceilings like waterfalls of fabric. The DJ is blasting the latest hits. Everyone's dressed beautifully and has a certain level of Hollywood sparkle to them. I roll my eyes around the room until they collide with Desmond's. I must pay a second glance in his direction.

He's dressed to arouse. Quintessential debonair attire. Black and caramel brown are his colors of choice for the evening. Black button-down shirt with the silk tie to match kept contain behind a tailor-made slim fit vest with the matching blazer. His slacks stress his muscular columnar legs and I'm sure I've seen his black suede shoes in a fashion mag I read at the hair salon. It's not fair he looks this fucking good. I can't even snatch my eyes off him quick enough before he catches me staring.

Until...

Pryce walks in.

The music stops and everyone becomes a blur when Pryce steps through the door... at least from my vantage point. Complete contrast to Desmond in everything except his height. That is the only thing they twin at. Pryce dressed casually. Ripped stonewashed jeans, green bomber jacket over a bone-colored hoody. On his feet are wheat-colored Timber-land boots. Tattoos peek up through the hoody, the ink prominent around his neck.

Few photogs are in attendance inside. The only ones allowed past the red carpet are the ones paid by the magazine. They flock to Pryce immediately. Camera bulbs flash but they are no competition for the blinding yet genuine white smile he flashes them in return.

I feel a bump against my shoulder that forces me to peel my eyes off him.

"You're drooling," Asha claims, with a stone face.

I touch the side of my mouth to find nothing. "No I'm not."

"You will be if you keep staring at Pryce like that." She rolls her eyes. "Especially when the man's *wife* is standing right beside him. Are you nuts?"

I turn my attention back on him and notice her standing next to him. I missed her the first time, so caught up on Pryce. And I'm not sure how I didn't see her. She has all the double take potential packed in her petite frame, more than others in the room combined, and I can't help but to hate the fact that I can't deny it. Leelah pulled her cloud of blonde curls into a slicked low chignon for the night. She's sporting this all white off-the-shoulder jumpsuit with long-sleeves made of lace. The bottom of her jumpsuit flares out at the hem, concealing her shoes that I'm sure are designer. The woman glows and her smile makes me want to self-combust. She appears like she has everything she wants. From the confident stride in her walk and relaxed shoulders in her posture. I hate her for more than being Pryce's wife. She's perfect and I'm not, and that fact burns me in a place I can't soothe.

I feel a bump again and I whip my head in Asha's direction once more.

"Stop it," she warns with enormous eyes. "*Stop* whatever you're thinking right now because it's showing on your face. And if I can see it, I'm sure *she* will too."

Truth is Pryce's wife has everything and I just want one of those things, Pryce. Even if it is only his attention for tonight.

"I'm going to go over and say hello."

"Mykal, no!"

"I'm the assistant editor," I insist. "It's only right I greet them. How would it look if I didn't?"

"It would look just fine," Asha answers. "Considering your *very* recent history with Pryce."

"No one knows about it. I doubt *she* even does."

"But *you* do." Asha grabs my arm gently. "Let's just go to the bar, have a few drinks, and have a good night. Turn up like we planned! My husband's at home with the kids so I can hang for an extra two hours. Come on. Let's make the most of it."

"After..." I pull my arm free. "... I go say hello."

"Mykal, please don't—"

I walk off before Asha can say anything else or interfere with my plans to approach the Williams's.

The both of them are in the middle of a conversation with one of the magazine's in-house stylists when I interrupt them.

"Pryce," I say to him, only glancing at his wife for a moment.

His eyes meet mine before they briefly trace the outline of my body. His attention to the details below my neck brings a smile to my lips.

"It's been a while," I add, inhaling the surrounding air. I pick up traces of Leelah's fragrance that smells like a sweet flowering plant mixed with top-of-the-line essential oils. Her scent makes it harder to ignore her.

"Yeah," Pryce acknowledges, taking his wife's hand and pulling her close. "Wifey has given me a good excuse to stay busy these days."

"Too busy for me, though?"

I pause for reaction, and I get it a little. Leelah jerks her neck slightly, her eyes moving from Pryce to me, then on Pryce again.

He forces a laugh. "Still the same ol' Mykal, huh?"

I lock eyes with him and crack a sexy smile. "You know me well."

Pryce clears his throat and gestures at me before glancing at his wife. "Baby, this is Mykal Jones, Amir's cousin and the new assistant editor at For The Culture." He looks to me, "Mykal, this is my beautiful wife, Leelah Waters-Williams."

Now I have to pay her attention and when I do, her presence costs me my confidence.

Her eyes drink me in slowly.

Leelah's got the grayest eyes I've ever seen. They appear almost silver with the lights reflecting off them. She's not a troll at all like I claimed and I knew she wasn't when I said that. She's breathtaking, and the one thing that would be an obvious boost to her beauty, her light eyes, proves she isn't just a pretty face. Her eyes aren't empty and dependent on being just pretty. There's sincerity behind her gaze. She exudes a silent empathetic and unspoken warmness in them, a characteristic that is probably what's got Pryce so damn smitten over her.

"It's nice to meet you, Mykal," she says. "I read your cover story on Pryce last year. You captured him excellently through words. Better than anyone else could... besides himself, of course."

Leelah moves in close beside him and takes him by the arm, tilting her head back so she can gaze up at him. He peers down at her and they share a glance before he lowers his lips to hers and pecks her right in front of me.

I inhale a deep silent breath.

I wonder if she knows how to fight because I don't, but I'm kind of willing to risk it all.

"Thank you," I say, forcing a smile. "He made it easy."

When his lips are off hers, he moves them to her forehead to leave another kiss. Something across the room steals his attention when he does that and I'm burning red inside that it isn't me.

"Oh! Corey just walked in," Pryce announces, glancing down at Leelah. "Let me introduce you to him. Mykal," he says to me, paying me not even a second more of a glance before taking Leelah by the hand again to walk off, "it was good seeing you."

He turns to exit our little huddle. Leelah peeks over her shoulder all casual-like when she exits our conversation. "Nice talking to you, Mykal. Enjoy your night."

Her hips sway as she follows Pryce close behind. He holds her hand so sweetly, and when he realizes they aren't close enough, he moves an arm around her waist and pulls her closer to him.

Watching him with her leaves a nasty taste in my mouth and there's nothing I can say about it. She is sweet and more than polite. Wholesome and genuine.

"Bitch," I still whisper to myself.

I went from feeling like a star on that red carpet to feeling like some kind of lesser in her presence. I don't like that at all and I refuse to accept defeat.

Pryce runs his hand up and down her back as they speak with Corey at the far end of the room. Of course, because of the distance between us and the music pumping loud out of the speakers, I can't hear them. But from what I can see, she's comfortable in Pryce's environment. What's supposed to be *my* environment. A party for the magazine I'm assistant editor, and she's more comfortable here than me. That pisses me off even more.

"Did you behave yourself?" Asha asks when she rejoins me.

I roll my eyes in her direction and stare at her from the side of my eyes. "As best I could. He kept it cute around his wife and I really can't fault him for that but I'm sure if we were alone again, he would show me someone different."

"Girl." Asha shakes her head. "You gotta let this go. Pryce is a married man and, as a married woman myself, I can tell you I'd be willing to catch a case over a woman like you not knowing how to chill the fuck out. *Leave* that man alone, *please*. I am begging you. If for nothing else, do it for your own peace."

I hear Asha's words, and honestly, she's giving sage advice. She's a friend and is doing what a friend would do, try to talk sense into me... but I'm not trying to hear any of it.

"You're right," I concede, turning to her to force a smile. "Let's go grab a drink at the bar."

She points at me and smiles big. "See *now*, you're talking my love language. Come on!"

I sneak another peek at the Williams's on my way over to the bar. Pryce is smiling from ear to ear when he turns away from the convo he's having and finds me staring. He glances my way as I walk past. It is brief, but I catch when his eyes do that thing again and he steals a peek at my ass before snatching his eyes off me.

And that tiny morsel of attention is all I need to defibrillate my efforts with him. Because I have no intention of giving up without really shooting my shot with Pryce.

What I lack in wholesomeness I more than overflow with in sensuality and sexuality, something Leelah couldn't touch me on, I am sure of that. If there's one thing I know I can do, it's fuck a man to my submission. If all fails, there's always sex and I'm willing to lower the bar just to prove my point.

Yeah, I said it.

The night is winding down, finally. As much fun as I'm having at this For The Culture anniversary party, I just want to return home and lie in my bed with a warm sexy body beside me.

It's later in the night but people are still entering the party for the first time. The owners, Corey and Amir, have both arrived and left. Corey had to travel to Miami for business and Amir needed to return home to his wife and their newborn son. All who remain at the party are magazine staff, their plus ones, photographers, and a few reporters from other publications covering the event. Most of the tables held empty glasses on their surface. The dance floor is lively now. People moving to the music, the DJ spins. I'm on one end of the room, my back to a wall after spending most of my night sitting in VIP. I'm not sure if anyone else can tell, but I'm ready to go.

"You really should try the champagne," Faith insists beside me, finishing her second glass. She's been good company tonight, but not enough of the distraction I was hoping she'd be.

I invited Faith to the party the day I learned about it. With this thing with Mykal turning into my new weakness, I wanted to ensure that I kept my distance from her, and the only way I knew to do that was by bringing Faith with me. I knew my penchant for not being rude would force me to keep my distance from Mykal so I could keep Faith company throughout the night, since she knew no one here.

What good that did.

For most of the night, my eyes would scan the room in search of Mykal. I tracked her conversation with Pryce and his wife, then her time at the bar before she and her coworker danced a little on the dance floor. After that, I lost sight of her and I've been trying to find her in this big room ever since.

"I think I'll stick with cognac," I answer Faith, while I visually searched the room for Mykal again. "Champagne, unless it's a particular brand, gives me a headache."

She shrugs a shoulder. "Well, I'm going to grab another glass at the bar. I'll be back soon."

I nod at Faith's exit and return to scanning. If there was a night, I needed a release, it was tonight. Mykal showed up here looking like sex in a dress. Chocolate poured into the color red. She's gorgeous every day but tonight exceptionally eye catching. I could mingle with everyone tonight except for her. And I'm feeling a way about that.

"You really brought a plus one huh?" I hear beside me. I lower my eyes quickly to find the woman occupying my thoughts, Mykal, standing next to me against the same wall.

"And you didn't," I reply, pushing my back off the wall to stand upright. I turn to face her.

She gives me a once over, and licks her lips. "One thing I have to give you, Desmond, is you know your way around your designers."

"My mother was a fan of fashion." I smile to myself. "I knew all the important labels by heart by the time I was five."

Though my years with my mother were brief, one thing I remembered was that fashion was her other religion. She loved to wear the latest and greatest, and to present herself to the world at her best. She'd always say to my father, "Just because I'm charitable doesn't mean I have to dress that way."

I chuckled to myself at the thought.

"What's funny?" Mykal asks.

"Nothing." I shake my head, still smiling. "Just had a random thought about her."

"Hmph," she huffs.

"Look good, feel good," I say next. "My mother's motto. She used to say that if she looked good, she'd feel good, and if she felt good, she'd do good and align herself more with helping others feel and do good too."

Mykal sputters a laugh. "She sounds like she was a saint."

"She was," I say lowly, to more so myself.

"So." Mykal moves in a step closer. "What are you getting into tonight?"

Our eyes meet and there's this familiar energy in her gaze. A penetrative stare that has had me deciding to do things I know better not to do since arriving at For The Culture. But they're decisions I've made, because to me, Mykal is irresistible in ways I must avoid.

"More like *who*; my date for the night, hopefully," I answer before taking a sip of my drink.

Her look of seduction morphs with my words.

"Her name is Faith," I tell Mykal. "I can introduce you to her if you like."

"I'd much rather slide down the edge of a hot razor blade naked and cool off in a pool of alcohol after." Mykal pushes herself off the wall beside me. "You seem bored with her, anyway. You should drop her home and spend your night wisely with someone who can make your next few hours worth it. Like with me."

The prospect makes my dick stiffen in my slacks. Because what I wouldn't do to have her red dress decorate an area of my apartment's floor tonight.

"Why would I do that when we've discussed this?" I ask.

"Because much like your date, it's also boring to be well-behaved most times."

"While I appreciate the invitation, Mykal," I retort. "I'm going to have to pass."

"I brought you more cognac," Faith announces as she approaches from behind.

I watch as Mykal's eyes move over my shoulder and then switch my way again.

I lift my current glass of cognac to my mouth and finish the drink, setting the empty glass on the white table in front of me and turning to Faith to accept the fresh one she's walked over.

"Faith, this is Mykal," I introduce. "Mykal, my friend Faith."

Mykal's eyes roll from the top of Faith's head and linger on Faith's mesh ruched baby blue mini dress and finally settle on the tip of Faith's silver pumps. She says nothing to Faith, so Faith takes initiative.

"Oh!" Faith lays a hand against my chest. "She's the woman you said hates your guts, right?"

Mykal's eyes stare at Faith's hand on my chest.

"Actually," Mykal starts, refocusing on Faith, "I'm the woman he's fucked twice... so far, at least."

Faith's jaw drops and so does mine before I cover my mouth with my fist and laugh into it.

"You two have a good night," Mykal remarks before walking off and switching her hips the entire way. I hate myself for turning my head to watch her ass rise and fall with her walk.

My hand is at my face now, fingers pinching the bridge of my nose.

"Wow." Faith chuckles lowly before taking a sip of her champagne. "I wish I can say her revelation surprises me but that would be the lie of all lies."

"Faye."

"I guess I see now why you've been missing in action lately." Faith shakes her head. "She's beautiful. A huge *bitch*, but beautiful. Exactly your type."

"Faith, I—"

"You told me she hates you but you left out the part about you fucking her." She turns to face me. "Twice, was it?"

"Let me explain—"

"Just, wow, Desmond. Wow."

"I apologize for her brashness, but why are you so bothered?"

She gasps.

"I thought we were cool." I bump my shoulder into hers.

"Yeah, I'm *cool*, but I'm not *that* cool, Desmond," she answers. "I prefer assuming you're sleeping with someone else over actually knowing and *meeting* the woman."

I sigh. "Can we just pretend that didn't happen?"

She rolls her eyes. "I'm a model, Dez, not an actress."

"Isn't it all the same thing, though?"

"*Take* me home, right now," she orders through her teeth. "And by home, I mean mine where you will not be."

I slowly shut my eyes and squeeze them tight.

There goes my night.

———

Faith was decided when she told me to take her home. I apologized from the venue to her building's curb and she accepted not a single apology.

"You embarrassed me, Desmond," she scolded as she unhooked her seatbelt.

"How?! I did nothing," I replied lowly.

"That's my damn point." She shook her head. "You didn't tell me you slept with your assistant editor, and you didn't put her in her place when she spilled your business to me. You did nothing."

I never took Mykal to be the messy type. If I did, I surely would have kept my distance tonight or thought twice about inviting Faith as my plus one.

I drive down the winding driveway and stop feet in front of the door of my father's property. It is still early in the night and I didn't feel like returning to the party or driving back to my apartment. So, I figured I'd visit my father's home to be in his company. He may not be cognizant, but his presence is all the comfort I needed tonight.

Usually, all the lights in the house are off, all except my father's master bedroom light, but tonight is the opposite. All the lights are off in the property, from my view outside, all except in his study.

I step through the door and enter in silence. Lights from soft white bulbs cast a warm glow through the crack in the door that leads to my father's study. The light's existence instantly furrow my brows. Instinctively, I look up the stairs to find nothing but darkness.

I want to call his nurse, Mali's name. Sure, she must be around somewhere, but I follow the warmth of the light like a moth to a flame. When I arrive within feet of the threshold to my father's study, I press my palm flat against the door's surface and push the door open slowly.

At his desk is my father. His reading glasses sit on the bridge of his nose and his hands hold up a newspaper. For a moment, I convince myself that I must be hallucinating. It's as if time has gone back and it has transported me several years in the past with my father seated at his desk reading.

"I found him in here earlier," I hear whispered over my shoulder. Mali's standing a few feet behind me when I glance that way. She closes her dark gray sweater over her blue scrubs and walks a little closer. "I brought him a newspaper and I just left him be."

I turn to look at him again.

"You better get in there," she insists with a smile. "Enjoy every bit of this moment."

I inhale sharply and nod, turning toward the threshold of the study's door.

"Se-senior?" I stutter.

My father glances up from the newspaper in his hand. He lowers the glasses from his nose to his chest, the specs hanging against his chest like a necklace thanks to his glasses's chain.

"How much, Desmond?" he quizzes, giving me his undivided attention.

His response almost knocks me off my feet.

The moment my father's doctors confirmed his dementia had entered middle stage Alzheimer's, I'd been calling him Senior. I'd been doing it for a reason. That wasn't my usual name for my father. It was a name I used whenever I needed something as a kid. It became an inside joke between the two of us. I'd mess up and need his help. And he'd know right away I messed up because instead of calling him dad, I'd call him Senior. His doctor encouraged it. Said it would assist with helping my father recollect in times of confusion or forgetfulness. I'd been using the title for over a year. I lost hope somewhere around the six-month mark. So, you can imagine my shock.

Still I asked, "What do you mean, *how much*?"

"What do I mean?" He chuckles to himself while leaning back in his seat. My heart swells with delight, seeing him in his preferred setting. My father used to live in his study. Brainstorming article ideas, typing most of them up in that chair and at that desk with several shelves of books behind him. I take a mental picture because I know in my heart of hearts this won't last long.

"Whenever you call me Senior, I just know I either have a problem to fix or something to pay."

I laugh, not recognizing my expression of amusement. That's because I can't decide if I want to laugh or cry and the ache in my voice is clear. Tears prickle at the sides of my eyes. I want to run to him, fall to my knees and hug him until the muscles in my arms hurt. It's been too long since I've felt like I could tell someone my problems, give them my troubles, and they solve it all for me. My father was that person, but after Alzheimer's set in, I've had to be my own strong friend.

"And since you didn't walk in here with your shoulders slumped like you did when you broke Mr. Dawson's living room window after batting your baseball through it when you were ten..."

I bark a laugh at the memory, holding my fist up at my mouth.

"I know you need money," he says through a laugh. "So, how much?"

I move my fist from my mouth and press my hand to my chest and say, "No money, dad, I just... I'm just happy to see you is all."

"Hmph," he huffs, chuckling to himself next.

I make my way into the room, my eyes fixed on him, refusing to break focus because I want to remember this moment long after today. "What are you reading there?"

"Today's paper." He closes it and sets it down on the desk. "The maid in the blue scrubs out there brought it in to me an hour ago when I stepped into the study."

I furrow my brows and peek behind me at Mali. She holds a hand up and mouths *"it's fine"* and offers a warm approving smile.

"You know, " my father says. I twist in my seat to face him again. "I don't know who they have editing these things lately. The errors are glaring. Almost makes me want to take on the job of beta editing just so I can have something decent to read. Horrible. I imagine this writer is a freelancer. You know how I feel about freelancers."

My joy slants my eyes as I relish this moment. "Well, you know, with the great Desmond Ellis II retired, help is at a minimum."

"They should publish nothing at all, if that's the case, I believe."

"I-I recently received a promotion to editor, if you can believe it," I tell him. "At a magazine called For The Culture. It's new. They just celebrated five years."

His brows shoot you.

"Black owned."

"All right now!" He smiles with all his teeth. Even at my father's age, his smile shaves off a good ten years. "Now that's amazing news. Congratulations, son. I'm proud of you."

I close my eyes and exhale all the air in me, allowing his words to travel through my ears and find a home in my memories. I want to remember this moment through and through so I can replay it in my mind at a later time.

"Thanks dad," I say. "I really appreciate it."

"Absolutely." He nods. "If I could do it again, I would've created my own."

"You will," I tell him, sitting up in my seat. "I'm planning to launch a newspaper in your name."

He sits back. "Say what now?"

"That's the whole reason I even accepted the promotion. To gain the experience working at a publication so I know how to handle the day-to-day operation of print media and delegate responsibilities accordingly."

He blinks in response.

I could tell him about the ghostwriting I've been doing to perfect my craft, or that I created a blog and have been ghostwriting under his name, providing commentary on current news events affecting the black community. But there's no time. I don't know how long he'll be cognizant and I won't chance it.

"It's a large feat, I know."

"Huge." He leans forward in his seat. "But you got this. I raised you to be capable. Journalism is in your DNA."

I nod, receiving every bit of his encouragement. Because I've been needing it, desperately.

"I'll be here for guidance whenever you need it."

I know this isn't true. I know that this moment we're having is only temporary, fleeting, and might never happen again. His doctors already told me about instances of cognizance. That it'll happen out of nowhere, in a flash sometimes, and go away just as quick. But I don't ruminate on that too much. I made a vow to myself to enjoy every moment with my father. For better or for worse. And I intend to do that now.

"But I doubt you'll need it," he assures next.

I'm filled with warmth on that alone, his confidence in me. Despite how much I've fucked up, I'm assured that I can still meet my goals.

"How about when it comes to matters of the heart?"

His question makes me blink hard. "Of the heart? What do you mean?"

"I've heard about work which you are clearly excelling at and I know you aren't short of admirers."

I chuckle.

"You've never been. Short of sense when it comes to them, yes, but never short of a flock. However, love is a man's balance. Work is essential and admirers are nice for things to do, but love helps you recharge and elevate. The right kind keeps you evolving and growing."

"There's someone, I think... although we've met under questionable circumstances that have somehow complicated things."

His brows wrinkle.

"She's convinced she hates me but I have reason, several reasons to believe otherwise."

"Your mother hated me too." He laughs. "She was the prim and proper queen and I the slick talking corner boy from Brooklyn. But she recognized my potential to be more."

"I remember the stories she told about you two."

"Well. " He chuckles some more. "This woman you speak of, does she have potential?"

I close my eyes and nod confidently, grateful I can answer honestly and with foreknowledge that this would make him happy. "She has *plenty* of the potential *we've* discussed."

"Then cultivate that," he instructs. "In whatever way that potential needs to be cultivated, facilitate that to meet the end goal. You're already creating a lifeline, this paper you mentioned. Cultivate her potential so it's aligned with your lifeline and make sure you help her do the same for you." He winks.

I nod again, understanding exactly what he means but not knowing in that instance how I would do such a thing with a woman like Mykal.

"Now," he says, folding his hands on his desk and scooting his chair closer. "Tell me more about this paper you're planning to launch. I want to know everything."

So I do. I tell my father every detail I have developed and the time-line of events that must occur to make it happen, and he listens to everything. We talk until the night sky gives way to morning and the time we spend together becomes the greatest hours of my life.

TWENTY-ONE

"**D**efense!"

Boom. Boom. Boom.

"Defense!"

Boom. Boom. Boom.

The crowd cheers from the television screen mounted behind the bar. I sit on a stool, my eyes glued to the screen. I gently grasp the dome of my wine glass.

My eyes burn from tiredness, and I blink my lids repeatedly, trying to water my eyes enough to soothe the ache.

The time is 7pm local time in Oakland, California, which is my current time zone until tomorrow. I'd just gotten off a flight from New York to Oakland two hours earlier.

I roll my head around my neck twice, then sit up in my seat. To say I am only jet lagged would be a lie.

I'm also nervous.

"Can I refill your glass?" The bartender questions. I'm on my second glass and already I'm experiencing lightheadedness.

"Any more wine you'll have to pay someone to carry me out of here."

He smirks. "I doubt I'll have to pay anyone to carry you anywhere. I know I'd do it for free."

I ball my lips to keep from smiling. "I'm flattered."

"As you should be."

I bat my lashes playfully and he laughs in response.

"Where are you visiting from?"

"How do you know I'm not a local?" I take a sip of my wine, swallowing slowly.

"Your accent," he answers, smiling. "It's got East Coast all over it."

I tilt my head to one side. "Really?"

"*Mm-hmm,*" he hums, nodding. "Noticed it when you ordered your first glass."

I giggle while shrugging a shoulder. "I never knew I had an accent."

"Well, it's there." He leans his forearm on the bar. "So, where you from?"

"New York."

"Yeah," he drawls out. "I can see it. With your chic trench coat and cute haircut. Probably live in the city, huh? Like Carrie Bradshaw?"

"I'd like to believe I'm more like Samantha, even though Carrie and I earn our money the same way."

"Samantha, huh?" His smile widens. "Don't tease now."

I toss my head back and laugh.

The bar has some square footage to the layout, but it's a tiny hole in the wall in downtown Oakland. Downtown Oakland was my first stop when I stepped out of the airport. The hotel I need to be at is located here.

"You're a writer," he guesses.

"How'd you figure that?"

"You said you earn your money the same way Carrie Bradshaw does. She was a writer in the show."

"And how do you know so much about Sex and the City, anyway? You're not their target market."

From appearance, he didn't seem like the romantic-comedy binge watching type. His bulging biceps and a forest for a beard said otherwise.

"My ex was a huge fan." He shook his head. "I'd watch it with her to seem sensitive. It was a pretty good show though."

"It was."

"Are you in town for work or pleasure?"

I point my eyes up at the screen. The cameraman pans the camera on Pryce Williams at the perfect time to capture him shooting a three-point shot. Pryce's new team, The Bronx Ballers, is playing his old team, the Oakland Flames, in Oakland tonight at a venue only a walking distance from the bar, and the game that started almost two hours ago is just about to end. This game is the whole reason I even boarded a flight to fly over 3,000 miles from home.

"I'm in town for both work and pleasure."

More the latter and less the former.

After the For The Culture anniversary party, I couldn't stop thinking about Pryce. It's not like I tried. Pryce and his wife, Leelah, only stayed at the party for an hour. And from the time he arrived and until he and his wife left, he didn't pay me an ounce of attention. I'd steal glances at him every so often while at the event, but he kept his eyes glued to Leelah. His lack of attention to me was frustrating. I figured he had to do that since she was with him and I just knew if things were different, if it were just the two of us, he'd be true to himself.

So... I created the possibility of us being alone.

"Nice," the bartender comments. "It's always nice to combine the two."

"I agree."

The Ballers win the game by ten points and I'm out of the bar five minutes later.

Pretty poignant too. Pryce playing his old team in his old hometown. Flying to Oakland was a decision I gave little thought to. Not when I decided I'd board a plane on a Thursday, not when I put in a request for two days off, not even after I got the deets on what hotel and room Pryce planned to stay while in Oakland.

I hoped he'd stay in his old place, a two-story Spanish Mediterranean home that a Cribs inspired TV series featured in one of their episodes. Seems he sold the house soon after he got married.

That's okay.

Although I'll have to adjust my plans a little, I'm sure I'll still be able to carry them out.

I push through the turnstile doors and enter The Laurel. It's a five-star hotel with outdoor seating in their garden of rich green palms and colorful flowers. Inside the lobby, hotel patrons walk about the area, heading either to the hotel's restaurant or to the bank of elevators to head up to their rooms.

I booked a room a few hours before flying out, although I have no intention of staying between those four walls. I needed access to the hotel so that I could conveniently make my way to Pryce's floor, which I navigate to when I step on the elevator.

I watch attentively as the floor numbers on the mini-tv screen changes with the elevation of the car. By the time the elevator car gets to the 30th floor and the doors open, I take a deep breath and step out.

I've planned to wait for Pryce for an hour, the most an hour and a half. I know that after every game, he interviews on the court, does press in the locker room, then needs time to shower and change before he leaves to head home or, in this case, to his hotel to rest.

My heart picks up the pace as I stand against the wall beside the door of his room. Found out his room number from his assistant, Darnell. I told Darnell that For The Culture wanted to send Pryce a thank you gift for his attendance at our anniversary event and, since he would be out of town, we could ship it to wherever his next game was. Because his assistant and I have dialogued before, Darnell thought nothing of it and not only told me the hotel Pryce would stay at but what room he booked under his name. For added measure, I inquired if Pryce's wife would accompany him because we want to send her something too. Darnell told me I could send her gift to their home in upstate New York because she would not join Pryce on his brief trip to Oakland.

I twist my wrist to glance at my timepiece as I wait. I planned up until this moment. I don't really have a plan, don't know what I'll do or say once Pryce arrives, but I doubt I'll need to do much. We have some history. He's seen me in my lingerie. That moment we shared at Chateau Luxure meant something. He never denied he wanted me and only turned me down because his head wasn't in it that night. I'm sure things are different and with us alone again, I doubt he'll turn me down twice.

The faint sound of the elevator arriving on the floor chimes from the far end of the hall. The Laurel is a large hotel. Pryce's room resides on a floor of suites likely all booked by the players on his team.

Pryce appears when he steps around the corner wall. His attention is down on his phone as he swaggers toward me and his room. On his shoulder swings the strap of a duffel bag and in the other hand a gallon of water. I exhale a sigh of relief when I see he's alone because I didn't have an idea what I would do if he had his bodyguards with him, or worse, someone who would recognize me. My relieving exhale pulls him from his phone and he double takes when he sees me standing on the other end of the hall.

He pauses in step for only a second.

"Mykal?" he questions low, jerking his head back next.

I lift a hand to wave innocently. My heart is hammering now. I played this scenario in my head dozens of times on the flight over and in the bar where I waited, but nothing could really prepare me for this.

He turns to glance over his shoulder, then faces forward, closing the rest of the distance between us.

He furrows his brows when he arrives in front of me. "What are you doing here? How did you even...?"

I take a deep breath and steady my trembling legs. "I figured we had some unfinished business."

I couldn't stop shaking. And his unchanging reaction is throwing me off.

"Unfinished business? Are you serious?" He runs his palm down his lips before balling his hand into a fist and holding it over his mouth. "I don't know what you mean by that but... yo, what the hell are you doing here right now, Mykal?"

"Pryce." I step forward and he takes a step back. I take a breath to recover from his reaction. "I play back that night we shared at Chateau Luxure last year *repeatedly* in my head."

He closes his eyes and shakes his head.

"That night was *ours*. And even though nothing happened between us, I've wanted you for a long time. A *really* long time. I've wanted you long before then and you know that. At this point, I acknowledge your *situation* and I'm willing to look past it, for tonight... if you are."

"My *situation*?!" He asks, his voice increasing in volume. "I don't have a *situation*. I have a marriage. I'm a married man. Happily. You met my wife." He bends his legs at the knees for only a moment, so we're eye to eye. "Remember that?"

I untie the belt of my trench from around my waist and peel open the coat by the lapels to reveal the same nude lace bra and panties set I wore the night he turned me down.

Pryce's eyes leave mine to venture south of my neck, taking in the nude lace clad to my curves underneath the trench.

He stands up straight again and takes another step back.

"Nah." He steps around me and his absence leaves a brush of air behind. "You need to get the fuck off my floor with this shit. You're tryna bring problems to me and I'm not with it. At all." He dips a hand into his black joggers' pocket to retrieve his room key. "I don't even want anyone to catch me standing here with you."

"Pryce—"

He turns quick to face me again.

"You out your *fucking* mind right now!" His warm breath hits my face as he stage whispers while pointing at me. His eyes are shooting daggers now. It's a scowl that stuns me, one I've never seen from him. The intensity behind his glare sobers me right the hell up.

"I am *married*, and this right here? This shit you did? Done brought to me? Is disrespectful on so many levels. I introduced you to my fucking *wife*, Mykal!"

"I don't give a shit about her," I shoot back.

"Well, I definitely do!" His chest rises and falls with so much force. His mouth morphs into a tight jaw before his top lip hikes on one side, and he stares at me in disgust. "Yo, with all due *disrespect*, get the hell away from my door before I have to call security."

I jerk my head back.

"Now!" He shouts, his voice echoing around us. I jump back. "Get the fuck off my floor and go fast, Mykal. For real."

I take a breath and hold the air in. Tears prick the side of my eyes. I refuse for him to see a tear fall, so I turn to leave. A part of me is saying for me not to glance back, but I've made enough poor decisions today. Why not make another, right? Believing I'll see Pryce at least looking my way, I turn in time to find the hall empty and his door closing as he enters his room.

I stop and purse my lips at his absence. All the planning and scheming to pull this off never brought about the possibility of this scenario. I want to run up to his room's door and draw him back out here, curse him every which way for disrespecting me, denying me, whatever, all, so he can feel what I'm feeling right now.

Rejection.

Inferiority.

Embarrassment.

I want him to feel something. But I do nothing except turn on my heels and make my way off his floor.

I stomp my way to the elevators, stabbing at the buttons when I'm there. I don't care if I go up or down, I just need off this floor before I lose it.

Here I was yet again.

Another scenario for the books where Mykal gets the short end of a situation. Left wanting something she can't have... and I have had enough of this shit.

TWENTY-TWO

Light listening music plays from unseen speakers. The chatter of patrons hums just above the music. People fill tables to the brim within eyeshot. Across from me is Mykal, whose eyes are moving around the room as she takes in the environment around her. It was a long shot inviting her to dinner tonight and her accepting. I'd only had the idea the day before, but had a feeling she would refuse. Shocked me when she agreed.

"You were right," she admits, breaking the silence between us. I give her my attention. "It's nice."

Something's been a little off with her lately. She'd requested time off days ago and had returned to work with less steam than usual. Quieter in meetings and to herself throughout the workday. We weren't the best of friends, considering her disdain for me. And because I had nothing really to go off besides my assumption, I've kept my concerns to myself, but something is definitely different with her.

I bow my head in acknowledgement of her comment.

We sit in SeaView, a restaurant on an anchored yacht on Long

Island. It sits on the East River that divides New York City from the island. At our window seats, we can see the skyscrapers in the distance lighting up the night.

"Romantic," she mumbled. "This is the place I would assume you'd bring someone you at least liked."

"Well." I chuckle. "I've already confessed to *liking* you, Mykal."

She exhales and sighs as she peers to her left to glance out her window. "You know what I mean."

I squint my eyes in observation. "Mykal, is everything... okay?"

She looks at me.

"I can't help but notice you've been a little less than Mykal lately."

"What do you mean?"

"Less snappy turtle." I crack a smile.

She arches a brow.

"For one I'm shocked you agreed to accompany me here tonight."

"You were offering free food, and you said you needed to talk to me regarding the unsung project." She shrugs a shoulder. "I needed to eat and get out of my apartment, so I thought, why not?"

"I offered to pick you up in my car," I add, "and you said yes with no convincing."

"I don't own a car and I definitely didn't want to rent one and pay a toll to drive here either."

I move my eyes off her for only a moment to mull her answers over in my head.

"It's not that deep. It's like you said, we still have to work together so, I'm *working* with you."

Completely out of anything else to say on the matter, I simply huff, "Hmph."

"Speaking of which." She shifts in her chair. "What about the project did you want to discuss?"

"Yes," I answer, leaning forward in my seat. "The team's articles for the unsung project have been beyond exceptional. It's exceeding my expectations and I have you to thank for that."

Nothing in reaction. Not even a crack of a smile.

"It looks like we'll complete this project early. I wanted to commend you for that and to celebrate a little with dinner."

"You didn't have to do this." She forces a smile. "Just doing my job."

"You're doing more than just your job." I nod for emphasis. "I know you're not the biggest fan of mine and I know how things started between us was unconventional, but you've not let that get in the way professionally and I'd like to thank you for that most of all. This could have been a disaster, but it wasn't. So, thank you."

She folds her cinnamon glossed lips into her mouth and rubs them together then simply nods.

Though she won't confirm it, something is weighing on her. I don't expect for her to tell me, nor will I ask her to. But I decide to do something about it.

"Pick a table of patrons you like."

She looks up at me. "Excuse me?"

"A couple, a group, anyone. Surveil the restaurant and choose the table of people you like. You're allowed to go off of just appearances and you can judge as much as you like. Just pick who you like."

"But, why?"

"Just do it."

She stares at me for a moment before taking a breath, blinking a few times, then peeling her attention off me to survey the room. SeaView is at capacity for the night. Reservations filled with not a single empty table available for seating.

"Them." She points discretely. I follow her line of vision to a couple. They're older, possibly mid-60s. They sit next to each other as they enjoy what's left of their meals. On the other side of the woman are a dozen red roses and a small box that sits on ripped white gift wrapping paper.

"Why them?" I ask.

She twists her head to squint my way. "I have to explain my answer?"

I smirk. "Oh, absolutely. Mykal Jones doesn't just like anyone, I've learned. So why them?"

She rolls her eyes and inhales the surrounding air before releasing it slowly.

"They're in love," she answers. "After whatever amount of years they've been together, they do more than tolerate each other. I can tell this because they sat beside each other instead of across from one another in a crowded restaurant, no less. The one opportunity they get to sit apart they decide against it."

I glance their way again and see their story through Mykal's eyes.

"I like that" She sips her wine. "So, I like them."

I focus forward and make eyes with the waitress in charge of our table, gesturing for her to approach Mykal and I. We've placed our orders, but it hasn't arrived, although that isn't what I want to talk to our waitress about.

"Your order will be out shortly," she confirms when she's in earshot.

"I appreciate the update, however, I have an uncommon request."

"Sure, what can I get for you?"

I gesture to the elderly couple. "Are you servicing at their table as well?"

She shoots a glance that way. "I am, yes."

"If they haven't paid for their dinner yet, my guest and I would like to settle their bill."

Mykal's brows shoot up.

The waitress's face lights up next. "Oh, wow. Well, no, they haven't covered their bill since they are still working on dinner."

I scoot forward in my seat to dip my hand in my slacks' back pocket to pull out my wallet.

While sliding out my credit card, I tell the waitress, "Please charge the cost of their meal and anything else they've ordered on this card, but do me one big favor."

"Sure," she says, accepting the card.

"Let them know someone has taken care of their bill, but do not tell them who took care of it. If they ask, just tell them someone who admired them."

The waitresses smile grows wider. "No problem. It's their anniversary too. They're celebrating thirty-years married, so I'm sure this will be a welcomed surprise to them."

The waitress leaves our table, and my focus returns to Mykal. She slightly slacks her jaw.

"That was mighty generous," she states, fighting back a smile.

"Wait till you see what happens next," I assure her.

A second or two later, the waitress returns my card to me before venturing over to the couple who has just finished their meal. They exchange a few words before the couple's heads are moving left to right, scanning the room.

"Look away," I tell Mykal, and she does so quickly. After a few moments pass, I instruct her to look again and just as I knew would happen, Mykal smiles, genuinely. From a place I knew needed to feel the energy of that smile.

The couple continue searching, the apples of their cheeks lifting from smiling so hard. The wife's eyes land on Mykal and the two lock eyes. The wife puts two and two together, taps her husband on his forearm, and then points our way. He holds a hand up in the sign of thanks and the wife presses her palms together and bows her head towards us. Although this isn't how I like to pay-it-forward, preferring anonymity, I acknowledge them and the gesture since it seems to lift Mykal's spirits.

"That felt—"

"Good?" I finish.

"Different, was the word I was going for," she admits, her eyes slightly slanting from her growing grin.

"Well," I say, leaning forward to pick up my glass of cognac. "It made your face do something I don't see often but that I insist you should allow it to do more of."

"And that's?"

"Smile."

She balls her lips to keep from smiling again.

"You really have a beautiful smile, Mykal. Please don't fight it."

Her eyes find mine and keep it company for a second too long. Dinner tonight was to be as cordial as cordial should get, but I've seen this look in Mykal's eyes before, and it's trouble... the kind I like.

My phone buzzes in my pocket, causing me to blink free of her stare.

I slide my hand into my pant pocket and pull out my phone, clearing my throat when I read the name on my phone's screen.

"Excuse me," I say to Mykal. "I have to take this."

I should excuse myself physically from the table too, but I answer instead in front of her.

It's the yelling in the background that makes me push my chair back without thinking.

"Mr. Ellis," my father's nurse says as calmly as she can, given the noise in the background. I know it's taking a lot of effort not to mirror all the bass-filled screaming and things shattering, but she doesn't, and I know her calm is more for me than anything else.

"I'll be right there," I promise immediately.

I'm up and on my feet a second later, seconds away from turning my feet toward the restaurant's exit when Mykal comes into view.

Shit.

"*Um.*" I pinch the space between my eyes. "I have to go."

Her eyes are moving from left to right, analyzing me.

It's hard to weigh my options.

"Okay," she pushes her chair back. "Should I call a cab, or...?"

Right.

"Shit." I sit back down. "*Uh*, yeah." I shake my head next. "No."

"Huh?"

"Dammit. *Um.*" My hand is back on my face, fingers pinching the bridge of my nose again.

I invited her out to Long Island and picked her up in my car. It just didn't seem right to abandon her like this, but my father needed me and I couldn't leave the nurse to handle him alone. Mali is already doing more than any live-in nurse should do.

"It's okay," Mykal assures low. "I can call a cab. This wouldn't be the first time I've had to find my way back home after a date."

Even though this isn't a date, I wouldn't correct her. That's the last thing on my mind to do, anyway.

I finally weigh my options and they all point to a decision I really don't want to make, but I have no choice.

I single out a one-hundred-dollar bill and drop it on the table. It's more than enough to cover our uneaten meals, the waitress's tip, and then some.

"Come on," I tell Mykal. "Let's go."

———

I tried to talk myself out of bringing Mykal to my father's house, but I didn't like the other options. Having her find her way back to the city at this late hour when I'd invited her all the way out to Long Island felt wrong. Driving her home would have added more time to me getting to my father to assist the nurse with talking him down from his latest episode.

My mind raced so much with how to explain what was happening to Mykal. I forgot she was beside me in my car until she gasped as we turned onto the paved path leading to my father's property.

"This is *ginormous*," she says lowly.

I swallow hard.

Privacy was something my father was very big on while cognizant. He and my mother purchased this five bedroom, 5600 square foot Colonial property in the quietest part of Long Island to escape any eyes that could recognize him. And here I am, bringing what he would consider the press to his front door.

We roll to a stop in front of the wrought-iron gate. On the driver's side is a post with a keypad mended to the surface.

"Ellis Estate," she reads on the mailbox. Mykal gasps once more. "Is this *your* home?!"

"Yes," I answer. It isn't a lie. I grew up here. This is where I still considered home.

"Geez," she replies. "Seems like a lot of house for just one man."

The gate splits in two and opens and I step on the gas to drive thru, causing the car to lurch forward. I peek to my right to see her eyes every-where. It's impossible to see a thing in the dark with only my headlights providing visibility. But she surveils the scenery anyway and her curiosity is making me uneasy.

No one besides me, my father's nurse, and close family members know of my father's condition. A lot of his good friends are deceased, work associates are too busy trying to stay afloat and evolve with the changing times in print media to even remember to check in with him, and with me starting and updating a blog in his name, everyone including the public believes things are just as they should be with him.

I bring the car to an abrupt stop a few feet in front of the estate's entrance.

Mykal turns to me to say something but I interject with, "I need you to wait out here."

She shuts her mouth. Her brows shoot up next.

"I'll be right back."

I don't wait for her response. I put the car in park, unhook my seat-belt, and push the door open to step out of the car.

She isn't on my mind anymore. My mind is on bringing my father back to himself.

All the lights in the house are on tonight, a clear sign everything is not all right.

"Get me the fuck out of here!" I hear him shout the moment I push the front door open. "I don't know who the hell you are, where I am, or what business you believe I have here with you, but you've better let me go right now."

"Mr. Desmond, please calm down."

"I'll calm down when you tell me where I am and who you are!"

Their voices are coming from upstairs, so I make my way there, climbing the stairs two at a time.

I'm at the top of the staircase when I realize I've left the photo album. The thought to head back downstairs crosses my mind for only a moment before I have to abandon the thought completely when glass crashing the floor in my father's room causes me to run in that direction.

"Get me out of here!" My father yells at his nurse as he hurls a ceramic saucer at her head.

That also lands on the wood floors with a crash.

I get to the threshold in time to see him lift his crystal vase to toss next.

"Senior!" I shout. "It's okay."

He squints my way and steps back. "And who the hell are you?!"

I exhale through my lips and close my eyes for only a moment to regroup. I'm really wishing I remembered to grab the photo album from the office now.

"A gentleman and a scholar," I try.

His eyes are still wild, chest heaving. I can't risk waiting for him to come to.

"Dad," I lead with this time while approaching him. "It's me, your son."

"My son?" He questions. My father's eyes bounce between his nurse and I. "Have you two kidnapped me?"

"Dad—"

"I don't know who the hell either of you are," he screams. "But I know you better get me the hell out of this home if you know what's good for you."

"Dad, please—"

"Quit calling me that!" He demands. "Who are you?"

"Your son. I'm your son."

"Where is Phyllis? Where is my wife?"

My heart sinks.

"Who are you people?" He lifts his hand to his head. "Where am I? I-I don't understand what is happening."

"Dad, it's okay."

"Who are you?" he asks again, but this time with tears in his eyes and as they brim his lower lids, I want to cry too.

But I don't because someone has to keep the level head here.

"All three of you better let me go right now before I call the cops." He points over my shoulder. "All of you!"

I turn to follow his gesture to find Mykal standing frozen at the threshold of the bedroom.

"I..." Mykal starts. Her eyes move between my father and I. "I needed to use the bathroom."

Nothing can come out of my mouth because my mind goes blank. An onslaught of thoughts, the feeling that everything around me is crumbling, almost swallows me whole. I want to stand there and explain myself, but I don't. I move toward the door instead and she moves out of my way immediately. My focus goes to the stairs which I jog down, heading to my father's study. There I pull open his desk's drawer, and grip the photo album, opening the book as I climb the steps to his bedroom two at a time again.

Mykal is at the top of the stairs when I arrive and I say nothing to her.

I just brush past her and make my way to my father and say, "Do you remember this?" while pointing at his and my mother's wedding photo.

With wild eyes, he trains his eyes on where I'm pointing. The lines between his brows relax. I turn the page.

"How about this?" I quiz.

He stares at the photo of me, as a baby, swaddled and cradled in my mother's arms. My father walks closer, brings his hand to the plastic covering the photo, running his finger down the shape of the Polaroid. He glances up at me and I force a smile. The red lines in his eyes are pronounced tonight, the bags beneath them puffier than usual.

He nods, his shoulders slump, and he releases a deep defeated exhale.

"Okay, son," he croaks through strained vocal cords, "I... I'm tired."

I exhale a sigh of relief.

"I need to lie down," he informs next.

I nod, taking him by the hand and guiding him to sit on his bed. "You lie down and I'll get you some water from downstairs."

An expression of concern mixed with bewilderment morphs his expression and sends his eyes analyzing his environment again.

"This has the same furniture as my home," he mumbles.

"This *is* your home," I assure him, pulling the covers up and over his legs.

"I'm sorry," he says lowly as his gaze lifts, struggling to meet mine. "I still don't know you but your eyes are familiar. They look like Phyllis's."

"It's okay, dad, you're okay." I pat his hand twice. "I had to skip my appointment with my barber yesterday. So, I completely understand why you don't recognize me with my beard in need of a trim." I smile assuredly hoping it'll suffice. "I'll be back."

I turn to the door to find Mykal still standing there. I don't expect her to be anywhere else but here. The thought of explaining what's going on has no place in this space. My concern and priority is my dad, and I hope she knows that as I head down the case of stairs.

"I can take water to him, Mr. Ellis," Mali offers with her usual warm smile as I enter the kitchen.

I nod, allowing a smile to pull at my lips as well. "Mali, thank you. You are sincerely a godsend."

"Aww, really it's okay." She waves her hand in the air in a sign of dismissal.

"I am so sorry about this. It's a lot. Too much. You need a raise," I insist. "I'll contact your agency first thing in the morning and will see to it that I increase your day pay—"

"It's absolutely okay, Mr. Ellis." Mali pats my shoulder. "These kind of breakdowns happen, and this is what I am here for. You're paying me more than enough already. Please don't beat yourself up over this."

Mali moves around me to grab a bottle of water to take up to my father and as I follow her with my eyes as she exits, I see Mykal standing at the kitchen's entrance.

She says nothing, and neither do I, but I can see questions clutter her mind just by looking in her eyes.

"A rare sighting," I start. "You know my father selected this property in this area to be alone with his family." I pull out a stool beneath the marble island and plop into a seat. "He always said my mother was the one with the money but he knew peace, and wanted to separate himself from any form of media and just in time for when he, Desmond Ellis II, this no-name reporter's name kept getting brought up around water coolers at work and at coffee tables in homes."

"But he runs a blog," she recalls, eyes moving about my floor, as she no doubt attempts to make sense of everything. "He's still writing, but how is he able to—"

"It's me," I confess, staring at the counter below me. "I created the blog. I have been ghostwriting blog posts under his byline. Upholding the mystique because I want to launch a paper in his name. It's a dream of his so a goal of mine."

I look up for only a moment to see her brows wrinkle then I make the counter my focus again.

"My reasoning for accepting the position of editor at For The Culture was to gain experience working at a print publication. I have no intention of staying there for more than a year."

I glance up again to see her jaw slacked this time.

It's the truth, it's my truth, and if there's anything I've learned tonight, it's that the more I work to hide what's happening with my father, the more jailed by the truth I feel.

"You've been wanting editor and you've told me you'll stop at nothing to get it," I tell her with a shrug. "Now you've got it. And what a story this'll be, too, huh? Famed journalist's secret is out. Desmond

Ellis II has Alzheimer's disease and his son has been ghostwriting articles under his byline to hide his father's illness from the public. More at ten."

"I won't tell," she assures lowly. "I will say nothing."

"You plan to save it for later?"

She shakes her head. "I *won't* tell."

"What's the catch, Mykal?" I ask, swiveling on the island stool to face her. "You've been wanting editor since I've walked through FTC's doors. And you've threatened to keep coming for my head until you have my position."

"I wouldn't want to be the one behind destroying a legacy." She pulls out the island stool and sits beside me. "I hate you but I don't hate you that much."

I sputter a laugh.

"Plus what you've done, what you've been doing... you're a saint."

"Ha!" I huff. "Far from it."

"Surely close enough." She stands to her feet. "And me telling everyone about your father would make me even more of a devil than I already am."

"Mykal—"

"I'm going to use the bathroom as planned, then I'll call a cab—"

"Give me ten minutes." I stand to my feet too. "Let me check on my father and I will drive you home."

"Desmond, it's fine." She holds up a hand. "You're needed here. I can get home alone."

"Not my style." I iron my hands down my shirt. "Let me get my father settled and I'll be back downstairs in a few minutes. The bathroom is down the hall and to the left." I gesture at the wine fridge beneath the counter behind me on my way out of the kitchen. "Pour yourself something to drink when you're done in the bathroom."

"You're a good person, Desmond," she mumbles as I leave the area to head upstairs. But her tone sounds more like acknowledgement and pity than observation and analysis.

And I don't blame her.

TWENTY-THREE

MYKAL

It's a slow news day.

In my office, I stare through the glass walls at the writers parked at their desks damn near twiddling their thumbs. Nothing is happening today in media to discuss or write about. The last writer has submitted their article for the unsung feature we've been working on for the past two months. Our in-house photographers have shot artist photos, fact-checkers have completed fact-checking, editing is handled, proofreads done. Now the stories are off to print. It is time to move on to the next feature, but the meeting about that isn't until tomorrow.

I blow raspberries with my lips and lean back in my seat. I contemplate pressing play on a Netflix film and watching from my computer until quitting time, but I don't even feel like doing that.

So I do the next best thing - I tap into social media.

I've always considered social media to be the cesspool in the land of make believe. No one is posting their failures, setbacks, or disappointments. It's a highlight reel and understandably so. When you go to someone's home, you don't see portraits of them unhappy or pictures of tragic events nailed to their walls. But damn. Can people, or at least the people on *my* timeline, show a little realism? They can't be this happy, right?

I scroll, liking everything out of a force of habit when I happen across a post from one of our rival magazines. They are strictly online and report on only celebrity gossip, but what they have posted flips my stomach and nearly stops my heart.

It's a photo of Pryce and his wife. They're walking out the doors of a New York City restaurant, hand-in-hand. It would seem like an otherwise regular photo, but this website clearly has journalist with eyes made of magnifying glasses. Because blown up and cropped into a circle beside the photo, is a zoomed in capture of Pryce's ring finger that bears no wedding band, but his wife's name tattooed down the length of it from the cuticle of his nail to the top of his knuckle. And his tattoo artist didn't tattoo the letters small on his skin. The letters are in all caps and tatted in big, bold, black ink. He wants her name to be seen. He's making a statement. Pryce has every right to do what he wants, but I can't help but to feel slighted.

Somehow... I'm offended.

And considering what happened between us only two weeks ago, I feel I'm the inspiration for his decision to put her name there. I slam my phone down on my metal desk, face first, and lean back in my chair. My exhales leave my nose harsh and my jaw throbs from how hard I'm clenching my teeth. I should let this go. It has nothing to do with me.

I'm being ridiculous.

I lean forward again and snatch my phone off my desk. The screen has not dimmed, so the image is still very much there.

I read the caption next.

Pryce Williams stepped out with his wife, Dr. Leelah Waters-Williams, for a night of dining at GrayArea. The newlyweds enjoyed a private dinner at the lounge and bar on Pryce's first night back in New York City. It seems during his travels he squeezed in an appointment to acquire a new tat because paparazzi captured The Ballers' center with his wife's name etched down his ring finger.

"*Dr. Leelah Waters-Williams,* my ass," I mock. "What kind of doctor has the time to hang on her husband's arm every other night?"

As usual, she glowed beside him and what is so irritating is she isn't even trying.

Wild curls pulled up in a messy bun with a sweatshirt, sweatpants combo and white converses on her feet.

She radiates happy energy, all over her.

That could've been me.

I tap out of the app and tap into my internet browser, typing her name in the search window. What started as just a quick search, turns into me finding her practice's location, clicking the phone symbol and eventually her office number.

"Hello, good afternoon. Dr. Waters-Williams's office," the voice said on the other end of the phone.

"*Uh*, yeah, I, *uh*," I stammer. I didn't visualize this to the end. "I need to speak with Ms. Waters."

"Dr. Waters-Williams," the voice corrects, and I grind my teeth in response. "I'm sorry. She's officially Waters-Williams now, and she's adamant about us recording that to memory." She giggles. I find nothing she's said funny. "Are you a new patient?"

"No," I answer, then immediately say, "I mean, yes! Yes, I am."

"Okay," she replies. "There is currently a waitlist to meet with Dr. Waters-Williams even for consultations."

I roll my eyes at the news and the constant repeating of Leelah's married name. If Pryce and I exchanged vows, I would've dropped my last name and took his without him even asking. No hyphen, no problem.

Mykal, what are you doing?

"Would you like for me to add you to the waiting list?"

"Yes," I reply, not mulling over the reality of everything. But ask me in this moment if what I'm doing makes sense, and I'd tell you it's genius. Scheduling an appointment to speak privately with Leelah at her place of employment where she must keep it cute would give me an opportunity to tell her about her husband and me in Oakland. Nothing happened, but she didn't need to know that. I'd tell her we were together in his hotel, which we were, but instead of clarifying anything, I would let her imagination fill in the blanks.

Pryce and Leelah always look so happy. Like their world is perfect and nothing exists outside of them.

Let's see how secure and happy they really are because I'm about to shake the love nest a little, and I don't give a shit.

I end the phone call and I'm semi-satisfied with what I've done. I know very little about therapy and what a waitlist for the visit is all about, so I'm shocked that only twelve minutes pass before my phone rings again and the same young lady I dialogued with earlier is on my phone again.

"Hi Ms. Jones," she starts, "I just spoke with Dr. Waters-Williams and she told me she can meet with you this evening at six."

I arch both brows. "She... can? This evening?"

"At six. Yes," she replies, and I can sense she's smiling. "Usually new patients are on the waitlist for at least a month, but after I added you to the system, and I alerted her to this, she asked me to put you in at our earliest convenience. Our earliest is at six this evening."

Suddenly, my heart picks up in pace.

"It's extremely short notice but If you want the time slot, it's yours," she stresses.

"*Uh*, su-sure, yeah," I stammer. "I'll take it. Six is fine, I think."

Was it, though?

"Perfect," the woman confirms. "Please arrive at least 15 minutes before your appointment to fill out new patient paperwork. We look forward to seeing you at six."

What the hell am I doing?!

"Great," I exchange instead. "Thank you."

———

Here's the thing about me - whether for good or bad, I keep my word and go through with things even if they are absolutely insane. My pride won't allow me to do otherwise.

Like sitting in the waiting room in Leelah's office.

The space is of a decent size and is nothing like how I imagined it.

Leelah's secretary, April I'd learn is her name, offered me something to drink the moment I stepped off the elevator. When I declined, she took her seat again behind the mammoth-sized work desk that sat in front of an in-wall water fountain. Stacks of magazines laid on the small table in front of me, not one For The Culture. The couch I sit on is comfortable and perfect for waiting.

The rest of my workday seemed to speed past as I waited to come here. I did not know what I planned to do once I spoke to Leelah. I just knew I had a point to prove, whatever that point was.

I lower my head into my hand and pinch the bridge of my nose.

I should get the hell out of here!

"Mykal," I hear less than a minute later.

I drop my hand, lift my gaze, and damn near shoot up off the couch when I see Leelah standing only a few inches away.

She slicked her hair into a chic topknot bun today. A camel brown pantsuit with a pure white bodysuit under the jacket is what I eye on her next. The expression on her face is even. Delightful. The disarming, easy glance of someone receiving a friend.

"Leelah." I swallow hard. "Good to see you again."

But it isn't.

Seeing her again just confirms my observations of her from the very start. The woman is stunning and regal. Her husband is the celebrity, but she exudes the allure of one with little effort.

Fuck.

"Please." She gestures to the frosted white door behind her. "Let's step into my office."

My knees feel like they want to knock.

I nod in acknowledgement and make my way to her, anyway. Leelah pushes open a door that leads to a hall and steps through before me, holding the door opened for me to step through too.

"Follow me," she instructs. And I do.

Her walk is authoritative. She walks like she owns the place, which she technically does since it's her office, but I'm sure she doesn't own the building. Damn sure not the block. I angle my chin up and follow behind her, only stopping when she turns left and opens her office door. She steps through and holds the door open for me, closing it the second I'm inside and she's on the other side of the threshold. Her office is simple, but still stylish. A single raw exposed brick wall, standard visitor

chairs, a view of SoHo from her window and green plants on the floor
and on her desk.

"I have to be honest with you, Mykal," she starts, walking behind her
desk and taking a seat. "It surprised me to see your name on my waitlist."

My eyes move off her office things and focus on hers. "Did it?"

She smirks and I have to blink twice to be sure that is what she does.

"Off top." She reaches in her desk drawer and retrieves a notepad, "I
have to let you know that I'm going to refer you to another therapist."

I wrinkle my brows.

"Her name is Dr. Liz Peters," she says, shifting her eyes off me and
focusing on the notepad as she writes. "She's incredible and frankly, I
have no doubt she's the only person skilled enough to deal with a case
like yours."

I jerk my neck back in time for her to finish writing and to look up
at me.

"Like, mine?" I question.

"Yes."

I'm stuck between a place of confusion and intrigue. "And what's a
case like mine?"

"Well, that's what's got me perplexed. Because I can't, for the life of
me, make sense of why you're here. So. I'm not too certain how extreme
your case is."

I say nothing, not because words have escaped me in this moment. I
say nothing out of curiosity about where she's going with this.

"Besides the difficult time I'm having figuring you out," Leelah
continues, leaning back in her seat and crossing her legs in her chair.
"For two very crucial reasons, I cannot treat you. One, because you tried
to sleep with my husband and I will find it impossible to maintain objec-
tivity with you as a result."

I blink hard and almost forget to breathe.

"And two, because, respectfully? I want to lay your ass out where
you stand because, well, you tried to sleep with my husband."

I part my lips to say something in response, but nothing comes out.

"Yeah." She nods. "Pryce told me all about you showing up on his
hotel room floor. The man called me an hour after it happened if you
could believe that."

She stunned me into silence.

"*Mm-Hmm*, I was just as stunned as you are right now. But you know what? It wasn't you trying to sleep with him knowing he's married that upset me because I can count on my fingers and toes the amount of women who have tried sleeping with him even after having foreknowledge that Pryce has a wife." She smiles sweetly, and it menaces me. "No, see, what pissed me off was the fear in his voice as he told me what *you* did and him admitting fault for *your* actions, which was quite bizarre to me."

My thoughts are blank. This is not how I imagined this going, so I'm speechless.

"Of course, I can't have you shoulder the blame for that because Pryce's fear has more to do with his and my history, but you put him in a position that was extremely selfish and unfair on your part. So yeah, I want to beat your ass for smiling in my face one moment, then trying to sleep with my man the next.

"As you can imagine," she adds, not appearing to have taken another breath, "beating your ass in my office would be bad for business. So, the mature and responsible thing to do here is to, of course, not turn you away because you clearly need help. Other than pursuing a married man, you showing up at my office for whatever sick twisted reason you're here for definitely needs to be evaluated, and Dr. Peters is the only person I know with the keen eye and patience who can get to the root of your self-sabotaging decisions. I'm not sure how long you've made them, but my guess is it's been for way too long since you didn't talk yourself out of making the bad decision of showing up here."

Her words are like jabs to my ego that I can't block. I feel naked standing there, glued to the spot. Her words are blunt and penetrating, but all the while her expression is nonjudgmental. She sees me and I don't want her to.

"Mykal?" She solicits my attention. And she doesn't continue speaking until I give it to her. "We're done. Please leave my office immediately and do me the favor of never returning here again, okay?"

The second she gets out her last word, I spin on my arches and hightail toward the door, yanking it open when I'm in front of it.

"Mykal, wait, your referral," she calls behind me, but I don't turn back. I'm too embarrassed to meet her eyes with mine.

I take enormous steps toward the exit, not even stopping when her secretary, April, calls after me.

I stab at the elevator's button, feeling like the air is thin. It's clear Leelah's office is a safe space for others, but for me it might as well be a gas chamber.

When the elevator arrives, I stumble in, push the button for the lobby, and stab some more at the door close button until the doors slide closed in front of me. I press my back to the wall of the car, fighting my hardest to hold back my tears but giving in to them the moment the first one escapes my eye.

I slap a hand to my wet eyes and slide down the elevator's wall, wanting to be any and everyone else so I don't have to be myself.

Twenty-Four

"This is nice," Faith compliments, lifting the bowl of her wine glass to her lips. "Dare I call this romantic?"

I chuckle, then sip my Bordeaux too. "Just wanted to make up for the other night."

Faith and I sit in front of my fireplace in my living room. The night is a chilly one, chillier than the previous nights. Autumn had been warmer than usual, so the change in weather was expected but definitely not craved on my part.

"That's because you're a good guy." She turns in her seat on the blanket I spread out on my rug. "I'd like to do more things like this. Just you and me."

I shift my eyes to hers.

"We've kept things as friends and that's been cool, but..." She shrugs a slender shoulder. "I don't know, I've just been wanting more lately and with you."

I tuck my lips into my mouth, wanting to tuck my head into my neck instead. What she wants isn't what I want. It has never been what

I've wanted with Faith. She's a noble woman but, our goals and interests have never aligned.

"Dez." She bumps her shoulder with mine. "Say something."

I'd never tell her exactly what my thoughts have revealed. My truth is too harsh and disappointing.

So, I'll tell her the watered-down version.

And that is what I prepare to do, but when I open my mouth again to respond, my intercom's bell buzzes.

I peek over at the com system, then down at the face of my watch. It's well past 11pm.

She tilts her head to one side. "Who's that?"

"I do not know." I stand to my feet; thankful my bell has saved me and make my way to it.

In front of it I ask, "Who?"

"It's Mykal."

I jerk my neck back.

"Mykal?!" Faith gasps behind me. "That woman you work with? Why is *she* here?"

I turn to Faith. "I don't have a clue."

My bell buzzes again.

"Well." Faith crosses her arms. "Tell her to leave."

My bell buzzes a third time.

"I can't just tell her to leave, it's late and—"

Faith releases a loud sigh. "She left her home at this hour so she can return home just fine at this hour too."

"Faith, I have to see why she's here."

With that, I buzz Mykal in, to Faith's horror.

"We're on a fucking date, Desmond!"

I want to correct her, but know I won't be able to do it without sounding like a jerk. So, I say nothing while making my way to my apartment's door.

"*Ugh*," Faith growls. "This is unbelievable."

I get to my door and open it in time to find Mykal already standing on the other side.

Her eyes are glassy, skin more flush than usual.

"Well, hello there," she drawls out.

From the first word, I can smell the liquor on her breath. The scent is so strong she didn't have to utter another word for me to smell it with her mouth closed.

"Mykal?" I question. I feel like I'm chasing her eyes because she struggles to meet them with mine. "How do you know where I live?"

"Same way you knew where I lived." She walks up to me and pushes me back so she can enter my apartment. "Employee directory. Thanks for the idea, Inspector Gadget."

"The fuck?!" Faith shrieks when Mykal waltzes in. "Are you kidding me?"

"A pop up at my apartment deserves a pop up in return." She enters the apartment more, her head moving from side to side. Mykal is clearly ignoring Faith or is so inebriated she doesn't even know Faith is there, despite Faith's vocal discontent at Mykal's arrival.

"This is nice," Mykal says, turning in place, losing her balance. I go to her when she looks like she's about to take a spill on my floor. "The prince of journalism lives modest, but you'd need to be a blind person not to see the money in this decor."

"Mykal, have you been drinking?"

She laughs cynically. "I haven't been drinking enough."

"Desmond," Faith nags from the living room. "Ask her to leave."

"*Desmond ask her to leave,*" Mykal mocks. "Oh, I'm sorry, Ms. Fashion Week, did I interrupt something here?"

"Yes," Faith replies. "You did. So can you go?"

"I can't," Mykal shoots back in a high-pitched voice, mimicking Faith's.

"Faith." I take steps toward her. "Let me call you a cab so I can handle this—"

"A *cab*?!" Faith's brows furrow. "When have you ever called me a fucking *cab*, Desmond? And at this hour, no less?"

I close my eyes and take a breath, knowing I've never and would never if this were any other circumstance, but having these two women in the same room is practically giving me heart palpitations.

"When he invited me to dinner in Long Island," Mykal slurred. "He refused for me to take a cab home even after he had to tend to an emergency."

I swallow hard, hoping she doesn't continue. The last thing I need is her revealing my father's condition in her drunken stupor."

"Mykal," I try with a warning tone.

"But you are not me, huh, Ms. Fashion Week?" Mykal taunts. "You're probably just a lazy fuck, like I predicted." Mykal shrugs then snorts a laugh before transitioning into a bellyful chortle.

"Bitch!" Faith spat, taking quick steps toward Mykal.

I run between the two in time to stop Faith.

"Get off me," Faith shoves. "You and these damn strays, Desmond. I swear." Faith shakes her head next, pulling free from me and stomping to the couch to gather her things.

"He's got a thing for strays, you know?" Faith informs, matter factly.

Mykal stops laughing and looks Faith's way.

"There's this cat that moseys her useless ass up to his fire escape every morning and instead of shooing the damn thing away, he feeds it, gives it attention when he shouldn't. For one, all the cat does is take, providing *nothing* in return. And two, the cat is no good for Desmond because he's allergic to her. And yet, he continues to give the stray a reason to return instead of cutting ties to the thing."

I only blink at her words, seeing where she's going with this.

Faith snorts a laugh and shakes her head after shrugging on her black fur coat. "The man loves his strays in animal and clearly human form because I'm looking at yet another one that has moseyed her useless ass up here too."

Mykal takes a step toward Faith and I loop my arm around Mykal's waist to stop her.

Faith guffaws and looks Mykal up and down before continuing to my apartment door, stepping out and leaving without uttering another word to neither of us.

Once we're alone, Mykal turns in my arm to face me. Up close, she looks even worse and smells ten times more awful.

"So," she whispers, and I hold my breath. "Shall we?"

Mykal creates distance between us, which I'm grateful for, but then she undoes the belt around her wool belted wrap coat, dropping the coat to the floor. She kicks her black pumps off next.

"Mykal—"

"*Shh,*" she shushes, pulling at the hem of her shirt next. "I know what you like. I can be that."

"Mykal." I shake my head. "I don't want that right now and not from you. Not when you're in this state."

"In what *state*?" She questions, but doesn't stop undressing. She's pinching the button of her jeans that holds it together. "Horny? Because that's what I am. And you and I together is the escape I need right now. So..." She pulls her jeans down to her knees, then wiggles the denim off the rest of the way before stepping out of them. "... let's do this."

"No," I refuse, looking her in the eyes. "What's the matter? What are you escaping? Talk to me."

I notice when her breath hitches and when she shakes her head to refocus on the task at hand. She approaches and I take a step back.

"You were fine earlier, before you left the office," I recall. "What happened?"

"Why does something have to happen for me to want sex?"

"It's not you wanting sex, it's you showing up here drunk and throwing yourself at me that's concerning."

"Oh, what's this? A moral compass now?!" She sighs a laugh that sounds more like a cry for help. "Desmond, just fuck me, okay? Just fuck me so I can do the thing I know I'm good at, please. Damn."

I wrinkle my brows in response to her words.

"Because," she stalls, exhaling audibly, then runs her fingers through her hair. "Because I'm not tall enough, light enough, smart enough, successful enough. I'm not enough anywhere else but with this..." She unhooks her bra, allowing her breasts to spill out from the lace. "I know I can do *this*, and I can do it really well." Mykal pulls down her panties and steps out of them, too. She stands naked in front of me in more ways than she's aware.

"Rejection has been a constant co-star in my life this month, and I need a fucking win somewhere. So, let's just..." She exhales a long sigh.

I walk past her and grab the blanket Faith and I lounged on in front of the fireplace earlier. The glow from the flames reflects off Mykal's skin, giving her tone a molten appeal. So beautiful, so stunning, even at her lowest.

I drape the blanket around her shoulders from the back and walk my way in front of her. She sniffs back her tears twice and on her third try to keep it all in, she finally lets them go. I wrap my arms around her and pull her close to my heart, allowing her to bawl against me, giving her the moment she needs to hold nothing back.

"You're enough Mykal," I tell her.

Her cries stop, but her body still rattles against me from her sniffling.

"Anyone who measures your worth based on what you can do *for* them isn't worthy of you doing anything *with* them."

I create space between us to lift her chin so she can look at me. "Sex is not a solution to your problems."

She stares at me with puffy eyes.

"Sex feels good, it feels great with you, that's true. But only when it's an act exchanging power, Mykal. Not wielding it."

She says nothing in response. I walk her to my couch and help her to sit. Mykal is quiet thereafter and I do most of the talking in her silence. No questions though because I know she's in no mood to answer them. She listens, nodding or shaking her head where applicable as she curls up next to me. Mykal becomes so comfortable, she eventually drifts off to sleep in my arms less than an hour later. And I hold her the whole time feeling just as comfortable with her there.

———

The espresso machine is no match for the blender, crushing ice with its blades.

The next morning, I battle a hangover headache as I sit across from Desmond. I ended up spending the night at his place, not by choice. After I'd awaken from sleep on his couch sober and alone two hours after falling asleep drunk in his arms, I tried to sneak out of his place. I felt way too embarrassed to remain there after interrupting his night and throwing myself at him, only to be talked down off the hoe ledge. No one had ever said the things he said to me. It felt good to hear his words. But I hated how necessary it was for me to hear them.

The moment I attempted to step off his couch and tiptoe to his front door, he walked from the shadows of his hallway to stop me.

"Cocoa and espresso with chocolate whipped cream," Desmond announced as he returned to our table. "A little too sweet for the morning, I maintain, but you like what you like."

We caught a yellow cab to Groundhouse for coffee, how poignant as this was the place we first met. There wasn't any work today, but he insisted we have the best coffee in New York City to start the day.

Desmond offered me his bedroom last night, and he slept on the couch. His place was so him from the fireplace and stone floors in his kitchen to the king sized canopy bed with posts made of white ivory in his bedroom. The wall of sneakers in his living room threw me off though, because I would never take him to be a sneaker fanatic. He was all about fine suits, pressed slacks, and shiny oxfords. So, it was interesting to spot sneakers on pedestals displayed like awards.

The coffee shop is quieter than usual. The hustle and bustle a little muted this morning.

Or maybe that's just me.

I showed up at Desmond's home the night before for reasons I would never repeat and how he responded was brand new to me but on brand for him. He's a class act.

"You sure you don't want a scone, a bagel, or anything to eat?" He asks.

Not once has he ever acted or treated me in the way other men of his caliber had in the past. Desmond instead is caring, gentle, extremely kind despite how I've been with him.

I shake my head, answering his question, lifting the paper cup to sip my coffee. He does the same, directing his attention out in front of him.

I stare at him in his element. The man is gorgeous. Even dressed down in a white tee, dark blue joggers, and white sneakers, he looks like a trillion bucks. He was too handsome to be this kind... at least kind to someone like me.

"Pick someone in line," he starts, pulling me out of my thoughts.

I was staring at him but spaced out and hadn't realized his head was now turned my way.

"Huh?"

"Pick someone in line so we can buy them coffee."

I wrinkle my brows, then relax them, remembering the last time we did this. "Why do you do that?"

"Do what?"

"Buy strangers things."

He chuckles.

"It's very Mary Poppins of you," I add.

He shrugs. "My mother was huge on paying-it-forward later in her life. Her grandparents, my great grandparents, were aristocrats and inventors with patents. So she grew up well off. And although she could have everything, she was always unhappy. That changed in her adult age when she found her joy in being selfless. Her fear I would later learn was no one remembering her when she passed on. So, giving and being of service to others became the peace she'd always wanted. Until I was seven, right before her death, she and I would go to the market to buy groceries and she'd always offer to pay for the person's groceries in front of us. She'd watch their stuff get rung up, their eyes staring at the screen attentively observing as the cost of their groceries went up. When the cashier told the shopper's their total, my mother would let the shopper know she'd cover the cost and that the shopper can just place their bagged groceries in their carts and head home." He smiles, then lets out a laugh. "The expression on their faces would be the brightest part of my day. They always expressed shock first, then disbelief, suspicion because no one ever does anything kind without a hidden agenda, right?" He shakes his head. "But then after a few moments of the act setting in, gratitude emerged, genuine gratitude. After she passed, I maintained that pay-it-forward attitude because everyone is going through something and need something good to happen to them. I try to be that good."

I couldn't help but to smile with him.

"People are so used to people being shitty to them that when someone shows love or kindness, they have to find the catch when one doesn't exist."

I look away, dropping my eyes into my lap before grabbing my cup to take a sip. I'm guilty of the same thing.

"Anyway," he continues after sipping his coffee too, "My mother always credited her time at a mental health retreat as where she discovered her purpose which was to serve and give back. She said beyond the meditation, hiking, fancy meals she ate, it was the individual therapy she received at the retreat that was most valuable because she learned to love herself and learned to love others without conditions."

"A mental health retreat?"

Desmond nods, sipping his coffee again. "She went before she had me. My mother and my father were on the verge of divorce. He was working long hours at the paper. She was feeling unfulfilled in her career as a stylist. She always had money but no guidance on how to make it work for her. My mother felt overwhelmed and a loss of identity. And finding the retreat then wasn't easy. According to my father, who told me this years later, anything dealing with therapy was hard to find. Internet wasn't a huge thing and mental health wasn't a priority where you could just ask for a referral from a doctor. But when you want something and put the effort into finding it, somehow, it finds you. Plus. he was an incredible investigative reporter."

The idea intrigued me to the point of fascination.

"So..." I lower my view below the table to play with my fingers. "How did she eventually find it?"

"My father asked around and one of his colleagues who contributed to the health and wellness section of Holidae Press told him about a story he wrote covering retreats around the U.S. My mother wasn't one for travel, so she picked one in Hudson Valley, NY. Left for six days and returned a brand-new person."

I huff dramatically. "That sounds too happily ever after to me."

"Life doesn't have to be hard with everything, Mykal."

I dart my eyes in his direction.

"Life can be good, you can have enough time, and you don't have to learn everything the hard way. There's life on the other side of chaos and disorder. It just takes effort and a realization that it exists. And even if it doesn't exist." He shrugs a shoulder. "Putting in the work to at least seek it out will surely bring you closer than sitting and doing nothing besides being skeptical."

I swallowed hard at his words making more sense than I wanted them to. "Even if there *were* still such a thing..."

"Not *if*, because there *are*," he corrects.

"It's not like someone like me can actually go to one of those things. I have work, a schedule to stick to—"

His brows shoot up. "*You're* interested in going to one?"

"I didn't say *I* was interested." I insist. "I was just saying—"

"Mykal, if you're interested in going, I'm positive your boss will understand," he interjects with a smirk. "You know what? Here." He leans back in his seat to pull his phone out of his pocket. "Let's do a quick search, nothing serious."

"Search for what?"

"For mental health retreats."

I shake my head. "Desmond—"

"We're just looking," he interjects. "If you were to go to one, would you want to go far or stay local?"

"*If* I were to go to one," I play along, "I'd want to go far, *far* away."

"How far are we talking? Out of the country?"

"No." I shake my head again. "I'd favor somewhere where the weather is warmer than here. If I'm going to be relaxing and getting my mind right like you claim people do at these things, I'd like to do it with fewer clothes on."

He lifts his head from his phone and moves his eyes to mine.

I fight back the smile that wants to pull at my lips at his reaction.

"A place for fewer clothes," he repeats, and I laugh. "Got you."

My heart feels something. I don't know what it is. Watching this man, I said I hated do something so selfless does something to me.

"Honolulu," he announces.

"What?"

"Honolulu," he repeats. "Hawaii. There's a mental health retreat scheduled to start in Honolulu, Hawaii next week Wednesday. They usually host retreats in upstate New York according to their website, but this year they're holding it in Hawaii. Lucky you." He winks an eye. "It runs for seven days. One-story villas by the beach, daily therapy with a

Dr. Liz Peters, all-inclusive meals. This is nice." He taps through a few pages of his phone's screen. "I've been to Honolulu. Very city-like, so you should feel right at home. They arrange shuttle pick up from the airport, room and board in your own villa..."

I tune out the rest when I hear her name.

"... Dr. Liz Peters... She's incredible and frankly, I have no doubt she's the only person skilled enough to deal with a case like yours."

Leelah's voice echoes from the corners of my mind and my heart drops with every word recollected.

"I think this retreat has your name written all over it," Desmond promises, pulling me out of my daze. "Yoga on the beach, sunrise meditations, a hike up Diamondback mountain—"

"No-no." I wave my hand as a sign of disapproval. "I can't go, I'm good."

"What?"

"I have work, I have my plans," I claim. None of those things matter, and truthfully, had it not been for the therapist being mentioned by Leelah first, I would have jumped all over the idea of this retreat.

"Work will still be here when you get back," Desmond tries. He shakes his head. "Mykal, you need to get away like you need air. I'm telling you."

I stare at him.

He drops his head for a moment before refocusing on me.

"What happened last night was... " He cringes. "It was *a lot*. Even for you. I can't ignore it. It was a loud and clear cry for help—"

"Oh stop it. I just drank too much—"

"You need a break," he cuts in. "You need time to regroup, time in a space that's different from what you're used to."

"And how do you know that?! Desmond, you barely even know me."

"But I'd like to," he imparts, looking into my eyes. "I'd like to get to know you. And I'd *love* to get to know you at your best."

All I can do is blink in response.

"I've seen you at your worse. I know what it feels like to be hated by you. And despite that, for reasons that now make sense to me, I am still very drawn to you, so..." He shrugs. "I want to see what it'll be like when

Mykal is good. And not good on the surface, but really, really good. Because, it's like I said, work will always be work, but this?" He gently caresses my right temple with his fingertips. "Is the real bag. If this isn't right, nothing else can be. Believe that."

"And what's the reason that makes sense now?"

He tries to fight his smile at first but surrenders to the tug at the corners of his lips instead. "You won't freak out?"

"I'm not promising anything," I shoot back

"I wouldn't imagine you responding with anything less." He smiles big. "You have potential."

It's my turn to wrinkle my brows. "Excuse you?"

He chuckles. "My father has always told me to find a woman with potential and I trust his guidance because it has never failed me. He'd always say she doesn't have to have it all because most of us don't, but a woman with potential, the drive to grow, can meet your potential and together you can build and grow if you're both willing to build and grow together. Not on some we complete each other rhetoric. We both should be complete individually which is why you need this retreat—"

"What's your end goal though?" I query. "You've already gotten the sex so it can't be that. So why are you so fixed on me and this so called *potential*?"

"Generational wealth is my end goal," he answers, reading me. "If I can be candid."

I quirk a brow. "Generational wealth? As in... children—"

"And business, property, investments – financial assets. Marriage. A future." he interjects. "Yes."

Well, damn, this is... different.

And that just opens up the floodgates. My head is spinning with questions now. *Why me? Do I want this? What about me shows him I'm even worthy of such a thing if I wanted this? Am I even capable?*

I form my lips to question this, but he stops me by leveling my head by my chin with just the tip of his finger.

"We're getting way ahead of ourselves, and I'm not trying to scare you away or overwhelm you with this long range, forward thinking. Right now, all I know is you are a force I want to align with. You are hugely talented, and a go-getter who sees no limits to their success, to anything really. You wanted editor as a fairly new staff writer and went for it, even though you were without a doubt under qualified, on paper."

I arch a brow.

"You absolutely were." He laughs "You're bold, stubborn, very sexy, and highly intelligent, and I am *extremely* attracted to all that. Now don't get me wrong, do I still want to fuck you? Absolutely. I am still a man and you are still very fine."

I give in to the smile pulling at my lips.

"But," he continues, "I require a little more than sex at my age. I need potential. You have potential. Specifically the kind of potential that appreciates over time."

I furrow my brows this time.

"Vision. Mykal, *you* have vision. You know what you want and you figure out how to attain it, regardless of how out of reach it may seem to others. It's slightly misdirected but you have a lot of it. The kind of vision I'd love to grow and build with, and I sincerely want to see where this goes beyond one night. But you've got to meet me halfway on this. You *have* to do the work, your own self-work. We both do. But I'm patient and I'm willing to wait if the wait is worth it. And I know it is because you're worth it."

I inhale the surrounding air, blinking away briefly. Tears prick at the corners of my eyes as I refocus on him and take another breath to keep the tears all in. No man, not even my own father, has ever told me anything like this. It's taking everything in me not to give in to my emotions.

"So." He extends his long legs so he can lean forward and dip his hand in his back pocket. "I'm going to book this retreat for you—"

"Desmond, I can pay for it myself."

"I owe you, remember?"

I squint at him, confused.

"You covered for me at FTC when I had that family emergency to attend to last month. You told me I owe you for covering, and I always repay my debts."

"I was being a jerk, I didn't really mean that."

"Would you be more accepting of this if I were offering to pay for a bag or a pair of shoes?"

I tilt my head to one side and roll my eyes up to the coffee shop's barreled ceiling, thinking.

"Because this is like the same thing. It's a gift. You can't wear it. But it's an experience that your spirit will wear forever." He smiles. "You can cover the flight if that'll make you feel any better."

I went from just having coffee with Desmond to him suggesting something that could change my life.

I observe Desmond as he busy himself with booking me for something I know will impact me. I just don't know how and in what way. But whatever happens, I understand he isn't like any man I've ever dealt with and I'm curious how things will change between us now that I can't deny that fact.

Twenty-Five

MYKAL

Desmond told me his first lie.

"Would you like another glass of champagne before we land?" The flight attendant asked. She wore her hair slicked back into a low chignon with Hawaiian flowers circling the circumference of her bun.

"Yes, please," I reply, matching her smile.

The lie Desmond told me was that I could cover the plane fare to Hawaii, but three days later, he talked me into canceling it.

Lush green trees become visible through my window view. I press the back of my head against the plush butter-brown airplane seat as I watch the scene change from my vantage point.

When I found out the flight to Hawaii would be ten hours long, I almost considered canceling it my damn self. But before I could back out of anything, including the flight, Desmond called me to tell me, "I know a friend who knows a friend." And that "friend" owns a private jet they were so gracious enough to lend to me, well, more so Desmond, to charter a private flight to Honolulu, Hawaii.

"Here you are," the flight attendant said to me as she extended her hand with the glass for me to take. "Is there anything else I can get for you before we land?"

"I'm fine, thank you," I say, smiling, turning my head to look toward my window view.

I wanted to soak up every bit of this moment.

Flying private was like night and day compared to commercial flying.

I expected a long line to check in, having to hope to find a seat in the terminal before boarding my flight, needing to wait my turn as I walked through a long passenger boarding bridge to board the aircraft. But I got the complete opposite.

I got the decked-out lounge area, with ample seating, that served a five-star breakfast and offered brunch drinks like Mimosa, Bloody Mary, and Peach Bellini, by request and on the house. A van shuttled me from the lounge to the private hangar, where I climbed the steps to the aircraft and the captain and two flight attendants greeted me by name. I didn't have to worry about sharing a row with strangers because the flight only had one passenger, me.

My cousin Amir flies private all the time, but I've never seen the need to. I don't have anywhere important to go and my pride is too big to ask, much less tag along just for the sake of being on a jet.

The mainland becomes more visible the closer to the runway the plane descends and when the wheels touch down; the landing is like butter, smooth and comfortable even after impact. Everything looks so magical from my view. There is so much I don't know. I'm not sure what to expect, but I'm curious to see what this trip will do for me.

"Aloha, and welcome to Hawaii, Ms. Jones," the captain radio's from the cockpit. "We ask that you remain seated. Once we have come to a complete stop and are clear to exit the aircraft, we will open the doors for you."

I allow my eyes to roam the interior cabin, taking in for the last time the wood paneling, plush seating, and ambient lighting. I'm not sure if this will be my first and last time flying private, but I want to remember everything just in case it is.

I considered reaching out to Desmond but opted to wait until I settled in the villa. And that's exactly where I go. Once the captain opens the plane door and lowers the steps, I'm on my way.

A Hawaiian welcoming committee, two women dressed in floral printed wrap dresses, greet me on arrival. They aloha my ear off and drape beaded leis and two fresh flower leis around my neck before escorting me to a white shuttle bus. Through views of palm trees and flowering bushes, I'm chauffeured through the streets of Honolulu with my eyes and hands to the shuttle's glass window like an excited child. Street signs that read like tropical cocktails, boxy apartment houses that remind me of dingbats in southern California, barefoot pedestrians who walk with surfboards clutched beneath their arms. I am most definitely not in New York City anymore and nothing makes that more clearer than when I arrive on the retreat grounds.

The shuttle bus drives through a gated community. Villas of the same size circle the block. I don't have to look past them too hard to find the view of turquoise water stretching for miles and the white sand that borders the lapping tides.

My driver drops me off at the main house. A staff of men dressed in all white collect my bags from the shuttle. Within moments, a woman greets me from the front desk as I approach.

The main house's chairs are made of wicker and gold and the front desk is carved entirely out of toasted marble. A seating area to the left of her comprising of wicker chairs and plush, inviting white cushions face the beach and the high sun.

After giving my name, checking in, and receiving the itinerary for my stay at the retreat, the men on staff escort me to my personal villa, a villa I would call home for the next week.

On an electric golf cart, another one of those men dressed in white drives me around the property, pointing out all the areas I needed to know. Like the beach, which I could access from my private deck, and the part of the area myself and other visitors would visit every morning, afternoon, and night for breakfast, lunch, and dinner. When he points out the villa where I'll attend therapy, I still in my seat. Out of all the things I look forward to doing on this island, therapy doesn't make the list at all. That's something I will deal with tomorrow though because in this instance, especially after we pull up in front of the villa assigned to me, all my mind can do is soak up this moment.

My bags are already inside when I open the villa's door with my keycard. The first thing I see is the beach straight ahead. Everything in my villa faces the beach. The king bed covered in soft white bedding and topped with freshly picked Hawaiian flowers. Even the bathroom, furnished with a stand-in shower and deep soaking tub, points toward the view of the beach. The kitchen shares the space with the dining area and has a floor plan that spills out onto the deck when the doors leading to the deck are opened. And the deck leads to the beach itself. I literally walk off of the platform and sink my white pedicure toes into the white sand, and smile at the warmth it provides while I inhale the ocean air.

I close my eyes and stay in this moment, not thinking about what I need to do.

And for once, it feels good.

———

When it's good, it's good, and it's important to enjoy the good for as long as you can, because when you're Mykal Jones, it won't last long.

It seems everyone else can have great days consecutively but me, I can be on a beautiful island, surrounded by beautiful things and misery will still find me.

Twenty-four hours after that glorious feeling following my arrival, I return to feeling like I don't belong.

It all went downhill after breakfast the next morning. Food was delicious, the staff the sweetest. But meditation at sunrise sent me spinning. I sat amongst six other women, who sat with their backs straight, legs comfortably crossed, eyes closed, and minds grounded in bliss. Not a person said a thing, they were just there, finding peace in their breaths.

"Allow yourself to be," the petite instructor insisted before we began.

Be what?

I did not know what that meant. I'd researched information about meditation for a celebrity trends piece I had to write a year ago, but the practice could never stick because quieting and clearing my mind was impossible.

Then there was yoga on the beach. I was clearly out of my damn element. The same women in meditation who understood how *to be*, whatever that was, could twist and hold positions that ached my joints, but they did it effortlessly and with relaxed faces.

"You can use the props and move at your own pace," the lean yoga teacher instructed, but I refused to be the only one at yoga using that shit. By the end, I felt annoyed, unmotivated, and defeated. I couldn't even relax correctly at a place specifically designed for relaxing.

And now I have therapy.

Great.

As soon as I walk through the door of the villa which is two properties down from mine, I'm greeted by a woman, an inch or two shorter than me. Her eyes are sincere and her face pleasant and framed by salt and pepper curls.

"Mykal," she greets, standing up from her seat on the armchair. "Welcome."

Her face is youthful but mature. She's dressed in a blue floral loose-fitting dress that moves with the breeze blowing in from the opened deck doors.

"I'm Dr. Liz Peters." She extends her hand for me to shake and I accept. "It's a pleasure to meet you."

"Thank you." It's literally all I can reply with because the feeling is not mutual and it isn't a pleasure to meet her.

The thought of meeting her is more intimidating than actually meeting her though. In fact, she isn't intimidating at all. The doctor has a welcoming vibe that appears authentic and untampered with. She's making it hard not to like her.

I debate with myself about if I should let her know her reputation proceeds her with me, but I don't want to answer the question why it does and I most definitely don't want to relive the moment Leelah mentioned her name to me.

"Please," she gestures at the loveseat across from one armchair. "Have a seat."

I go there and do as instructed, my eyes briefly roaming around the villa. When they return to Dr. Peters, she smiles warmly.

She parts her lips to say something when her phone chimes in the armchair beside her, keeping her from continuing. The phone lies on a black notebook, which she lifts to silence the call.

"My apologies." She pecks at her screen with her thumbs. "It's my son," she giggles. "He calls me every day at the same time."

I smile back.

"He never forgets to call," she adds.

I'm not sure why, but this normalizes her, to me at least. I love my mother to the moon and back and call her as often as I can as well.

"He must be an only child," I comment lowly.

"No." She shakes her head as she sends the message she's typed. The chime indicates this. "My son Everett has a younger sister, Eryn. They both live in California and are inseparable. She doesn't call as much, though. She's much more independent, so *she* thinks." She rolls her eyes playfully. "Anyway, he's on California time and probably forgot I'm not in New York for the next few days. I'll silence my phone, so no one interrupts us during our session."

I blink away.

What I wouldn't do for several more interruptions for the duration of this session.

"You're from New York too, based on what you told me in your questionnaire."

I filled out the thing the day after Desmond booked me for the retreat. The trip excited me and I thought the questionnaire was harmless, but I wonder if I should have been less honest with my answers.

"Yes, I am."

"What part of New York?"

"In the city. My apartment is in downtown Manhattan and I work in Midtown."

"Lovely," she replies. "My practice is in Brooklyn. I live a floor above it."

"You look *Brooklyn*," I say.

She laughs. "And what does *Brooklyn* look like to you?"

"Comfortable, laid-back, unpretentious."

"And Manhattan is.."

"Hustle and bustle from sunup to sundown," I answer. "Mostly, jaded and unimpressed. Because if you aren't hustling or bustling, you're falling behind, always."

She smiles and reaches for the black book her phone previously laid on. Dr. Peters lifts the cover and removes the pen from the pen loop, and starts writing.

She asks, with her eyes still down on the page she's writing on, "How was meditation and yoga this morning?"

I push air through my closed lips and it makes a mocking sound before I can stop myself.

She glances up.

I fix my face the best way I know how to and say, "It was cool."

"Do you meditate and do yoga in New York?"

"I don't have the time. It seems time-consuming and only something I can do when time permits, which is never. Plus, I'm not calm enough or flexible like people usually are who do those kinds of things, anyway."

She nods, and offers a warm smile again. "You're a journalist, right? That sounds exciting."

I shrug. "It has its moments of excitement, I guess."

"What do you write?"

"Entertainment pieces. We recently completed work on a series of articles highlighting the artists and musicians who don't get the attention more popular acts in their fields do."

"Ooh, that sounds like a great read."

"I'm excited to see the finished product once the magazine hits the stands."

"Have you always wanted to be a writer?"

I shrug again. "In some ways, yes, I guess."

"In some ways?"

She hangs onto every word, huh?

I roll my tongue around my mouth, debating on elaborating.

She taps her pen on her notebook's page and chuckles lowly. "I get two types of people whenever I do therapy at these retreats, and Mykal, I do plenty of therapy. And it is always and *only* two types of people I encounter. I either get the types who tell me everything before their butts can touch the couch or the ones who dread this part of their stay, choosing to remain tight-lipped in every session because of it and can't wait for the sessions to be over before they can even begin."

I tighten my lips to keep from smiling.

"The ones who are tight-lipped at first always have one regret at the end of the retreat."

I sit silently waiting for her to continue.

"They all regret not opening up sooner in their sessions so they could have gotten more of the help they needed in the time available to them."

I bite inside my cheek, listening.

"Now, I flew from New York, like you did. And the flight was not a short one."

"At all," I add.

"At all," she parrots, laughing a little. "So I want for your travel time to be well worth it. I want you to get the most out of your sessions so you can return to life at home better than you left it. And how we can do that is by you answering honestly always. This is a judgement-free zone, and I mean that. My brand of therapy stands by that. I am here to help in any way I can. Take advantage of this, Mykal, and refuse to hold back. Be more than honest. Be transparent."

I swallow hard.

"I saw a little of that transparency peek through earlier in our conversation. Let's keep it going because transparency fuels transformation." She winks.

I'm hesitant to do it at first, but I nod my understanding.

"Now." She lifts her pen again, "about writing, let me pose the question differently; if you could do anything you wanted to do, and money wasn't an issue. You completely paid off everything that needed paying off, and you have enough money to cover any necessities you'd ever need. With all of that handled and if you could do whatever you wanted to do, what would Mykal do?"

I thought I didn't even have to think about it. The answer has always been...

"Journalism."

"So if you didn't get paid to write the articles you write, to conduct the research you conduct and to transcribe interviews word for word, you'd be fine with it?"

I sit with her words once again, reimagining myself doing all the things she mentioned with the knowledge I wouldn't receive a check for it. And I'm fine with that. But only if I did something else, too.

"Well, when you put it like that, not exactly. I would still want to be a journalist. But I would feel something is missing though."

"Then your answer is only half correct. Be patient with yourself. Dig deeper and think again. Think limitless."

And so I do. I take her advice and dig deep to test my choice. I loved researching, and I loved the sound of my fingers drumming against my keyboard, typing up at least one thousand words or more. I don't like that it's stories about celebrities who hated people like me, though. But I loved seeing my byline on a glossy page. Interviewing celebrities honestly helped with me living vicariously through them, but I didn't really love it. Interviewing celebrities definitely isn't something I would do without compensation. But writing, I love that through and through. Watching my thoughts materialize into actual words is like magic. I write articles, but I don't eagerly get up every day to do that. The only time I did it was when I was going for editor. Now editor is what I want, truly. To shape a magazine in the vision I have for it based on my thoughts and ideas, I want that. At first, the only reason I wanted editor was because it seemed like something I could brag about, especially to my father. But eventually, it became more. It became my way of having control over what people consumed and at this point, I wouldn't make it about celebrities at all.

I didn't want to be just an editor, though. Not anymore. I wanted to be an editor and something else. Something that has given me joy and that I would absolutely do for free.

My eyes widen at the realization.

"I'd write scripts. Musicals." I smile and briefly drop my head in my hand, a little embarrassed, but it is the truth. "I'd still be a journalist, an editor to be specific. I'd do that for free, but not writing celebrity-based anything. I'd want to cover topics worth something, but I wouldn't just be an editor. I'd write scripts too, if I could. Yes, that's what I would do." I lift my head once more. "I would be the Tyler Perry or the Spike Lee of musicals. So I guess the Wesley Sparks or Lin-Manuel Miranda."

"Okay!" She smiled big. "Can you elaborate on what you mean by that?"

I sit up in my seat, excitedly. "I would write musicals and write me in them so I always have a part."

Dr. Peters nods, then writes again.

"But that's unrealistic. I can't be an editor *and* a script writer, right? Especially when I hate singing and acting, sometimes. Plus, with script writing at least, I'm not patient enough to write everyone's lines and the music. I do not know how to write music, actually. Just thinking about it is making my head spin." I laugh nervously. "I'm also not trained enough to commit wholly to portraying the parts in a musical the way some of my favorites are. You couldn't tell me Lin-Manuel wasn't a seasoned actor based on his performance in Hamilton. I went to a high school for the Performing Arts, but I just never followed through on that. I lacked the discipline to stick with it, but writing has always been a passion—"

"What are you then?" She interjects.

I squint my eyes in response. "What?"

"What are you then?"

"I don't understand the question."

She places her pen between the inside spine of her notebook. "You've told me all the things you're not, so what are you?"

I'm confused by her question, is what I am. I don't say that though.

I ask instead, "I've told you what I'm not?"

"Several times since we've started talking."

My brows relax.

"So, now I want to know the things you are. Let's hear them."

I roll my eyes from corner to corner, searching for the answer to a question that should be simple to answer, but my mind is drawing blanks.

"I could sit here and tell you, *'Mykal, you're enough.'* That seems like the right thing to say, right? What a therapist should say, I'm sure. But enough of what? You've told me all that you are *not* enough of, so what are you enough of then?

I open my mouth to respond and come up empty. The words swirl in my mind, though.

I'm amazing, I'm beautiful, I'm talented... I think.

But I don't honestly want to say that.

"You could tell me at least five things you *are not* since you've arrived, but you can't bring yourself to tell me one thing you are?"

"I'm great," I try. "I guess."

"You guess?"

"I don't know..." I shrug, frustrated. "Yeah?"

She offers another one of her warm smiles.

"Here's a question I want you to sit with," she starts. "Don't answer it as soon as I ask, just sit with it."

"Okay..."

"Why do you think you are so uneasy speaking about what you are, but so comfortable discussing what you aren't?"

I inhale deeply.

"What are you protecting yourself from by discussing what you lack?"

"It's just easier." I shrug once more. "I hear it all the time from my dad. What I can't do, what I'm not good at, I just see them more clearly than anything else. It's really not that big of a deal for me."

"The way you speak to yourself matters though. It translates into everything in your life. It sets the limits in your mind in motion and forms the foundation for what you believe you're capable of. Your words determine your altitude in your life, Mykal."

I swallow hard.

"You're telling me what you aren't based on what other people are." She moves her notebook to the chair beside her. "You are comparing and that can lead to a lot of misguidances in terms of self."

I blink in response.

"You mentioned your father. What are his parents like?"

"*Um,* I wouldn't know. My dad's parents both died before he and my mother ever got together, so I never got to meet them. But based on things my father says whenever he's comparing himself to me or my generation, they were pretty strict."

"Is your father strict?"

"Very." I lean back in my seat and let my eyes follow the rise and fall of the ocean waves outside. "If tough love was a person, it would definitely be my dad."

"Trauma bonding can sometimes be mistaken for tough love from parents."

I bring my eyes back into focus and onto hers.

"Some parents make the mistake sometimes of thinking because what they call *tough love* didn't kill them when they were younger, and because their parents did it too, that it must be right even when they know themselves it didn't feel right when they experienced it. So intentionally and often unintentionally it gets passed down generation to generation and viewed as normal, but often it isn't."

I move my eyes again, focusing on the wicker chair beside her. Doing so helps me digest what she's just said and apply it to my life to see if it's true.

"It's important we teach people how to love us and to set boundaries, including for our parents, sometimes. It isn't easy and it may seem like something you feel you don't need to do, but to be happy you will have to do it and as soon as possible."

I inhale a long, deep breath and let it out slowly through my lips. In this short time with Dr. Peters, we've unpacked so much and I'm exhausted, but not uncomfortable about any of it. With each answered question, weight lifts off my shoulders I didn't even know were there. I'm curious about what else we can discover and address.

"We've covered work and family but have yet to discuss your love life."

I snort a laugh. "I don't—"

I catch myself from dwelling on the *nots* and *don'ts* as advised.

Instead I tell her, "I assure you, my dating life is as confusing if not more confusing than my work and family life."

She smiles, no doubt waiting for me to continue.

I clear my throat, roll my eyes, and laugh at what I'm about to admit.

"The guy," I start, "who I can now admit I like very much, I also thought I hated, but the hate has never been mutual because he purchased this trip for me despite how I've treated him. He's kind and amazing, and likes me for some strange reason, but I'm so screwed up, and focused on what I don't have that I've completely ignored what I do have."

"And what's that?"

"A man who really likes me for me," I say smiling. "And as crazy as it sounds, I didn't realize this until just now."

Twenty-Six

The vehicle's wheels slowly roll over the course brick road as my driver gently brings the car to a stop.

Sun rays shine through the windshield and backseat windows. I lean forward and take in the view with squinted eyes.

"We're here sir," my driver informs behind the wheel, unhooking his seatbelt. "I can get your door for you."

"I got it, thank you," I tell him, sliding my wallet out my back pocket and singling out a fifty-dollar bill. "This is for you."

He turns in his seat to accept the bill, then glances up at me through the rear-view mirror with smiling eyes. "*Mahalo*, thank you."

I smile at his gratitude.

The last time I was in Hawaii was when I was twelve, so the sound of his native 'thank you' encourages a welcomed memory.

I step out of the vehicle and inhale the air, eyes moving all around me, taking in the scenery.

I flew in on a red eye last night. Would have flown in sooner, but I didn't want to set off red flags at the office. Both the editor and assistant editor couldn't be away for too long and at the same time without people putting two and two together. So, I picked the weekend to travel.

Villas circle the paved path leading to the beach. This place looked amazing in person. The photos online did it little justice.

I walk toward the villa that has the welcome sign pitched on the lawn, instructing guests to check in there.

"*Aloha*," the woman with wavy black hair greets me at the front desk. "How may I assist you?"

"Hi, I'm visiting a friend." I smile. "Only for an hour or two and would like to locate her villa."

"Absolutely." She smiles back. "Their name, please?"

"Needing the jet again, huh?" My friend Gabriel teased when I asked to borrow his to fly out to Hawaii. "This woman must be something else to have you skipping time zones to see for only a couple of days. I hope the jet lag will be worth it."

"Mykal Jones," I answer the concierge.

I hadn't heard from Mykal since she arrived, nor did I reach out. Definitely could have waited for her to return to New York, but then again, I couldn't.

I missed her. Her smile she consistently fought to hide from me, the sharp wit she dealt me with little effort, her analytical eyes that attempted always to find the catch. All the things that would drive someone mad, intrigued me and drew me to her. I'd known this woman for all of three months and she was gone for only three days and already, I missed her.

I approach the wicker front door of Mykal's villa. The directions given by the concierge were simple, so it's easy to find the property.

I played in my mind what Mykal's reaction will be when she sees me here. I didn't know her well, and she isn't the most predictable person, so there is no telling if me being here will flatter or annoy her. I don't care. I want to be supportive, and this is what I know supportive to be.

I ball my hand into a fist and tap the door with my knuckles. There's a brief wait until I see the knob turn and she opens the door.

She's dressed in three quarter black leggings with a bikini top of the same color. Her face volleys between wrinkled brows and blinking eyes.

I hold a hand up to wave because it's the only thing I can think to do and I joke, "Would you believe me if I said I was in the area."

She exhales through her lips.

"Or would it be too creepy to admit I flew close to ten hours just to see you?"

Mykal inhaled a stuttered breath before taking two steps toward me and when she arrives in my space, she swings her arms around me and holds me tight in a hug that makes my heart leap in my chest.

"It's not creepy at all," she whispers against me. "It's so you."

I wrap my arms around her as well and hold her close for however long she wants me to. Close to a minute later, she steps out of her hug.

She lifts her eyes up at me and smiles. It's a smile I've never seen. Actually, her entire demeanor is one that's new to me.

And I didn't think it was possible to like her even more than I already did, but in this moment I do.

She takes my hand and pulls me over the threshold, guiding me inside her villa.

The space is as gorgeous if not more gorgeous than the pictures online. A sprawling living space with a direct view of the beach. They wrapped everything in white or accessorized it in wicker. Hawaiian music plays from an unseen speaker, offering a festive vibe in this setting. The ocean water outside scents the air surrounding us. It's beautiful. She's beautiful standing there looking at me with her hands gripping each side of her naturally cinched waist.

"Nice, right?" She asks, scanning the room as if seeing it for the first time. "I almost don't want to leave. I probably won't."

It's my turn to wrinkle my brows and blink my eyes. "Come again?"

She giggles, and it's the most effervescent giggle I've ever heard come from her.

"I quit," she announces next with the biggest smile on her face.

"You quit, what?"

"The magazine." She shrugs a shoulder. "Well, I'm *going* to quit the magazine and go for an editor position somewhere else. I've handwritten my letter of resignation that I plan to send to HR by Monday."

I just stare. It's all I can do after hearing this news. "What? Why?"

"It's this place." She spins on the arches of her feet while gesturing around herself. "There's just something in the air here that makes everything feel right with my life and the direction that's right for it is so clear when I'm on this island."

I move in closer. "What happened?"

She shakes her head like she's searching for the words and when she finally finds them, she says, "I realize that for a majority of my life I have been trying to chase other people's joy and that is why I was so unhappy. I've been here thinking if I had those cars, and that man while working in this specific position, writing about these specific famous people, I would be fulfilled. Or if I lived in a certain part of Manhattan with a walk-in large enough to live in, I could be as happy as the people who had those things. But it turns out it wasn't any of those things I wanted. All of those things are great, but I wanted the joy people exuded while having those things which really have nothing to do with those things at all. Those people were just happy. Not happy because of. They were just happy, *period*, Desmond."

I shift my eyes along her face, taking in her words.

"I want to write but not articles about celebrities, transcribing their words and centering my universe around them. I want to be an editor and work on topics that matter. And..." She takes a breath. "I want to write musicals and act and sing in them. I want to write musicals and be an editor. I want to do both, as unrealistic as that might sound. But I don't care. I want that. And if it never yields me anything that's okay because I will be doing something I deeply love."

She smiles even bigger than before and her face lights up. My heart can't help but to melt over that.

"I want to create from a place of wonderment and imagination because somehow, while I've been here, I realize that's what would make me the happiest, Desmond. That is what's missing for me."

She licks her lips and takes strides toward me. "I want to know what it feels like to make love to a man who wants to get to know me past what I present to him on the surface. A man who can say 'I got it' for more than a pair of shoes or a designer handbag. Although I still want a man who will say he got it on those things too. Let's be real here."

I chuckle.

"I want to love a man who sees value in what's going on inside of

Mykal that others can't see. I think I've found him. No, I *know* I've found him. And he's been here, right *here* for the past three months and I didn't even see it, until now."

I follow her with my eyes, lowering them to hers when she's close.

"See, a man like that is worthy of praise and devotion because that type of love is raw and kind, the best kind of love."

I run the back of my hand down her cheek and she closes her eyes at my touch. I have to take a breath to keep from diving headfirst into the depths of her like I want to in this moment.

She balances herself on the arches of her feet to lift and press her mouth to mine. I wrap an arm around her waist and guide her close.

On her lips I whisper, "You swore you didn't like me."

"I was lying the whole time," she whispers before kissing me.

And I join her, interlocking my tongue with hers and sending our kiss deeper.

I'm tired, jet lagged for sure, but my body comes alive with her this close, so I lift her in my arms and ask her to direct me to the bedroom.

When we get there, no words need to be spoken. Only clothing removed and we do that, with lips still locked and our hands very busy. We pull, tug, and push our clothes to the villa's floor, our bodies never too far apart, eager arms constantly drawing ourselves back to each other. The only time she moves her lips off mine is to drop to her knees to take me in her mouth whole.

I want to stop her, not thinking I can last another moment inside of her mouth, but she's bobbing and wrapping her lips so tight around me I can hardly find the words to speak. Her hands are on either side of me as she slides me in and out of her mouth with fervor. I drop my head back when it feels like it's spinning. My hand finds a home in her hair, which I stroke as she plays a disappearing act with her mouth. I feel myself about to come and pull myself free before I lose myself too much, and this soon. I lift her into my arms to lay her in bed so I can return the favor. She's damn near dripping for me when I bury my lips between her lower lips. I go straight for her pink pearl that is swollen and pulsing, waiting to be polished by the tip of my tongue. I look up to catch her back arching off the bed and the sight sets something off in me that has me burying my face even deeper between her thighs, wanting to taste every part of her with every inch of my tongue. Her moans ricochet off the walls and are like music to my ears. I challenge myself to make her moan louder and for longer. Her thighs cuff my ears when I slide my tongue from left to right. Her body vibrates next, and when I peek up to see the effects of my actions, I find her eyes rolling as her hand rests against the top of my head. She reaches the end of her release, and her arms fall at her sides, but I give her no opportunity of reprieve before I'm on my knees and over her. I sink in slowly between her legs, burying myself so deep inside her, her back arches off the bed again.

The natural light from outside shines through the floor to ceiling windows as I pump into her slowly at first, feeling as her previous release lubricates my work on her. She's boneless already, eyes finding it difficult to stay on mine, but I watch her. I watch her because she's the most stunning woman I've ever met with a personality that frustrates and captivates me at the same time. A woman who took my breath away at first sight, whose drive, stubbornness, and unwillingness to bend is a turn on for me.

She grips my backside with both hands and wines her waist beneath me. She doesn't guide my movements, she only enjoys the ride, and it's a marvelous sight.

Inside her, I can forget everything. My father's condition, my lofty goal of starting a newspaper, that I'm falling for a woman I never planned to fall for.

I use my arm to push myself back, grabbing her by the hip to turn her over and to slide in from the back. She grips the sheets and shudders when I glide in once more, burying myself to the root inside her. And she accepts every inch, lifting her ass by the waist to consume even more of me, and I go wild.

I pound what last of the energy I have into her and she takes it. Moaning to the point her voice grows hoarse, and she loses control over herself and her body. I have to hold her down to anchor her to the bed so I can keep stroking while she spirals down from her high. As she reaches her end I start my descent, burying my nose into her short hair and inhaling her as I give into my release. I grunt and thrust until I'm consumed by the moment and finally collapse on top of her completely.

She lifts an arm and holds my head against the nape of her neck as we catch our breaths together.

I roll off her, hooking my arm around her waist and pulling her close to me. My eyes are heavy, and sleep is near, but I notice when she settles against me. I wrap my arm around her tighter.

"Sex with you is always great," she whispers. "But you pulling me close like this so I can catch my breath in your arms hits a different spot... and I love that."

I smile with my eyes still closed. "So, is it safe to say this isn't just another hookup?"

Mykal turns in my arms and I secure her in place, wrapping my arms around her waist.

"It's safe to say this is much more, Mr. Ellis," she answers on my lips. "And I love that, too."

Epilogue

1-year later... November 30, 2021

DESMOND

I stare down at the printed newspaper with The Ellis Daily sprawled in big bold letters at the top of the front page. There are columns of words to the left and right framing the large photo of the front page story, full coverage on the up-and-coming black owned village in upstate New York - Greene Gardens. The building project for the village was financed by billionaire Bryant Greene. With commercial property and residential buildings starting to take form in the village, I made it my priority to document the efforts and make it the paper's first front page story. Bryant Greene was making history and a difference, and so was I, so the collaboration between the two of us made perfect sense.

I've worked tirelessly for this moment. Many sleepless nights and blunders with the printing press. The paper's operation is smaller than I would like, but to start, it's perfect. And for a small local paper, everything looked great. Our first story was a toss up between giving new subscribers a glimpse into our operation, introducing the paper in its infant stage and showing its growth from the ground up or taking on a story very little media was paying attention to. Greene Gardens it was. My father was like a pioneer in journalism for reporting on the unreported, so I knew which story he would applaud.

"You have to be willing to do the things others won't to achieve the things others can't," he'd tell me when I was younger. "Never take the easy way out. If it doesn't challenge you, it doesn't change you. True pioneers don't discover things that have already been discovered. Remember that. Always take the risk."

I run my fingers down the newspaper and over the black words. I lift the paper and press it to my nose, inhaling the newspaper print paper smell, relishing in the moment.

After serving another six months at For The Culture, I took the leap and invested in two warehouses in Dumbo, Brooklyn. I put out a call for experienced writers, editors, copy editors, photographers, and printing press professionals, both new and seasoned. I worked with building the culture from the ground up, insisting on supplying my printing press, and now here I stood, in my corner office holding the very first paper under The Ellis Daily imprint that is scheduled to hit newsstands tomorrow morning at 4am.

When Biggie said it was all a dream, he spoke from a place of relativity because although I knew what my goal was, to start one of the only black-owned local newspapers reporting on black-related topics only, never did I imagine I'd do it in a year's time.

I just wished I worked faster so my father could have witnessed it firsthand.

"Mr. Ellis," my secretary called from her desk. The space in the office is considerably smaller than For The Culture's. But what we lacked in size, we more than made up for in effort and quality. "Ms. Jones confirmed your dinner date at six this evening."

I smile at the mention of her name.

Mykal and my relationship evolved after the day we spent in Hawaii. Brown limbs tangled beneath the white sheets, the ocean waves outside her villa serving as the soundtrack to our time together. We reminisce together about our time in Honolulu often because we cultivated something on that island that far surpassed intimacy. I finally got to know the woman of my dreams. A relationship wasn't something I even thought I had time for, but what I learned quickly after we made things official is that we will make time for the things we value, and I valued her very much.

So much, I made sure she had an office in the newspaper's HQ as well. I had plans to get her here full-time but I needed that to be more her decision than mine. She didn't work here but I remember her mentioning wanting to work on articles that mattered, so I offered her a space to do that as a credited beta editor, which she accepted. This was untraditional in print media, but I wanted Mykal to be a part of something great in whatever way possible. Her position allowed her to work here during her time off and her doing so not interfere with her other plans. It was her suggestions and keen eye that made The Ellis Daily a completed reality. Her potential to build and grow was starting to appreciate, as I predicted and I couldn't wait to do more of the same for her.

"Excellent, thank you, Cassie."

Mykal and I took things slowly after our hookup in Hawaii. At the suggestion of her therapist, Mykal and I determined what we were early. Blurred lines and gray areas were something Mykal insisted on avoiding, not interested in ending up in anything complicated, which would've undone all the progress she's made in therapy.

"Uh, Cassie?"

"Yes, Mr. Ellis?"

"Two things. First, please arrange for a dozen long stem roses to be sent to Mykal." I smile. "As luck would have it, she's also celebrating something monumental."

"Absolutely Mr. Ellis. I'll get right on that."

"And second, please hold all of my calls and send any important ones to my office voicemail," I instructed. "I'm going to take the rest of the day off to celebrate with her and the first print of Ellis Daily tomorrow."

"No problem at all, Mr. Ellis. Please enjoy the rest of your day off."

I grabbed the printed paper and stepped out.

Handing in my resignation to Corey was nerve-wracking. I knew what I had to do, but I also didn't want to leave my position as an editor at For The Culture considering how gracious he and Amir were with promoting me. Cushioning the blow, I suggested an option I knew they'd approve. I was at peace knowing that the new editor would serve the position with the best practices in mind.

In my car, I drove through The Cross Island Parkway headed to Long Island. To my father's.

On arrival, I drive through the wrought-iron gates and roll down the same paved road that has always stretched from the gate to my father's front door. But I wouldn't go inside today.

Instead I drive to the far end at the back of the property to where a slate gravestone lays over a manicured section of grass.

My father always told me to bury him so he could return to the earth and near the house he built with his life, so I honored his wishes. When we started the process of signing over trusts, he made me promise to never sell the property even after he passed. I have every intention to honor that as well.

"Hey dad," I greet over his plot. I fan dried leaves off the headstone, revealing his name and the date of his sunrise and sunset. The first print of The Ellis Daily is secure in my grip.

I squat down and lay the paper by his headstone.

"I did it." I lift the paper again as if my father is there with me for me to show him. "First press of The Ellis Daily. God, I wish you could have seen it."

My father passed in his sleep only three months ago. Shortly before his death, I'd transported him to the warehouse unseen when there was no one onsite to recognize him. I wanted him to see the setup and daily operation. To really get a feel of his vision happening in real time. He was cognizant enough to know what was happening, and that I owned it, that *we* owned it, and the light that gleamed in his eyes at that fact will stay with me forever.

The months leading up to his death; he spoke little. His illness worsened and affected his speech, so his communication was at a minimum, but I saw the joy in his eyes when he recognized the family name etched on the building's front door.

"And you got a full page on the second page. The life and times of Desmond Ellis II." I smile with pride. "We did it."

I never revealed my father's health condition to anyone outside of my family, even after his death. His obituary simply stated he died of natural causes and my family nor I spilled any info to media or the like. It was a family secret that I had every intention in keeping. My father would have wanted it that way. Mykal kept her word. She never told a soul either. I guess that's another reason, unspoken, as to why she had a recurring role in my life, why she would continue to with what I had planned.

At the thought of her, I pull out my phone and dial her up, lifting the phone to my ear.

"Hello handsome," she says when she answers.

"Hello beautiful," I countered, leaning forward in my squat to dust the dirt off my father's headstone. "Busy?"

"Never for you, what's up?"

"I know we have dinner plans tonight but I was wondering if you wanted to grab lunch in an hour to celebrate a little early."

"Your first print?"

"And you completing the first draft of your script this morning."

"Okay, yeah, sure!" she replies. In the background, I can hear her fingers typing on her keyboard. "I just need to finish up a little editing and then I'm all yours. You can show me your soon-to-be first print in person."

"Got it right here," I assure. "I'm just at my father's grave showing him the finished product."

"I wouldn't imagine you being anywhere else."

I nod slowly at her acknowledgement, inside excited to get her in my arms soon.

Mykal and my relationship is one we've taken slow. We hadn't become exclusive until a month after my father's passing. She committed herself to therapy, continuing to go at least once a week, and has devoted most of her energy to getting to know herself by pouring love and acceptance inward. To say she's transformed into a woman whose company is more than enough would be an understatement. I couldn't wait to ask her to bear the Ellis name and for her to accept.

In due time.

For now, I am enjoying the organic growth of our fairly new relationship.

"So one hour," she adds, the sound of typing continues.

"All right, I'll see you at your office within the hour."

"Okay, I love you."

I jerk my neck back.

"Oops, *uh...*" The typing stops and there's a two second awkward pause on the line because I can't find the words to say either after hearing her say that.

"I didn't mean that," she tries. "I mean, *I meant it* but... I just didn't... oh my God. I can't believe I just said that. *Um...*"

"Mykal—"

"Just... bye."

Before I could say anything else, she hangs up and I'm left with the biggest smile on my face.

———

MYKAL

I drop my phone on my desk and lift my hand to my face to cover my eyes.

"Oh my God," I repeat for the second time. "I can't believe I said it first."

My therapist, Dr. Peters, would be so pleased. She and I had been going back and forth about me sharing with Desmond how I felt for weeks, but I'd been telling her I wasn't ready. Seems my mind was.

I shake my head and try to refocus on work.

A knock at my door grabs my attention.

"Hey, boo," Asha announces as she saunters in. "Lunchtime?"

I sigh while shaking my head.

"What?" She asks walking closer. "What happened?"

"I just told Desmond I loved him."

Her jaw drops.

"Yeah." I shut my eyes and drop my head back between my shoulders.

Asha plops down in her seat. "But you love him, right?"

"Of course."

"So..." She throws her hands up. "Help me out with seeing the problem."

"I said it first." I cringe. "I can't believe I said it first."

"Where are we, in high school? So *what* you said it first?"

I level my head, only to drop it in my hands to pinch the bridge of my nose.

"The man changed your life and not in some he gave you the best dick of your life kind of way. Although I can only assume he did that, too."

I point. "Hey."

She holds her hand up in a surrender pose. "I'm just pointing out he changed your life in a way that is meaningful. If there's anyone deserving of hearing *I love you* first, it's him, Mykal. For sure."

I twist my lips to one side and nod. "Points are being made."

"So, lunchtime? I'm starved."

"I can't," I inform, turning to face my computer again. "I have lunch with him in an hour."

"Are you two actually going to eat or are *you* lunch? Because I can bring you something back."

I throw my pen at her, and she ducks out the way in time, laughing. "*We* are eating, thank you very much. But I don't know." I shrug. "I never know for sure with him."

"And I know it's fire, but you're always so tight-lipped about it."

"Desmond isn't just a random hookup anymore, darling. He's my man and you ain't hearing shit about it. Now up and out you go. I have to work so I'm done by the time he arrives."

After telling Desmond a year ago that I wanted to quit For The Culture to focus on writing musicals, he talked some sense into me.

"Don't quit," he told me while I laid in his arms after we made love for the third time. He'd surprised me by visiting me in Hawaii and I was so beside myself, I let my heart lead instead of getting in my own way. That day changed everything. Our relationship, how I felt about him, and even my impromptu plan to leave FTC to pursue my dream that I hadn't realized was still a dream.

"Continue to earn a living while studying your craft," he advised. "It'll be great leverage after you've got your completed script. Picture it: Former For The Culture editor and co-editor at budding daily newspaper makes her Broadway debut in a musical she wrote," he noted and I blushed. "Have the script in your hand and before you jump ship. Trust me on this. It's hard to be creative if your mind is cluttered with thoughts surrounding how you're going to pay for things."

"Says the prince of journalism, whose name is its own resume," I teased.

"I still know the struggle and what it's like doing what you love, but the money not being there. Plus, I know a few theater directors you can speak to once you have something they can work with." He wrapped his arm around me. "Take your time, use your leverage at FTC to advance yourself. Your creativity will thank you for it."

"Wait." I sat up when I replayed his words in my head. "You said former editor and co-editor of what?!"

"I won't be editor for too much longer. This is what I tried to tell you from the beginning." He turned to wrap his arm around my waist again to pull me down to him. "There was no reason to hate me, Mykal, because I only accepted editor for my own strategic reasoning. The editor position was always yours and I have plans for something I want you to be a part of, only if you agree that it aligns with your plans. As for me, I'm close to making my father's dream come true. That has always been my motivation behind my choices." Desmond kissed me on the cheek, then buried his lips on my neck. "So don't quit."

It was the best advice because six months later, Desmond resigned as editor, and they promoted me to his position. A week after that, he asked me to be what he called a beta editor at his newspaper and offered an editor position there whenever I was ready to leave For The Culture. I went from not being editor to becoming an editor of two publications. What is life?

"Fine, bye. Be like that." Asha stands to her feet. "I'll bring you back a little something just in case lunch ends up really being you."

I laugh while swiveling in my seat to face my computer again.

I got the office, well two offices, the view, the positions, and I'm working on my dream.

The one thing that was the pain in my life was telling my parents about it, more specifically, my father. I dreaded it so much I put it off for almost a year. My fear eventually spilled out in therapy and Dr. Peters insisted I face my fear head on and tell them.

"My father will think I'm crazy and unstable," I whined to her. "Tell him I'm going to focus on writing musicals? He'll laugh right in my face."

"Remember, it doesn't matter what others feel about you," Dr. Peters *assured from her seat across from me while we sat in her basement office in Brooklyn. "What matters is how you feel about yourself."*

Simple words, but those were the words that gave me courage as I sat at the dinner table with another one of my favorite meals, that my mother prepared, in jeopardy of being the meal I eventually hated.

"So I have news," I started as I sliced into my lasagna.

My mother was the only one who looked up from her plate and focused on me.

"I've decided to return to school for my MFA," I said, smiling big. *"I want to write musicals."*

My father scoffed.

"It'll be an accelerated program lasting a little over a year..."

"Unbelievable," my father added. He chuckled maniacally before shaking his head.

"I'll still work as editor at For The Culture because working at the magazine has always been my dream, but so has writing musicals. I'm confident I'll get through the program on top."

My father glanced at me and said, "Here we go again. Are we really here again? And why am I not surprised? You have the focus of a fruit fly and you are as predictable as the letters in the alphabet." He turned to my mother. "Didn't I tell you she'd change her mind again? Your daughter is so damn flighty it's exhausting. Now she wants to write musicals. My goodness. How embarrassing."

"I've always wanted to write musicals, daddy. Since high school."

"Oh, yeah, of course," he teased. "Like you've always wanted to be a model? Always wanted to write for a magazine? The latest lie you told your cousin. I told him not to give you this chance."

I dropped my fork in my plate and the clatter the handle made against the ceramic rim quieted the table. "You know what, daddy? I'm sorry."

He only stared at me.

"I'm sorry I'm not the daughter you've always wanted, or the son, because I swear you make me pay for being a woman every time you have to share space with me. And I hate to be the bearer of bad news but science has proven that the father chooses the gender, so me being female will always be your fault."

I tossed back my glass of wine and gulped before I continued. "I'm sorry that I can accomplish the same things someone else you know accomplishes, but it doesn't make you as proud when I do it. I'm sorry I don't make you smile whenever I visit after staying away for so long because I despise returning home, even if it's just for an hour. I'm sorry that I haven't been worthy enough for you to tell me you at least love me."

I stopped to shake my head and take a breath. Tears brimmed my lower lids, but I refused to let them fall.

"I'm sorry I have a father like you who is so unsupportive and who treats me like he wishes his wife swallowed me instead of gave birth to me."

My mother shrieked. "My God, Mykal!"

"I'm also sorry that I love you so much that what you thought of me mattered more than what I thought of myself. At one point, your opinion was paramount to my existence... but not anymore. Not today. Because today, do you want to know what I'm not sorry about, daddy?"

I don't get a response, nor am I surprised by that.

"I'm not sorry for discovering who the hell I am. I'm not sorry for finding what makes me amazing and not compared to what makes

someone else the amazing they are. I'm not sorry for knowing that I can always change my mind and do whatever I want, literally. But most of all, daddy, I'm not sorry that I finally don't give a fuck what you think about any of what I said."

His eyes ballooned at my final words and he opened his mouth to say something, but shut it instead and said nothing.

And I smiled at his response because it's a small defeat in a world of disappointments. I inhaled a valiant breath and refocused on my food. I stole a peek at my mother from the corner of my eye to see her tucking her lips into her mouth.

I turned to her.

I could have given her round two of it all, because I had plenty of fire left, but I don't. Truth be told, she's been my father's accomplice, but it's like Dr. Peters told me in one of our sessions, "You can't expect people to give what they don't have."

My mother lacks the courage to stand up to my father for herself so I can't expect for her to find the courage to do it for me. I just have to accept that.

I sigh and force a smile. "Mom, this food is delicious, thank you."

"You're very welcome, baby," she replies with a smile and a wink.

Since that day, dinners were less awkward and way less intimidating. My father and I exchanged even fewer words than before, but when we spoke, his words did not muddy me in criticism. I'd come to terms with the fact that our relationship may never be like the father-daughter relationships I saw on TV, and I'm okay with that. I have no choice but to be. This is my life, and I have learned to change the things I can change and love and accept the things I can't.

Besides, my father's inability to be impressed by me, fuels my ambition. His lack of applause sharpened my drive and my vision, qualities that attracted the most amazing man I have ever met into my life. So, I guess that will have to be my lemonade.

Life as editor is exactly how I imagined it. The pay is great, the hours are long, and the responsibility of running a magazine is not easy at all. But I'm here, not only doing it to finance my way through school, which is going fabulous by the way, but kicking ass as I do it and loving every minute of

being editor-in-chief. The owners and the readers have applauded my ideas
and direction for the magazine. My writers are skilled and I'm mentoring
one of our best so she's a shoo-in for promotion to editor, once I resign to
head over to work at The Ellis Daily full-time. The old me would never, but
I've transformed my view on there needing to be a loser if one of us wins to
there's enough room at the top for us all to win. Like one of Asha's internet
quotes suggested, the sky would be so dark if there were only one star.

Our latest magazine issues have been incredible because I ran the
publication with the understanding that we're all a team and each have
something to gain. Honestly, everything is perfect. I completed the
rough draft of my script this morning. I'm acing my creative arts
program in school, and I can't wait to hold my degree in one hand along
with my finished script in the other. I'm moving toward what I love,
what brings me genuine joy, and that, to me, is enough.

Light raps on my glass, tries to distract me.

"Asha, go away," I quip, refusing to take my eyes off my computer's
screen.

"Ahem."

The familiar deep voice pulls me away from what I'm doing, and I
do a double take when I see Desmond standing at the threshold.

He's dressed down in a plain white tee, gray joggers, and white
tennis sneakers on his feet. Had it been any other weekday, his getup
would have thrown me off because this is his weekend look, but I know
he's been at his new printing plant right next door to his office over-
seeing the first newspaper printing of The Ellis Daily.

"I told you one hour," I say, refocusing on my computer screen. I
force my eyes away from his, still totally in my head over saying *I love you*
first. "I'm far from done—"

"I love you too." His words float from his mouth with ease and enter
my ears, sounding sweeter than anything I've ever heard. If honey had a
voice.

I snatch my eyes off my computer screen this time. "Wh-what?"

"I said," he replies, stepping into the office that was once his months
ago, and closes the door behind him. "I love you too."

I lean back in my seat.

"Your slip of the tongue inspired me to hop in my car and to drive all the way over here to say that to your face."

I can't fight the smile pulling at my lips.

"I didn't want to wait. Didn't think it would be right to," Desmond continues, rounding my desk and only stopping once he's in front of me. "Because I just couldn't wait to tell you I love you too so you could see for yourself how serious I am about us."

He grabs me gently by the hand and pulls me out of my seat to stand.

The office is still made entirely of glass. I took down the drapes he installed because it didn't go with my office decor. So everyone can see us, but I don't care and neither does he. With Desmond these days, I'm not shy about what we have which has transitioned into us saying these three words. And he didn't have to confirm his love. His actions have always been clear. He loves me, beyond my wildest imaginings and the shit feels damn good.

"I love you more," I whisper as he wraps his arms around me.

A smile slowly appears on his lips and he leans forward to peck me on the lips once. "Isn't it ironic though?"

I lean my head back to focus entirely on him. "What is?"

"The office you first told me you hated me in ends up being the same office you tell me you love me."

I chuckle while pulling him closer. "Growth is a beautiful thing, ain't it?"

"Indeed it is." He pats me on the ass once and instructs me to, "Finish up. I'll go chat it up with a few of the writers while I wait for you so we can head out to lunch. Our reservation for six this evening is set, as you know, and we need to be on time for that one because my bed needs us both in it tonight." He winks.

"Oh, well, we can't disappointment your bed." I lick my lips. "It's been way too good to us."

"*Way* too good." Desmond smirks. "I'm out here."

I bite my bottom lip distracted by his smooth gait as he exits my office.

I can't believe I actually did it. I got the job, the man, and the seed of my dream waiting to bloom. I may not be where I want to be yet, but

I'm looking forward to where I'm going. And this waiting room I've created before I get there, has to be the best on the planet.

Turns out the life I always wanted has always been mine. It just needed a little love to light up the path that envy kept dark. My life is finally enough... good enough for someone else to envy, I'm sure.

The End.

Final Words

Dear Reader:

Thank you for reading *ENVY*. *ENVY* is the fourth book in the Love is Cure, Vol. 1 – Vices & Virtues series. After this, there are only three stories left to tell, and I can't wait for you to dive into those storylines.

For now, let's talk about Mykal and Desmond.

The theme of this series is to put vices with their virtues. Complete opposites on the surface with seemingly little in common and the only thing bringing them together is the potential to fall in love. The saints in each story can see something in the sinners that we can't, and they advocate for the sinners because they see the good and fall in love with that good. Love is the cure because love cures all, especially in this series. And no one is as opposite as Mykal and Desmond.

These two are literally polar opposites. Desmond is positive, Mykal negative. Mykal has an awful relationship with her dad, whereas Desmond has a great one with his father. Desmond is well-off, Mykal not so much. And on and on I could go, but I think you get it and caught a few more in the story.

I loved these two together. I absolutely adored Desmond. Honestly, he's a favorite of mine. The kindness, the compassion, the sacrifice and immense respect for his father and his father's legacy. Desmond was perfect, but flawed at the same time.

And then there's Mykal. Envious, unhappy with her life and circumstances. Life dropped the potential to love right in her lap, but she was so focused on other people's grass she didn't notice the rose growing in her own garden. She had a good thing right there in her face in Desmond and all she could see was a life she thought would make her happy, with Pryce - a married man who wanted no parts of her after securing his happily ever after.

And how interesting that Mykal envies Pryce and Leelah's relationship, which if you read *LUST*, you already know there wasn't anything to envy before that book with them. Envy does that though, I've realized. It narrows vision and creates tunnel vision of reality. Envy makes it harder to see what actually is, to satisfy the belief that everyone has it better than ourselves. When in actuality, we all have our mountains to move.

Isn't it also interesting that Mykal hated the two people (Leelah and Desmond) who had healthy relationships with their fathers?

It was so trippy going from writing about a loving father in My First, My Last, to writing a story about a father who was a complete asshole. Whew, chile.

When people you love, love and accept you, you glow differently and that was what Mykal truly envied until she found her own brand of life to live.

I loved everything about this story and I hope you did too.

This isn't the last you'll see of Mykal and Desmond. They may appear in one of the three books left in the series. Who knows, you might catch their glimpse on my readers website BkBookLounge.com.

Shameless plug lol.

No, but seriously, the best way to stay in the loop of all of that is to subscribe to my newsletter. BK Insiders get all the must-know info.

For now, though, thank you for reading.

If this is your first book by me, I hope you enjoyed the read. If you enjoyed it, I like to say you're a Brookelynite now. So, welcome!

If you've been rocking with me from a book or several books ago, I thank you, as always, for your support. You already know my love for you is bigger than these pages will allow me to show!

See you at the end of the next book.

Love,

Brookelyn.

P.S. if you want to know what happened the day Pryce got the tattoo of his wife's name on his ring finger, I captured the scene in a glimpse on BK Book Lounge. Visit BKBookLounge.com

Book Club Questions

1. What was your first impression of Mykal Jones?
2. What was your first impression of Desmond Ellis III?
3. What did you think about Mykal and Desmond's first meeting in the coffee shop?
4. What did you think about Mykal and Desmond's dynamic?
5. What are your thoughts on Mykal's father, Jedidiah?
6. How much of an influence do you think Jedidiah's disdain for Mykal have on her envy of others?
7. What did you like most about Desmond?
8. What did you like least about Mykal?
9. How do you feel about the ending?
10. What did you think about Mykal's growth throughout ENVY?

About Brookelyn Mosley

Brookelyn wrote her first short story when she was a sophomore in high school. Back then she discovered how using her experience as a teen living in Brooklyn to create romantic shorts was just as exciting to her as retail shopping and going on dates. After starting her first semester of college two years later, Brookelyn's creative writing became more of a hobby and something to escape the stress of midterms and finals.

Now in her 30s as a freelance writer, penning short stories and novellas is her everything. While her experience with writing has evolved for the better, her undying love for creating fiction remains unchanged. Brookelyn's focus is on creating contemporary women's fiction with characters based in urban settings. Her stories chronicle the emotional journeys and erotic experiences of women today through her characters and the scenarios they're thrown into.

The motivation behind her brand of writing has a lot to do with what she discovered storytelling provided for her - an escape. Her goal with her work is to create characters and urban worlds that offer a great escape for fiction readers looking for a break from the daily grind of adulting and who prefer to relax with good books and short stories. When she's not freelance copywriting, doing yoga, or showing her husband, son, and daughter lots of love, she can be found sitting at her computer desk, with her legs folded, and a cup of coffee (or a glass of wine) at arm's reach as she types or edits her latest short or novella.

Connect With Me Online!

Twitter: @brookelynmosley
Facebook: http://facebook.com/brookelynmosley
Facebook Reading Group: Brookelynites Book Lounge
Instagram: @Brookelynmosley
My Website: BrookelynMosley.com (FREE short stories!)

Made In Brooklyn.